*A shocking scandal
leads to passion, which can
only lead to one destination...
between the sheets!*

*T*his wasn't the way she had wanted it done. She'd dreamed of being swept off her feet. She'd dreamed of—

His mouth came down on hers.

Protest vanished.

He kissed her long and hard and, Heaven help her, she kissed him back.

As the kiss ended, Justin said, "There, that's answer enough for both of us now." He turned and walked to the door. "I'll see what I must do for the license." He placed his hand on the door before saying, "You're mine, Francesca."

BEDDING THE HEIRESS

Cathy Maxwell

BEDDING THE HEIRESS

AVON BOOKS
An Imprint of HarperCollinsPublishers

This is a work of fiction. Names, characters, places, and incidents are products of the author's imagination or are used fictitiously and are not to be construed as real. Any resemblance to actual events, locales, organizations, or persons, living or dead, is entirely coincidental.

AVON BOOKS
An Imprint of HarperCollins*Publishers*
10 East 53rd Street
New York, New York 10022-5299

For Lucia Macro,
trusted editor,
in celebration of our tenth book together.

The Title

*H*ome Secretary Lord Hawkesbury ignored the one twin brother standing in the shadows of the room, turning instead to the man who was his friend as well as one of the most respected diplomats in all England.

"Are you certain you wish to do this, Your Grace?" he asked Phillip Maddox, Duke of Colster.

Colster's answer was a glare, the sort only a true duke knew how to use to his advantage. "The title is rightfully my twin's," he answered. "It is not Justin's fault he was kidnapped at birth. These papers will correct a terrible wrong."

"As you say," Hawkesbury murmured, lightly touching the neatly stacked documents and their copies on the desk in front of him. One document would rescind the Letters of Patent conferring the title of Duke of Colster to Phillip Maddox. The other would grant the title to Justin Maddox, who was the elder by a mere fourteen minutes.

Hawkesbury himself was not the sort to give up power and couldn't understand any man who would. Still, even as "Lord Phillip," the current duke would be powerful. He had the skill, whereas the Scottish blacksmith who'd been proven to be the rightful duke would never have the authority or the alliances in Parliament to accomplish much. The best Hawkesbury could wish for was that the Scot would stay out of the way.

At first glance, the twins seemed identical. However, on further study, one could see where the disparate circumstances of their lives had carved differences in their features. Yes, they both were tall with dark hair and straight brows, but Justin was more muscular from years of working as a smithy. His hands seemed twice the size of Phillip's and bore the calluses of his trade. He also had a scar on his right cheek above the jawline. Nor did he have Phillip's touch of distinguished gray at the temples. Perhaps the gray was there and Hawkesbury couldn't see it, because Justin chose to wear his hair longer. Or perhaps because he lacked Phillip's mental acuity.

After all, how much education could a blacksmith have?

A knock on the door sounded. Without waiting for a response, the door opened and the Prince of Wales entered, along with his personal secretary, a man named Trudith. "Are we ready for the king?"

Hawkesbury came to his feet and bowed, as did the duke and his twin. "We are, Your Highness."

"Good. I'll bring him in. He's in good spirits today. We shall have this matter done in minutes." The prince looked to Colster, ignoring the Scottish brother as Hawkesbury had done. "I'll be glad to see this business done, Colster. Shocking mess."

"Yes, Your Highness," the duke answered.

The prince nodded to Trudith, who left to escort the king into the room.

The king did appear well this evening, although he had chosen not to wear his customary wig and there were deep circles, a sign of sleeplessness, under his eyes. Hawkesbury held up a pen. The king crossed the room, took it from him, and quickly scribbled "George R," *George Rex*, on the signature line of each document . . . and it was done. The transfer of power from one duke to another had been duly noted and signed.

The Prince of Wales, his expression solemn, escorted his father out of the room. For once, the frivolous prince was obviously as dismayed by the turn of events as Hawkesbury and the majority of Parliament.

However, Hawkesbury knew his protocol. He knew what was expected of him. He turned to the man who still held back in the shadows. "Congratulations, Your Grace," he said the title deliberately, wanting to impress upon Justin Maddox the solemnity of this moment.

The new Duke of Colster's response was to look at his twin as if completely stunned by what had been done.

And well he should be, Hawkesbury thought. *It was a damnable mess, and it was all his fault . . .*

The Sword

The man who held the Sword of the Mac-Kenna had the power to lead a rebellion.

Justin Maddox, newly named Duke of Colster, sat alone in the London home that had been owned by a long line of dukes of Colster before him. This evening, with a stroke of a pen, it had become his.

The hour was late. His brother, Phillip, had long ago taken his wife, Charlotte, and gone to his bed. Phillip appeared completely at peace with the decision.

Justin wasn't. He couldn't sleep. His mind was restless with worries until, at last, he'd had no choice but to take out the sword, holding it in his hand and testing its weight.

He was no duke. He'd been a blacksmith. The truth of his trade was now shown in his admiration for this weapon. Fire from the hearth played across the sword's wickedly sharp blade. Here was a weapon worthy of Vulcan's art. A perfectly balanced instrument of death.

Nor was he an Englishman. No swipe of the pen could erase years of living among the Highlanders.

And now here he was—betwixt and between: An Englishman who thought like a Scot. A blacksmith who was expected to be a duke . . . and he'd never be one. Not truly. It had taken a lifetime for Phillip to learn what he must know.

Justin closed his fingers around the scarlet leather handle, conscious of the greatness of the men who had wielded this sword. They'd been good men, honest, brave, and willing to lay down their lives for freedom's cause.

The bloodred rubies decorating the hilt winked at him in the firelight. They asked who he thought he was to take up such a weapon.

Justin didn't know.

He was certain that if he let this sword out of his possession, it could mean the destruction of Scotland—and that must never happen. He'd cut his teeth on the dream of rebellion. His heart pounded not only for freedom but also for justice.

Even as a blacksmith, he had practiced a warrior's code. He had lived and trained for the day he could prove himself in battle.

But life had delivered a strange twist.

He was now an English duke. He lived in London, amid the Sassenach. He saw how powerful they truly were and knew his beloved Highlanders would never stand a chance. The brutality known as the Clearances, by which families were run off their ancestral lands, burned out, or murdered if necessary, for the sake of money, would be nothing compared with what the English would do in response to rebellion.

This sword was nothing but cold metal, and yet the Scots' imagination had made it a legend, an icon. Men would kill to possess this sword, but even more would be killed if it fell into the wrong hands.

Phillip pretended it wasn't important, but Justin knew it was on his mind. His twin, ever the diplomat, was just biding his time before he'd ask for it. Phillip had no divided loyalties.

For that reason, Justin carefully placed the Sword of the MacKenna on a velvet cloth and wrapped it tight. He had to find a place to hide it, a place where no one would think to look—and it must be done tonight.

He searched the room. There was nothing here. He walked from one room to the next, searching until he found the right place. A new hearth was being built in the study. At one time this room had been a kitchen. Over the years and many re-modelings, it had been turned into the handsome, book-lined study it was today.

However, the hearth had retained its over-large size, a reminder that it had once been filled with bubbling pots and pans.

The marble mantel Phillip had imported from Italy had been carved specifically for the room's large hearth. It was so heavy, the workers had to assemble it in pieces.

Justin decided to finish the job for them.

In the end, it was relatively simple. He had the skill to create the hiding place and the strength to lift the mantel's shelf and seal it in place.

By morning, no one entering this room would notice anything amiss.

The Sword of the MacKenna's whereabouts would be his secret, its fate his burden.

Chapter 1

The London residence of
  Mr. and Mrs. Maximus Dunroy
October 1, 1807

*F*rancesca Dunroy waited for Lord Penthorpe, the most disreputable rake in London, in the darkness of the terrace outside her
father's library, the only relatively private place in
a house bursting with guests, laughter, and music. She'd sent him a note, imploring His Lordship
to meet her. He was late. He was making her cool
her heels, knowing, as she did, that with one word
he could ruin her.

For the hundredth time she wondered *why* she
had been foolish enough to trust him, and knew
the answer—because her father would never have
approved of him.

Her life until now had been very sheltered.
She'd truly been unprepared for the onslaught of

feelings Penthorpe's secret, dashing, whirlwind courtship had inspired. He was the very opposite of the prosaic young men who wanted her hand for no other reason than her inheritance. He made her feel beautiful. He had all the right words . . . and she'd even imagined herself in love with him. His attentions had been a ray of shining hope in a world too long confused and saddened by her mother Grace's long sickness and eventual death.

Caring for her mother, honoring her, had delayed Francesca's presentation to society. At four and twenty, an age when most unmarried women are ready for the shelf, she'd found herself being presented with girls some five years younger than she. Francesca had felt awkward and alone. The marriage mart was a competitive experience. The other girls, no matter what their age, had not liked the competition of an heiress.

Of course, her father had made it easy for them to shut her out.

Max Dunroy was considered personally unacceptable among the hostesses of the *ton*. Grace had been one of their most respected and admired members. They had been scandalized that Max hadn't waited even a month to marry Regina, who was a year younger than Francesca.

To demonstrate their displeasure, those powerful hostesses, led by Lady Bastone, had closed their doors against Max and Regina, who so dearly wanted to be one of their number. This ostracism also included Francesca.

Was it any wonder then that she had fallen into Penthorpe's trap?

After all, he knew how to charm a woman. He spoke to her as if she had the freedom and intelligence to make her own choices. It was heady stuff. And so, when he'd suggested she visit his private apartments where they could speak freely and without prying ears and eyes, Francesca had recklessly agreed.

Two days ago, thinking herself safe because it was the middle of the afternoon, she had disguised herself in boy's clothes and, with the help of her maid and a footman, snuck out of her house without alarm. She'd anticipated a lark, an adventure.

Instead she'd met disaster.

Penthorpe had not wanted some innocent meeting. He'd wanted to elope, a step she hadn't been ready to take. Perhaps she would have run away with him if he'd been willing to wait a week or a month or even a year or two.

He hadn't been willing to delay two seconds.

He'd wanted her fortune.

And when she'd refused to leave with him, he'd attempted rape to force her.

Only her quick wits and a well-aimed kick had protected her virtue.

Now Francesca rubbed a finger along the smooth granite of the terrace balustrade, aware of what risk she took in meeting him alone again, especially under her father's roof . . . but she had no choice. She'd had to find safe ground to confront him and ask him to return her mother's necklace.

It was a gold chain with a black pearl pendant. The pearl was priceless and made even more so because it was the first gift her father had given her mother. Her mother had passed it on to her only daughter the night of her death, and Francesca had not taken it off since that moment.

Apparently, during the struggle with Penthorpe, the chain had broken. Francesca hadn't discovered its loss until she'd returned home.

She had to have it back. Not only was it her most cherished possession, it was also proof that she had been in Penthorpe's private rooms.

A burst of laughter from the garden beyond had her stepping back into the corner of the terrace where the shadows were deeper and reminded her the house was full of people.

Originally this evening had threatened to be a ruin. Regina had taken a flea in her ear that if the matrons of society would not invite her to their homes, she would invite them. She'd decided to hold a ball that would outshine anything London had ever witnessed before. She'd chosen the Arabian Nights as her theme, and Francesca's father had poured barrels of his money into making the evening a success.

However, the women of the *ton* were a formidable force. Led by Francesca's mother's dear friend Lady Bastone, they had looked down their noses at Regina's invitation. One after another had sent their regrets until it had appeared as if no one would attend. Regina had been an absolute demon to live with as she'd faced the possibility of being completely humiliated.

And then Lord Phillip, the man who had recently given up the title of duke to his long-lost twin brother, had responded that he, his new wife, and the newly named duke would attend.

It was the coup of the Little Season.

For the past month, the *ton* had been abuzz with speculation about this Scottish duke. Few had set eyes on him. And now, for whatever reason, he had accepted Regina's invitation. Suddenly her Arabian Nights ball was *the* event. Those who had sent regrets begged to be included. Those who had not been invited came knocking on Regina's door, hoping to receive an invitation.

Max Dunroy and his wife had been so busy basking in their new popularity, it had been easy for Francesca to slip away to meet Penthorpe. Too easy, indeed.

At least Lady Bastone had still refused to attend. Francesca's mother had one friend who was incorruptible ... although Francesca missed the company of this woman who was also her godmother—

The door in the library opened.

Penthorpe had come. At last. Panic welled in her throat at seeing him again.

The door closed.

She sensed his progress through the library. She heard the faint movement of his steps across the room's thick Indian carpet. He didn't walk out to the terrace immediately but paused in front of the fire. On this side of the house, away from the merriment of the ball, there was no light other than that small blaze in the hearth inside and the slip of a moon in the sky outside.

Her heart pounded. She stepped back into the shadows, toward the ivy-covered brick where the terrace railing met the house. Her original plan had been to firmly demand the pearl, threatening to have the servants toss him out if he refused.

Now she realized such a plan wouldn't work. He knew she wouldn't call the footmen because then her father would learn the truth.

Francesca was surprised to realize that, in spite of her anger at her father for betraying her mother's memory and marrying so quickly, she didn't want to disappoint him with her own foolishness. Nor did she want anyone else to know how stupidly she had behaved over a rake.

No, she was going to have to cajole the necklace from Penthorpe. She must appeal to his vanity, make him believe she'd had a change of heart. She would have to seduce him into giving her the pearl. It was the only way that would work.

There was a footfall. He was coming toward the terrace door.

Her breath caught in her throat. She took another step back into the corner, not wanting him to see her first.

A cloud covered the moon. His shadow darkened the door, blocking the light from the hearth. Framed as he was, he appeared taller and larger than she remembered.

He stepped out onto the stone terrace.

Francesca didn't dare breathe.

He moved toward the balustrade. He was dressed in black, relieved only by the snowy white of his neck cloth. Tension radiated from him. He braced the railing with both hands and appeared for a moment as if he wished for nothing more than to jump over it and escape into the night. It was as if something weighed heavily on his mind. Perhaps he regretted what had happened between them—?

Her moment had arrived. *God give me strength.*

She moved forward, her kid dancing slippers making barely a whisper of sound—and yet he'd heard her.

He started to turn.

Quickly she slipped her arms through his and around his waist to hold him in place. Pressing her breasts against his back, she whispered, "At last you've come"—even as she realized his shoulders really were broader than she remembered.

And it hadn't been her imagination. He *was* taller. And more muscled . . . and even smelled differently.

Penthorpe preferred perfume water and cologne. This man smelled of himself, spicy, warm . . . masculine.

This man *wasn't* Penthorpe.

The realization so stunned Francesca, she couldn't think fast enough to untangle her arms before he turned, taking *her* in *his* arms.

His head a silhouette against the night sky, his face a shadow, he said, "If I'd known you were waiting for me, lass, I'd have been here sooner." His rolling Scots brogue confirmed her worst fear.

Before she could issue protest or apology, his lips came down over hers.

Chapter 2

*F*rancesca's first instinct was to push him away.

This was not what she'd wanted, what she'd planned. She attempted to lift her arms, but found herself trapped in his embrace. She couldn't even manage to protest. This man's mouth was hungry, demanding . . . and knew how to kiss.

That last realization burrowed its way into her consciousness, *tempting* her.

She'd been kissed before. Penthorpe had kissed her every chance he could. His had been sloppy, overeager kisses that she had thought she'd liked rather well—until this kiss.

Francesca found she couldn't resist lingering

just a moment for a sample. It was wicked of her, and her undoing.

This man's lips were firm and yet soft, yielding without being eager or anxious. He expected her to come to him, and, inexplicably, she did so.

Their mouths fit.

Their bodies fit.

Their tongues met.

At the first sensation of being this close, this intimate, Francesca surprised herself by not panicking. Instead she was instilled with an awareness that this was right. This was as it should be.

His hand slipped lower, past her waist to cup her hip, bringing her closer to his heat. Her breasts grew full, tight, hard. It felt good to rest their weight against the flat planes of his chest.

She turned her head, the better to explore and taste him. His mouth tasted of her father's iced champagne. His legs were strong, his arms protective.

Here was the forbidden male flesh. It was all the more intriguing because of the night air and the moonlight. They were alone, and yet not alone. The sounds of music punctuated by conversation and laughter were close and yet far away from this private expanse of terrace. It was almost as if she'd discovered her own secret Garden of Eden.

His lips left hers. She started to protest but then

he found her ear—and Francesca thought she would shoot straight to the heavens from the sensation. Who would have thought a mundane, serviceable ear could be such a lightning rod for bliss? She would stand here all night if he would kiss and touch her this way. She'd do more than stand. She'd beg, plead, sob—

"Justin?" The authoritative male voice from the other room was her first warning that she and her newfound lover were not alone. She'd been so involved in what he'd been doing to her, she'd not even heard the library door open.

Her companion broke off the kiss with a quiet sound of irritation. He resented the intrusion as much as she and pulled her into deep shadows, returning her to the corner where she'd only moments ago waited for Penthorpe.

"Don't speak," the soft burr of his voice whispered against her ear. "Don't even breathe."

Francesca was happy to obey. She had no desire to be caught out on the terrace kissing a stranger. However, here, in the haven of this man's body heat, she felt almost invisible. No harm would could come to her in his arms.

On the other side of the wall, their unwelcome guest moved toward the door. If he stepped out on the terrace he would be able to stretch out his arm and touch them. But he didn't take that one step.

Instead he stopped in the threshold. He waited a

beat in silence before saying with no small amount of exasperation, "I know you are here somewhere, Justin. I can sense your presence."

The man holding her went so still, she knew he was Justin.

Francesca leaned her head against his shoulder, wrapping her arms around his waist. She could hear the beat of his heart. Its quickened rhythm matched her own. Neither of them wished discovery.

The man in the room released his frustration. "Damn it all. This is nonsense. Complete rubbish. If you are angry, *talk* to me. I hate your damn Scots brooding." He paused. When there was no response, he changed tactics. "You are right. I shouldn't have brought up the subject of you remarrying when I did. Charlotte told me to leave the subject alone, and a man—a *wise* man—should always listen to his wife. And I know this is hard," he said, turning back toward the library as if thinking Justin hid there. "I can't help that there are boorish idiots in that ballroom who ask questions and say things that are none of their business. I'd thought this would be a much smaller affair, and that's why I'd accepted this invitation. I had not thought to throw you into the lion's den. But together we can brazen this out, Justin. Together we can make them respect you. Besides, there are people—*men*," he quickly amended, "no, women, in that ballroom you must meet. I want to introduce you to them."

He paused, waiting for an answer.

Justin didn't move. If Francesca hadn't been holding him, she could have imagined him turned to stone.

A long silence followed. The man in the library seemed to plumb the air with his mind . . . only now she sensed he wasn't as certain Justin was here.

He broke the silence, speaking to himself. "God, I don't know why I bother. He can be a stubborn bastard." And yet he wasn't a man to give up. Raising his voice, he said, "I suggested you might *think* about marriage. It wasn't one of those orders you complain about me giving all the time. But you can't continue to tomcat your way around. It doesn't suit you, Justin. You're a better man than that. There, that's all I have to say," he concluded as if remembering he had promised not to press. He began walking toward the library door, and the tension in Justin's body relaxed.

Well, parts of him relaxed. The "tomcat" comment made Francesca aware of more than Justin's kisses. He was hard. She could feel the shape and length of him even as his hand moved up to her breast.

Francesca captured that wandering hand before it went too far. His lips curved into a smile against her skin, and he raised his thumb and circled her nipple.

She gasped, the sound freezing in her throat when the library door opened. They were not yet alone.

And yet, instead of the gentleman in the other room leaving, a new voice spoke.

Penthorpe's voice.

"I beg pardon—" Penthorpe broke off as recognition arrived. "Lord Phillip, I didn't mean to almost bowl you down. I wasn't expecting anyone to be on this side of the house. Everyone is enjoying themselves in the ballroom."

Penthorpe was here—and she could do nothing to call attention to herself without revealing her identity to Justin or what she'd been doing with him out on the terrace to Lord Phillip and Penthorpe.

It also dawned on her exactly who Justin was. He was the Duke of Colster, her stepmother's prize guest. And his thumb was dueling with her nipple.

Where had her good sense gone? If she was discovered, her father would be furious. He might even send her away.

She was shocked at herself.

Lord Phillip knew Penthorpe. There was a coldness in his voice as he said, "No harm was done. I stepped back before the door hit me. Now if you will excuse me?"

But Penthorpe was unwilling to let the other man leave. "That was a dramatic turn of events, you discovering you had a twin brother." Francesca could picture him standing his ground in front of the door, refusing to let Lord Phillip escape. "Devilish bad luck to lose the title to him. I hope he didn't take all the money, too."

"I don't discuss my brother's business," was the terse reply.

"But to give up a dukedom—?" Penthorpe let his own wistful wishes finish the thought. "Damning bad luck."

"A man of honor does what is right," Lord Phillip answered.

"He's my neighbor, you know," Penthorpe said.

"My brother?"

"Yes, we have the two apartments in the building. We're on the same floor." When Lord Phillip didn't comment, Penthorpe continued awkwardly, "He owns the building, you know."

"I do know," Lord Phillip answered. "I'm very aware of the Duke of Colster's holdings, although not as informed as I should be as to who the tenants are." His response was a direct slap at Penthorpe. He added thoughtfully, as if struck by a new thought. "Do you have business in the library?"

"Business? Um, no."

"You weren't coming here to meet my brother?" Lord Phillip didn't wait for an answer but charged forward. "Stay away from my brother, Penthorpe. Keep yourself and your gaming cronies far from him or you'll answer to me."

Penthorpe laughed. "Your brother is a duke now. He can take care of himself."

"So he tells me. But you and I know how disreputable you are. Step out of line with him and I'll crush you."

Justin was not pleased with the threat. His hand had curved into a fist. For a second, Francesca thought he would storm into the library. She tugged on his jacket, begging him not to reveal they were there. He eased back.

Lord Phillip followed his threat with a pleasant "Shall we return to the ballroom? Our hosts will wonder what has become of us."

"I believe I'll enjoy a moment alone in the quiet," Penthorpe answered stiffly.

There was a beat of silence. Francesca could tell that Lord Phillip believed that even his suggestions should be obeyed.

But then, he had no sway over Penthorpe. "Very well. If you will excuse me—" This time Lord Phillip made it out the door. He shut it firmly behind him.

Penthorpe didn't waste time letting his true feelings be known. "Bastard. You look down your nose at me. You are the bloody idiot who gave up a dukedom." The sound of footsteps moved in the direction of the fireplace. She heard the scrape of objects against the carved marble mantel and could imagine him appraising the bronze obelisks sitting there.

And then he began walking toward the terrace door.

She shrank back into the corner. Justin leaned close as if hiding her from view. There was no coyness about him now. He truly was protecting her.

"Where are you, Francesca?" Penthorpe asked, more to himself than expecting her to answer. He was at the terrace door . . . but he did not step out. Instead he leaned against the door frame as if enjoying the night but unwilling to go out in it. She could see his sleeve, part of a leg and foot, his nose.

She closed her eyes as if to ward off the possibility of his taking one more step and coming outside.

Justin held her tight.

Penthorpe released his breath with a sound of annoyance. "Is she playing me dirty or could she not slip away?" He drummed his fingers on the door frame, debating the question. "Well, I may have to go to her."

To Francesca's relief he pushed away from the door, going back inside. His footsteps were muffled by the carpet as he walked to the door.

The door opened.

Francesca caught her breath, waiting.

The door closed.

There was no further sound.

"Finally we're alone," Justin said. He lowered his head toward hers—but Francesca was ready for this. She ducked and slipped under his arm. He reached to pull her back by the waist but she turned, escaping his hold, and hurried into the library.

She started to raise a hand to check her hairstyle for loose pins and then realized her hair wasn't a worry, not with the laces undone down the back of her gown.

How had he done that so fast? While he was kissing her, his fingers had unlaced down to her waist. Frantically she reached to pull her laces tight.

"Do you need help, Francesca?"

Startled, she whirled to face him.

He stood in the doorway, the soft light from the hearth highlighting his strong jaw and straight nose. His eyes were dark and his hair as black as night. He was a handsome man, not as pretty as Penthorpe but far more appealing. He smiled. *The devil was in that smile.*

"How did you know my name?" she demanded.

"Wasn't it Penthorpe you were to meet? I heard him call you by name. I felt your reaction, too, lass."

"I—I wasn't here to meet him," she lied.

He shrugged as if it made no difference. "Your hair is like red gold," he purred, his voice husky. "Are your eyes green like jealousy, or the blue of a summer's day? I can't tell in the firelight. Come closer, lass, and let me see. There is nothing beyond this room for either of us that won't wait until we've enjoyed a bit of pleasure."

Shame flooded through her—especially because she was tempted. "Stay back," she ordered while her fingers became tangled in the bow she was attempting to tie behind her back.

He held up his hands, a sign he had no tricks. "I've not come forward. You come to me."

Francesca's throat went dry. She swallowed. "I can't. I shouldn't."

"Of course you should, Francesca. We were just beginning to know each other."

Her mother would never have behaved as she had out on the terrace. Her mother had been the perfect model of a lady. She hadn't had untamable curly hair, or an independent spirit, or a desire, no, a *need* to be in control of her own life. Her mother had always deferred to her husband, even when he was unreasonable, whereas Francesca and her father battled at every turn, especially since he'd married Regina.

And the worst part was, Francesca would like nothing better than to walk back into the Duke of Colster's inviting arms. She wanted him to kiss her ear and nibble her neck and undress her completely—

It was the brogue, she decided. It made anything he said the sound of seduction itself.

It made him *dangerous.*

"I have to go," she answered, her voice barely able to speak beyond that dry throat. She stepped back, her fingers finally able to tie the bow of her laces tight. "Perhaps another time." She bumped the door and then quickly turned and yanked it open before she changed her mind.

She charged out into the hallway, anxious to escape—and walked right into Penthorpe.

Chapter 3

I knew you were in there," Penthorpe said with a note of triumph. He leaned one hand against the door frame, preventing her escape. "Were you hiding from me?"

Francesca leaned against the door, grabbing the handle with one hand behind her back, afraid Justin would attempt to come out. She prayed there was enough sense and kindness in him to realize they mustn't be caught having been alone.

"You were late," she answered, turning the tables on Penthorpe with accusations of her own. She just wished her voice wasn't so breathless. It made her sound guilty.

"That other gentleman, Lord Phillip, came in," she said, "and I didn't believe it wise we be caught meeting together. After all, I should be on the other side of the house greeting the guests."

"Why didn't you come out once you knew I was alone?"

She didn't need to lie for this answer. "You sounded angry. I thought it not wise."

Penthorpe's brows came together. He didn't trust her any more than she trusted him. It was painful to be confronted by what a bad judge of character she was. She had allowed his "handsomeness" to blind her to his many flaws—

The door handle she held with her hand behind her back began to turn.

She gripped it tighter. *Please wait.*

The handle stopped turning. The duke understood.

She could have dropped to her knees in thankfulness.

"Is something the matter?" Penthorpe asked. "You appear . . ." He paused for the right word. "Strained."

"What could be the matter?" she answered tartly, trying to relax her features. All she could manage was a "strained" smile. "Other than that we shouldn't be seen together.

"Then let's go in the library—"

"No," she said too quickly. She wet her lips. She had to keep her wits. "I should return to the ballroom." She nodded in the direction of the music and laughter at the far end of the hall. "I've been away too long—waiting for you, I might add—and Father will notice that I'm missing. Come, let's join the others." She didn't wait for his response but started to move down the hall when he stopped her in her tracks by saying, "What of the pearl? Is it no longer of importance to you?"

"It's mine," she said. "You have no claim to it."

A speculative gleam appeared in Penthorpe's eye. "And I'd be most happy to return it . . . for a price."

Francesca felt the color drain from her face. "I will not elope with you."

"After the vicious way you attacked me, I'd never offer marriage. But that doesn't mean you don't have something else I want."

She thought of Justin on the other side of the door. She prayed he couldn't hear any of this. Lowering her voice, she asked, "Then what do you want?" She feared the answer.

He smiled, the expression only making his silver eyes colder. "It's not what you believe. I've decided I'm not fond of redheads."

"I don't know how I ever thought you a gentleman or that I had any feeling for you," she replied, infusing each word with her dislike and disappointment in him.

Penthorpe laughed softly. "I'm not a gentleman,

Francesca. You've had plenty of warning, although you should have noticed that yourself from the beginning."

He was right. "What is your price?"

The rake considered her thoughtfully before answering, "One thousand pounds."

"One thousand—" she repeated, dumbfounded. She turned toward the wall, toward the door, toward the hall that led to the ballroom. "I don't have a thousand pounds," she whispered when she could speak again.

"Your father does."

"I could never ask for it." He would expect a reason for the request, and Francesca didn't know if she could bear the scrutiny.

"Then pay me yourself," Penthorpe said easily. "Won't you inherit tens of thousands upon marriage? Marry. I'm a patient man. I'll wait for my money. Of course, if you don't pay me soon, the price may rise. The longer you make me wait for my money, the more it will cost you." He smiled, taking no pity on her. "Actually, you are fortunate I'm not already doubling the figure after the way you almost gelded me the last time we were together."

"I wish I had," she answered.

Penthorpe laughed, obviously enjoying having her at his command. "Don't make this so difficult,

Francesca. After all, your father has spent twenty times my number on this evening's festivities. He would never notice a thousand missing."

"You would ask me to steal from my own father?" How could she ever have thought Penthorpe attractive?

"Or you could let me have the necklace?" His Lordship suggested. "I've no jeweler's eye but I imagine it is worth a fortune more than what I ask in ransom."

He was right.

And she must have the necklace back. Her father had already noticed she wasn't wearing it. She'd told him the chain was broken . . . but she knew that soon, especially once the hubbub of the ball was over, he would realize she had several gold chains she could have used to wear it. Or he would insist on having it repaired—

"I'll need a bit of time," she said. Time would give her a chance to think and not give in to the hysterics she was feeling.

Penthorpe took a step closer. "I'm happy to give you time," he said. "What say we discuss this matter again in a week?" He ran the backs of his fingers down the side of her face. "You can come to my apartments. You know where they are located."

Francesca struggled to hide her revulsion. "I thought you didn't admire redheads."

"I can overcome an aversion when I meet one who needs a bit of taming."

Instinctively Francesca raised her knee, but Penthorpe evaded the move, mocking her with his soft laughter. "I'm wiser around you now, Francesca. I know your tricks. That wisdom adds a bit of challenge to our dealings. Until next week then." He moved past her, heading to the end of the hall and the ballroom.

At that moment a group of gentlemen came into view at the end of the hall. Some had their hats, prepared to leave.

"Penthorpe," one called, "we've been looking for you. There's a game at Garrison's tonight. High stakes. Are you in?"

"Of course I'm in," Penthorpe answered. "I'm feeling lucky tonight." He glanced back at Francesca, who turned away, embarrassed to be seen in his company. "What time are we gathering?" he asked his cronies.

"In a few hours. What say, one? I have to find Brackett. He said he wanted to join us if we met."

Francesca shut her ears to any response. Penthorpe had just turned her life inside out, and she didn't know what she could do about it.

The gentlemen moved on toward the house's grand foyer, steered there by Penthorpe. Of course, she realized bitterly, he didn't want others to link the two of them together. He couldn't blackmail her if the truth came out.

For a second she debated going to her father and telling all—and then dismissed the idea. Her pride rivaled his. She'd said harsh things about his marriage to Regina, had accused him of making a mockery of them all, and hadn't always behaved well to her stepmother. She didn't want him to know she was guilty of the same foolishness. It would be too humiliating.

And she wasn't entirely certain that, if he learned she had spent time alone in Penthorpe's apartments, he wouldn't make her marry the rake.

She'd take her own life before she let Penthorpe bed her—or come close to her inheritance.

It was true that she would be missed in the ballroom. She had been gone too long, but first she needed to talk to the duke. It was important to know what he'd overheard and what *his* silence would cost her.

Francesca opened the library door. "Your Grace?" she whispered, half anticipating that he'd be standing right on the other side.

He wasn't. Nor did he answer.

She went inside, searching the room with her eyes. The fire burned low in the grate. The soft, flickering light highlighted the furniture and walls. There was no sign of a tall man. She crossed to the terrace door and stepped outside.

The moon had come out from behind its bank of clouds, turning the terrace silver in its light. Francesca looked to the ivy shadows, expecting him to be there.

He wasn't. She was alone.

He'd gone . . . but she knew she would see him again. The question was when and where.

She wasn't certain she would like the answer.

Francesca went back inside, knowing the only other place she could look was the ballroom.

Chapter 4

Francesca. Even her name was seductive.

Justin had jumped the balustrade around the library terrace and now moved through Dunroy's garden toward the side of the house where paper lanterns were hanging in the trees outside the ballroom.

Earlier, he'd been determined to leave this house by any means necessary. This was his first London party and he hadn't liked it. It hadn't been like any dance he'd known in Scotland. There wasn't foot stomping and whiskey drinking. No, it was a collection of strangers pretending to be polite while they postured for one another. Several times this evening, his twin, Phillip, had warned in his ear to be careful of what he said in front of this one or that. Even the dancing was tame compared with a good night in Nathraichean.

And through it all, Justin had been aware that the other guests were watching and studying him. He was an oddity. The blacksmith who'd been named a duke. They all knew he didn't deserve the title. Phillip was the twin they respected.

Then, when Phillip had once again raised the subject of his making an advantageous marriage, Justin had lost it. He'd had to escape.

That's when he'd met Francesca on the terrace.

The evening had now changed. Justin had a reason to stay. He had to find Francesca and finish what they'd started.

In fact, Justin hadn't felt so energized and randy about a woman since he was fourteen. Phillip could accuse him of sleeping with women but the truth was, Justin had been very faithful to his wife. It was Moira who had left him.

She'd run off with Laird MacKenna's heir, Bruce. She'd fallen for his promises to make her a lady, and so he had. But even then, Justin had loved her enough to want her back. It had been Laird Mac-Kenna who had pushed him to divorce her, something he'd done against his will.

Of course, if she'd stayed with Justin, she could have been a duchess, an irony that had haunted him . . . until now. Until Francesca.

He had to see her again.

Justin wanted to touch her, to smell her, to hold her. He had to know if the connection of desire between them was as strong and real in candlelight as it had been out on the terrace under the moon.

And so he returned to the ballroom.

It bothered him a bit that she was one of Penthorpe's conquests. He and Penny were neighbors, but not friends. The man was too much of a rogue for Justin's comfort. However, the fact that Francesca had obviously planned on a clandestine meeting with the rake boded well for Justin's chances of bedding her.

Justin could have cleared a hedge in one leap in anticipation. Francesca knew how to kiss. Her unbridled response made him wonder what else she did well.

The garden on this side of the house was crowded with guests in search of a breath of fresh air or a private moment in the leafy shadows. Still, that didn't mean they didn't notice him.

Heading for the stairs leading up to the terrace outside the ballroom, Justin was conscious of the trail of whispers following him. He was walking back into gossip and curiosity surrounding him and his brother. It made him uncomfortable to be the center of so much attention.

He hoped Francesca was worth it.

Justin took the stairs and caught sight of Phillip

and his wife, Charlotte, standing with their heads together not far from the door. They were probably discussing him. It seemed to be their usual topic—and that, too, was irritating.

Excusing his way through the crowd of people congregating at the doorway, Justin made his way toward them.

Charlotte was a beautiful woman with blond hair, blue eyes, and an independent spirit, developed from her American childhood, that was more than a match for her husband's. Justin liked her . . . although since they'd arrived in London, she often took Phillip's side in every confrontation.

Well, that was to be expected . . . in a faithful wife. Moira had rarely agreed with him on anything.

"Do you know a young woman named Francesca?" Justin demanded without preamble.

"So you decided to return," his twin answered, annoyed.

"I thought that is what you wanted," Justin replied with his own touch of annoyance. Forget looks. The true difference between him and his brother was their temperaments. Justin thought of himself as more agreeable and even-tempered than his brother. Phillip expected his orders to be instantly obeyed. He assumed he would be obeyed. Consequently, Justin enjoyed thumbing his nose at his brother's high-and-mighty ways every chance he could—except for right now. Right now he was on the prowl for Francesca. "Do you know a Francesca?" he repeated.

This time his twin heard the name. His eyes widened in surprise. "Francesca?"

"Yes, Francesca. I don't know her last name," Justin said impatiently. "You know everyone. Have you heard of her?"

"Why, yes," Phillip answered, appearing completely puzzled. "I wanted to introduce you to her earlier."

"Introduce me?" Justin glanced at Charlotte. "I don't remember you saying the name Francesca."

Phillip released a sigh as if asking the heavens for patience. "I wouldn't call her by her given name. She's our host's daughter. The one I mentioned"— he paused as if realizing he trod on delicate ground—"might be a suitable wife for you. She is the reason I accepted this invitation for you. Of course, I had not expected this evening to be such a crush—"

"*Wife?*" Justin held up a hand to interrupt him. One of Penthorpe's women a suitable wife for a duke?

Several groups of the other guests congregating on the terrace looked up at his question. Justin lowered his voice, not wanting to be overheard. "This world is an odd one."

"What do you mean?" Charlotte asked.

Justin waved a hand to encompass the ballroom crowded with dancers and guests in their finery. They were all enjoying themselves on their host's champagne and punch, and the air was growing increasingly raucous. "You see them here," he said. "They've rules for everything. *Don't* do this. *Must* do that. And yet none of those rules apply to them if they have enough power and they wish to break them."

"You have enough power," Phillip reminded him.

"And no money." The fortune making the Duke of Colster one of the wealthiest men in England had been built by Phillip through wise investments. Justin had refused to accept any of that personal fortune. If his twin had been able to amass a fortune of his own making, then Justin would also.

"Remember, brother," Phillip said, moving closer so that he would not be overheard, "my first wife was an heiress."

"And this Francesca is?"

"Yes. She's Max Dunroy's daughter. He's our host."

Justin shook his head. He wanted to bed Francesca, not marry her—especially if she was one of Penthorpe's castoffs. That she would chase her lover under her father's own roof made his skin crawl. His lust for her died. "I'll earn my money, my way."

"But you should at least be introduced to Miss Dunroy," Phillip insisted. "After all, a moment ago you were searching for her."

"I've changed my mind," Justin answered

"But—" Phillip started, only to be interrupted by his wife.

"This is his first outing into society," Charlotte reminded her husband gently. "Perhaps it is best if we leave now and not do anything too ambitious yet."

"Exactly," Justin agreed. "I don't want to be ambitious, and I am tired." He feigned a yawn. "Let's leave now."

"We still must say good night to our hosts," Phillip reminded them, always the gentleman.

"They won't notice us missing with all these people swarming around," Justin assured him.

"You are the duke," Phillip said. "Everyone has had their eyes on you. We must say good night."

"Then let us make it quick," Justin responded gracelessly.

His twin made an annoyed sound but took his wife's arm and turned to survey the ballroom.

Justin wasn't about to wait. He started through the crowd, heading in the direction of the doorway. If Dunroy and his wife, whom he'd met when he'd first arrived, crossed his path, so be it. Otherwise he would be gone. He had no wish to cross paths with Francesca again. He'd already had one faithless wife in his life. He'd not have another.

"Where is that sister of yours?" he asked Charlotte as they wove their way through the guests.

"Which one?" she said. "Miranda and her husband, Alex, are supposedly returning from the Orient. Of course, we can't be certain exactly where they are."

"No, the unmarried one. The one you visited in Scotland."

"Constance?" Charlotte's smile widened. "She's still there. At Madame Lavaliere's Academy for Young Women. She makes it sound as if she's been imprisoned—"

"I would, too, if I was where she is," he murmured.

"She's fine," Charlotte insisted. "It's the safest place for her. They will teach her what she needs to know in order to be a great lady."

"Just as you and Phillip are attempting to do with me? Would it not be easier for you if you could send me off?"

Charlotte placed a hand on his arm, bringing him to a halt. Her voice low, she said, "I understand how challenging this must be for you." She glanced over her shoulder to see that her husband had been waylaid by a group of gentlemen. This was what always happened when Phillip went out. People sought his company. They only stared at Justin.

Seeing her husband occupied, Charlotte confided, "Sometimes Phillip is heavy-handed. It's just that he understands this world. He only wishes to smooth the path for you."

"He can't. If I am accepted, it must be for who I am, not for who my brother is."

"I understand," Charlotte said, "but then, I have siblings. Phillip is feeling his way, too, Justin. He's never had to consider someone other than himself. He's trying. He wants to be close to you."

Justin shook his head, not trusting himself to speak.

Charlotte understood. "Be patient with him. Please. I understand where his heart is because all too often I annoy my sisters for exactly the same reasons he is irritating you. I want what is best for my family, and, yes, I'll nag, cajole, and threaten my sisters to see they have the very best I can give them—which is one of the reasons I want you to move home."

"I like my apartments. I like my freedom."

"But we are family. Justin, your kidnapping was a crime, but those who did it continue to succeed as long as you and your brother remain at odds. Don't let MacKenna win. Return home. The house is yours. *You* should be living in it. Not us."

Her words touched him. *Family.* He understood the meaning of the word. He would have laid down his life for any of his clansmen, clansmen who had turned against him when they'd realized he was a Maddox and kin to the Duke of Colster.

But his brother would never turn against him . . . and perhaps that was why Justin tested him. And protected him.

He bent his head close to hers. "I didn't leave out of anger."

Her eyes widened in surprise. "You didn't? I thought after that argument you and Phillip had—"

"Phillip and I argue all the time." And then Justin realized he'd said enough. He wasn't going to tell her the truth, that he'd left to draw the attention of those who might be searching for the Sword of the MacKenna away from her and Phillip. His twin had already suffered enough because of him. "I needed my privacy. I needed space to breathe, to think."

Charlotte released a sound of relief. "I'd feared you'd left because of us."

"Well, it is difficult to listen to the two of you cooing over each other all the time," Justin said, only half teasing.

Her answer was a laughing frown for his impertinence, but then she turned the conversation back her way. Charlotte could be remarkably single-minded, and it was obvious she was determined to do what she could to bring the twins together. "Which is what Phillip suspected. Justin, when he talks of you remarrying, it is only because we both want you to find the happiness we've found."

"I had that once, Charlotte," he assured her.

"You could have it again—"

"One wife is enough for any man during his lifetime."

"Phillip had a first wife," she reminded him.

"Yes, but then you are a rare prize, Charlotte. There's not another woman on the face of this earth with your courage or your beauty. I understand why Phillip snatched you up—speaking of which, let's see if we can pull him away from those fellows. I want to leave."

But Charlotte couldn't be dissuaded from speaking her mind by a few compliments. "Don't you want children?" she asked quietly. "Don't you yearn to pass your title down through your line?"

Children. There had been a time, when he was married, that he'd prayed nightly for them. Fortunately, considering the turn of events, it had not happened. "I'll leave that to you and Phillip. The way you are going, I won't be surprised if I'm not an uncle within the next year."

"Justin," she chastised him, laughter in her eyes—and he felt a pang of jealousy so strong, it threatened to bring him to his knees.

Phillip did indeed have it all—an intelligent

wife who adored him, the respect of important men, and a future full of bairns.

He had to escape. *Now*. Phillip *did* have an uncanny way of reading his thoughts, something Justin constantly denied, and he didn't want his twin to know how much he envied him.

Justin turned and would have taken a step, except that in that moment the crowd parted to reveal Maximus Dunroy and his very young wife approaching. Dunroy was a tall, thin man with a shock of silver hair on his head and bushy brows over his eyes. His wife was a wide-eyed, syrupy sweet thing with blond hair.

They stopped, one bowing, the other curtsying. Justin didn't know if he'd ever become accustomed to the formalities. He felt awkward nodding back at them.

But before he could speak and say his good-byes, Dunroy said, "Have you met my daughter yet, Your Grace?" He didn't wait for an answer but stepped back to reveal Francesca standing behind him—and words died in Justin's throat.

Standing in the light of a thousand candles, Francesca Dunroy was absolutely stunning. Her mass of red-gold hair reflected the candles' soft glow. Her almond-shaped eyes were framed by dark, thick lashes. Her nose was straight but perfectly feminine, and her mouth was generous, her lips full, her smile wide.

No wonder she'd been able to kiss so well.

Justin felt rooted to the spot. He couldn't have moved if wild cannibals had been after him.

Her smile grew fixed. She wasn't pleased to see him, either.

"Your Grace," Dunroy said, "this is my daughter, Miss Francesca Dunroy. Francesca, the Duke of Colster."

She jolted into a curtsy as if remembering she must do so and Justin was mesmerized by the sight of her creamy breasts swelling over the virginally white muslin dress she wore. He imagined her nipples were pink, the sort a man could make rosy with his mouth.

Dunroy would run him through if he could read his mind.

It took him a moment before he realized everyone was waiting for a response from him. Mentally kicking himself, he took her gloved hand and helped her rise. As he did so, she gave his fingers a squeeze, a silent, urgent plea. For what? To be her accomplice to her indiscretions?

At that moment Phillip spoke. Justin had been so momentarily taken aback by Francesca's presence, he'd not even realized his brother had returned. "This has been an excellent evening, Dunroy, Mrs. Dunroy," Phillip said. "But we must make our farewells."

"So soon?" Dunroy questioned, his disappointment clear. "I was hoping that His Grace would have the opportunity to dance with my daughter."

Phillip opened his mouth. He was going to say the words that would allow them to gracefully take their leave.

However, Justin now had other plans. "I would like nothing better than to escort Miss Dunroy on the dance floor."

His twin cocked his head in surprise. But Justin didn't offer explanations. Instead he tucked Francesca's hand in the crook of his arm and swept her toward the dance floor.

After all, their earlier kiss had only whetted his appetite for more.

And if she thought Penthorpe a generous patron, wait until she learned what Justin could do for her.

Chapter 5

*F*rancesca was absolutely certain it was not wise for her to go off anywhere with Justin—

No, the Duke of Colster, she amended.

She had to think of him by his title. It reminded her that this wasn't just any man. He was her father and stepmother's guest of honor. His presence had saved them from public humiliation and made their ball a success.

And there wasn't one person in this mad crush of people who wasn't eyeing them as he led her out for a dance.

Except he didn't take her to the dance floor. He walked right by it, leading her toward the door going out into the garden.

"Aren't we going to dance?" she whispered.

"I don't dance. At least not like everyone is doing here," he answered without even so much as a look in her direction.

"But you asked me to dance."

"How else was I to have you alone?" he countered, his brogue rolling through her and making her catch her breath in her chest.

"Alone? Why?"

Now he looked at her, and in his dark eyes, she found her answer.

Francesca's first reaction was to reach out and place the flat of her hand against the jamb of the door leading out onto the garden terrace.

His Grace paused. Smiled. His smile transformed his face, made him appear younger . . . and more than a bit devilish.

She found herself following.

He moved with intent purpose and she had no choice but to walk by his side, aware of how many people on the terrace watched them make their way down the stairs and toward the garden.

It was well lit here. Regina had placed colorful paper lanterns in the trees. Small tables had also been set up, and a goodly number of guests nibbled on plates of delicacies from the supper room. A servant walked by with a tray of iced champagne and Francesca reached for one, needing it for fortitude and to have something, anything to keep between herself and the duke.

He moved toward the clump of pines by the corner of the garden wall. It was private there and dark. Too dark. She dug in her heels, conscious that Regina and her father had come out on the garden terrace to keep an eye on them. "We've gone far enough."

To her relief, he stopped.

She gripped the stem of her wineglass. "I fear you may have a wrong impression of me."

"And what impression would I have, lass?" he asked.

Francesca forced herself to be sensible. "We both know."

"Good. Then there isn't any need for games between the two of us," he said before, to her horror, he leaned down to kiss her.

She managed to duck that kiss, buying time by draining her champagne.

The problem was, she wouldn't have minded kissing him again. There wasn't a part of her that wasn't attracted to him. Not even Penthorpe had this effect on her.

At the thought of Penthorpe, she remembered his blackmail. Her attraction to the duke shriveled like dead leaves. She would not be played for a fool again. "I believe we should return," she said.

"Too many people are watching." She nodded toward the terrace where her father was in a discussion with Lord Phillip and several others, and would have turned away, but he had other ideas.

He laced his fingers in her own, stopping her from leaving. "Green," he said decisively.

The word caught her off guard. "What?"

"Green," he repeated.

"What's green?"

"Your eyes." He pulled her closer to him. "When I first met you, I imagined them blue. Instead, you've eyes the color of a spring meadow. You have lovely eyes, Francesca." His brogue made her name sparkle like water flowing from a fountain.

It took all her fortitude to keep her wits about her—especially when he started moving deeper into the shadows. Francesca stood her ground. "Why didn't you tell me you were the Duke of Colster?"

He stopped, their clasped hands stretched out between them. "You didn't ask."

"You didn't give me the opportunity to ask." Accusations felt good. They eased her own guilt over her behavior.

He laughed silently and moved back to her. "Who took advantage of whom? I went out for a breath of fresh air, and was delighted with the results. Could I help it if Penthorpe isn't an attentive lover?"

Francesca felt the color drain from her face. So he'd overheard her and Penthorpe in the hallway. No wonder he was being so aggressive in his intentions. He thought her just another of Penthorpe's conquests.

And here she was, out in the garden with him, confirming his worst thoughts of her.

Panic welled inside her. Her stomach tightened, and her first instinct was to escape. "I beg your pardon, Your Grace. I'm suddenly unwell." *Think,* she had to find some place to think clearly. She hadn't yet had a chance. Regina had found her after she'd left the library and insisted she return to the ball. There was someone her father had wanted her to meet.

Francesca could have laughed hysterically at what her father would think if he heard the duke now. Instead she turned to leave, but Colster still held her hand. "Let go of me," she ordered.

He frowned. "What's happened? Less than an hour ago, you were happy in my arms."

Her temper snapped. "You are just like him, aren't you? You think to blackmail me."

The duke released her hand. "Blackmail?" he repeated, sounding genuinely shocked by the word.

Francesca realized then that she might have revealed more than she should. Perhaps he hadn't heard *everything* Penthorpe had said. She pressed her lips together, turned to leave without saying more—

His hand caught her wrist, forming a tight band around it. She glanced toward the terrace to see if her father or anyone else noticed. They didn't. They were all involved in their own conversations.

"What is this about blackmail?" the duke demanded.

Francesca wasn't about to reveal more. One answer would lead to more questions. She didn't want the Duke of Colster prying into her affairs . . . especially when it was her own foolishness that had led her into trouble. "Let me go," she said quietly.

"Is Penthorpe threatening you?"

"No. Why should he do that?" she said quickly. "Please, we should return to the ballroom. We've been out here long enough."

But the duke wasn't interested in protocol. "Not until you answer my questions. You were meeting Penthorpe in that library. Why?"

Rebellion rose inside Francesca. She'd had enough of heavy-handed males. She was tired of her father's expectations of immediate obedience in spite of his own transgressions. She now had to cope with Penthorpe's ordering her around, knowing that if she didn't obey, he could disgrace her.

But she didn't have to answer to the Duke of

Colster. And she wouldn't. She felt great pleasure in saying, "It isn't your business."

A flash of anger lit his eyes. "It is if I make it so, lass."

"I am not your concern, Your Grace. And I won't ever be." The words were bold, but filled her with a sense of independence she'd not known before.

He scowled at her defiance. "What game do you play, lass? Do you pretend to be the milk-and-honey miss while betraying your father and taunting your lovers?"

Francesca jerked her wrist from his grasp. "How dare you?"

"How dare I? I'm not the one meeting scoundrels like Penthorpe under my father's roof. I'm not playing the debutante while offering my favors behind closed doors to any man who steps out on the terrace with me—"

Francesca slapped him. The sound of the flat of her hand striking his jaw resounded in the night air.

Perhaps if she'd been thinking more clearly, she would have questioned slapping a duke in such an open forum. As it was, she'd struck out, wanting not only to deny the conclusions he'd assumed but also to erase her own sense of guilt.

As it was, the sounds of several gasps not far from them made her realize they weren't as alone as she'd thought. Other couples had been out in the shadows of the garden with them. She'd been so involved with the duke, she hadn't registered their presence.

She did now.

Startled, she turned to see their expressions of surprise even as the duke raised his hand up to his jaw. He looked past her. She followed his sight and saw both his brother and her father charging down the steps toward them.

Colster's anger was a real and vital force as he said, "I didn't deserve that, Miss Dunroy."

He was right.

But Francesca didn't have the courage to admit it to him. She could barely face the truth herself.

Instead she took the only option available. She ran. Without speaking, she dashed past her father. She skirted the crowd in the ballroom as much as physically possible, ignoring Regina.

She didn't stop until she'd reached her room and shut the door.

Still, she wasn't safe there. This was a damnable mess. The duke wasn't responsible, nor was Penthorpe.

No, the reflection of the person accountable stared back at Francesca in the mirror over her dressing table.

Unfortunately, this was also the only person who could save her, too.

Francesca walked toward her reflection and set down the wineglass she'd carried all the way upstairs with her. She reached out to the slick glass and touched her face. The woman in the mirror appeared young . . . and uncertain. She couldn't be Francesca. Francesca felt so old—and angry.

Regardless of what had happened this evening, she wasn't beaten. If it was the last thing she did on this earth, she would retrieve that necklace from Penthorpe. She'd make him sorry he'd attempted to blackmail her. One way or the other, she would take his prize away from him.

And as for the Duke of Colster . . . ?

The Thames would freeze over before she would ever speak to him again.

Chapter 6

*J*ustin rubbed his jaw, watching Francesca run off like some frightened rabbit—and couldn't help admiring the fact that she had been the first person with *honest* emotion since he'd arrived in London.

Penthorpe. How could his irresponsible scoundrel of a neighbor catch something as lovely and graceful as Francesca Dunroy?

Women were idiots.

And apparently the ones who most attracted him were also whores.

Moira had left him for Bruce, a self-serving bastard if ever there was one, and here was Francesca waiting with bated breath upon Penthorpe's beck and call.

Dunroy reached him first. "Your Grace," he said, "are you all right? I don't understand what came over my daughter. She's usually the most biddable of young women."

Justin almost laughed. Only a fool would describe Francesca as "biddable." Then again, the man's eagerness to please irritated him. "If my daughter had slapped a man, I'd wonder what he'd done to deserve it."

"I'm certain you didn't do anything," Dunroy said.

"I'm standing in the garden with your daughter, man. Don't be daft."

Phillip arrived, overhearing the exchange and smoothly interjecting himself. "I'm certain it was a small misunderstanding."

"Absolutely," Dunroy agreed eagerly.

"What if it wasn't?" Justin said. "What if I deserved the slap?"

Dunroy's toadying smile turned to a frown, but it was Phillip who answered. "Then you apologize and assure our *host* no offense was meant."

"I'm sorry, Mr. Dunroy," Justin said, aping a broader brogue than usual because he was being irrational and knew it. "I regret any offense to your daughter."

"No harm done, I'm certain," was her father's reply.

Before Justin could take him to task, Phillip

said, "Dunroy, you need to see to your guests. Rumors will already have started, and we don't want the names of your daughter or my brother in the midst of speculation."

"What shall I do?" Dunroy asked, this concern apparently terrifying a man known for his ruthlessness in business.

"Act as if nothing is the matter," Phillip answered. "Here, shake my brother's hand, so all those craning their necks to watch us will see it. Then go inside and dance with your wife."

"And what shall he say about his daughter?" Justin wanted to know.

"He doesn't have to say much," Phillip said. "He can mention she wasn't feeling well and has taken to her room. Young women grow overwrought all the time. If the champagne keeps pouring, everyone will forget this *supposed* incident."

"You are right," Dunroy agreed, his expression grave. "I shall do it. We hold our heads high and carry on." He turned and walked back toward his party like a man heading off to do noble battle.

Justin could have gagged. "The man worries more about pleasing me than defending his daughter."

"I don't," Phillip answered and faced him. "I warned you that this wasn't one of your country dances."

Justin's temper, already dangerously close to the surface, bubbled over.

"What? You don't think I could have my face slapped in the country, too?" He shook his head. He'd always been a gentleman to the ladies. But something about Francesca favoring Penthorpe had brought out jealousy in him. A jealousy that still lingered . . . and he didn't like it. "Did you know she is one of Penthorpe's conquests?"

Phillip reared back. "Miss Dunroy? She couldn't be." He shook his head, denying the statement. "She is gently bred. An heiress. I'm certain she is watched."

"Oh yes, they are all bloody virgins in there," Justin said, waving a hand toward the ballroom. "Personally I prefer the ones with the chastity belts. It's more challenging."

"Be quiet. You've only slept with the widows. Don't think I haven't noticed. And you haven't taken one step close to a woman with a title or connections."

"Only because I haven't been introduced to any of them, brother," Justin informed him snidely. "Remember? It's only tonight, and for this function, you deemed me worthy."

"I thought it would be a smaller affair than what it is," Phillip admitted.

"And you did want me to meet the heiress. Well, I've met Miss Dunroy and I am unimpressed."

Justin felt good saying those words. Noble even. It was about time he looked down *his* nose at someone.

He just wish he'd meant them.

The irony was that Phillip, the twin who believed the two of them could mentally perceive what the other was thinking, agreed with him. "The two of you seem to have formed an immediate dislike."

"I'm glad you noticed."

Something about Justin's tone almost gave him away. Phillip cocked his head. His gaze narrowed. Justin changed the subject, attacking this society he was supposed to embrace.

"I don't like being here. I don't belong. I'm *not* one of them." He indicated the other guests with a nod toward the house.

"As you grow more accustomed to the way things are, you will find it more enjoyable," Phillip assured him.

"I don't *want* to enjoy it," Justin answered. "I am what I am, brother. You can put gloves on my hands, give me dancing lessons, tutor me for hours on politics and manners, but I will still be the same. I'm a man who works with my hands, not my brains."

"That's not true," Phillip answered. "You are very intelligent, and there are other marriageable young women. And I'll help you build your fortune. Together we can do it."

"To what purpose?" Justin asked, letting his exasperation be known. "You can train a monkey to do what I've been learning, and to do it better. I want more, Phillip. I want to believe that all I've been through means something."

"It will," his twin insisted. "But you must be patient." He paused a beat before adding, "It would also help if you would return home."

"Yes, so you can supervise my every move and thought—"

"I'm only attempting to help—"

"Then let me be. Give me my lead. Perhaps what I'm supposed to do as duke isn't what you did."

"What I did is what a man owes his title. It's what Father expected."

"Well, I didn't know him, so I couldn't say," Justin answered.

The reminder of how different their childhoods were made Phillip flinch as if he'd been physically struck—and Justin realized this was the heart of the matter.

"We don't speak about this, do we?" he asked Phillip. "We pretend as if all could be made right. It can't, Phillip. We may be twins but the differences between us are too distinct."

"That's not true—"

"*The devil it isn't.*" Justin shook his head, taking a step back. "We've avoided discussing this—and I don't know if we should now."

"You are my brother," Phillip stated.

"I'm the man who has denied you your title, your whole reason for being," Justin insisted. "You should be bloody mad at me. Especially when you can do this all so much better than I."

"I've done what is right," Phillip said, and Justin had an irrational desire to strike at him.

"Aye, it may be right but you were still cheated."

"No more than you were."

Justin shook his head, struggling to keep his temper intact. "Here's the gist of it, man. If you can accept this, then you are either a saint or a martyr. As for myself, I don't know who I am anymore." His brogue was growing broader, but Justin didn't care.

He glanced at the lit house, saw Charlotte anxiously waiting for them on the terrace, and knew he couldn't go back in there. There was a stepping-stone path leading into the trees. Justin would stake a bet they led to a back gate for the walled garden. He turned and started following them.

"Where are you going?" his brother demanded.

"Back to my apartments."

"Shouldn't you say good night to our hosts?"

"I should," Justin said without looking back. He'd been right. He caught a glimpse of a door in the high brick wall. "But I won't. You say it for me. You know the right words." The last he'd said for no other reason than to irritate his brother. It was petty . . . unnecessary, but said nonetheless. Perhaps if Phillip had called him on it, he would apologize.

Instead his brother said, "What of your hat?"

"I don't need it." The last thing Justin cared about was a bleeding hat.

"Are you going to take the carriage? How will Charlotte and I return?"

Justin turned long enough to say, "Don't worry, then. I'll walk."

Phillip swore softly under his breath. The words didn't surprise Justin as much as how long it had taken for his brother to reach this point. "You can't walk all the way to your apartments. That's at least five miles. Wait, and Charlotte and I will return with you. It will give us a chance to discuss the evening."

Justin paused. "Phillip?"

"Yes?"

"Sod off."

With that, Justin unhooked the latch and let himself out. On the other side of the gate, his first act was to loosen the knot in his neck cloth. He wanted a drink and he wanted something more than French fizzy water.

He wanted a good whiskey.

Justin walked to the end of the alley behind the row of palatial houses. This was an older section of the city, and the properties were larger here.

Out on the street, the coaches of Dunroy's guests were lined up, waiting for their masters.

Clarens, the Colster coachman, saw him approach. He hopped up into the box while Danny, the Colster footman, opened the coach door.

"I'm walking," Justin told them as he passed.

"To your apartments, Your Grace?" Clarens asked.

"Possibly," Justin answered. "But first I want to find a tavern house with a whiskey sharp enough to cut your tongue in half."

"Aye then, you'll be wantin' to go to the Three Princes," Danny said.

Justin came to a halt. "Is it close?"

"We can drive you there and be back before Lord Phillip even knows we are gone," Clarens promised.

Justin shut the coach door and grabbed ahold of the edge of the box. He climbed the steps and swung himself into the seat beside Clarens. "Then let's be off," he ordered.

"Yes, Your Grace," Clarens answered. "Danny, you stay here in case Lord Phillip comes out looking for the coach." With a flick of the reins, they were off.

Sitting up on the seat, Justin enjoyed the feel of the wind in his hair and realized this was one of the few times it was good to be duke.

"That whiskey had better be good," he informed Clarens.

"It is, Your Grace. I've been needing to take you there since you first arrived in London."

Was it Justin's imagination, or did he hear a hint of the Highlands in the coachman's speech?

He shook the suspicion from his mind. He was so homesick, he was hearing things. Instead he glanced over his shoulder, back toward the Dunroy residence. *You are a coward, Francesca,* he silently told her. *A bloody coward.*

Francesca was in her night rail and pretending to be asleep when a knock sounded on her bedroom door. She wasn't going to answer. She'd sent her maid away with strict orders that she did not want to be disturbed.

As it was, Regina came charging in, a candle in one hand, without waiting for an invitation. She slammed the door shut as if to be certain the unmoving Francesca knew she was there. "The ball is still in progress."

"I'm not feeling well," Francesca answered, hugging her pillow and refusing to look at the woman. "Nor am I in the mood for you right now."

"You don't have a choice, *right now*," Regina countered, mimicking her. She moved to the edge of the bed, standing so that Francesca would have to roll over to avoid looking at her. "I've had enough of your high-handed ways, Francesca. I know you don't like me. I understand you think I'm too young to be your stepmother."

Francesca sat up. If she wanted this discussion, well, Francesca was in the mood to throw it back at her. "You may not be too young to be my stepmother," Francesca agreed. "But you are too young to order me around. I'm older than you and I refuse to listen."

"Well, if you are so mature," Regina said, "why are you pouting?"

"I'm not pouting. I was mourning," Francesca corrected. "You and Father have made a laughingstock of Mother's memory. All those people downstairs? They want a glimpse of the Duke of Colster. They don't care about you. Or me."

Regina didn't back down. "And slapping the duke in front of everyone was intended to do—what? Impress our guests? Show our breeding? Make him angry?"

Her point found its mark. Regret didn't set well with Francesca. She hid her doubts behind bravado. "He'll recover," she answered.

"Your father might not. You can think what you will of me, Francesca, but he deserves your respect."

Francesca feigned a yawn. "Obviously he

doesn't. Not if he didn't ask for my approval of his marriage."

The lines of Regina's face hardened. "You are so mean."

"You wanted me to stop pouting," Francesca reminded her.

Her stepmother turned, as if ready to flounce out of the room, but then she paused. "Continue with your airs, Francesca. Keep doing exactly what you are doing. We are of the same age, but I am your father's wife. No one can take that away from me, especially after tomorrow."

Francesca frowned. "Tomorrow? What's tomorrow?"

Regina smiled, the expression confident. "You'll have to wait and see, won't you? But let me tell you this, Francesca, I will win. Especially if you continue behaving like some spoiled, petted schoolgirl. It's your behavior that has made it so that your father barely hears you."

That was true. Hidden by the bedclothes, Francesca closed her hands into fists. "He was wrong to marry so quickly—"

"And so you are going to punish him for the rest of what—? His life? He's happy, Francesca. You are the one who is miserable."

There was an uncomfortable amount of truth in her stepmother's words. And what would Regina say if she learned about Penthorpe?

"I'm tired," she told her stepmother. "I wish to sleep."

"Oh yes, you can sleep," Regina said. "And then tomorrow we'll be up bright and early to pay a call on His Grace, the Duke of Colster."

"Why would I want to do that?"

"To apologize for creating a scene. Your father agrees. He said he'll see that you do it. He also noticed you weren't wearing his pearl pendant, and he is displeased."

"It isn't *his* pendant," Francesca said. "He gave it to Mother and she gave it to me. It's mine to wear when I please."

Regina shook her head as if Francesca were a child. What's worse, Regina made her feel like one, especially when she said, "You know what that pearl means to him. You are deliberately hurting him. I won't let you do that, Francesca. Think of me what you will, but I do love my husband. He's a kind man and doesn't deserve your spitefulness any more than he does Lady Bastone's."

"Lady Bastone was my mother's friend." She was also one of the few members of the *ton* who was not here this evening. The others had been too curious to see this new Duke of Colster. "It's hard for us, Regina, to understand why Father couldn't wait a decent mourning period before marrying you. Was that too much to ask?"

Now it was Regina's turn to look away . . . but

then she shrugged. "Your father isn't a young man. We didn't want to wait. We didn't feel we had time. After all, over the past five years, Max has lost both a son and a wife and I both my parents. Life is too short for mourning."

Francesca clutched the bedclothes. "But Father observed a decent mourning for David," she reminded Regina quietly. David had been two years older than Francesca. He'd gone out sailing with friends and had not come back. His death had thrown both her parents into despair. Her mother had fallen ill in her distress and never recovered, no matter how tirelessly Francesca had nursed her. "He didn't have to offend everyone over Mother. Then again, he had you to replace her."

There it was. She'd said it. Her deepest doubts about her father's remarriage.

"I don't replace anyone," Regina snapped. "And if you wish to behave like a spoiled, petted—"

"I am not spoiled."

"You aren't very wise about the world," Regina countered. "You have much to learn, Francesca. But I won't be the one to teach it to you. Go on then, bear your grudge against me and your father, but be careful. Your judgmental ways may leave you a spinster."

She spoke that last word as if it were a death sentence, and didn't wait for a response, but opened the door and left.

Francesca rose from the bed, marched over to the door, and slammed it shut.

The witch. Too restless for sleep, Francesca paced the room. She didn't know who made her angrier, Regina, the duke, or Penthorpe. She decided Penthorpe.

Francesca had once believed he'd honestly cared about her. His devotion had been a pretense. He wanted money. Well, he wasn't going to receive even so much as a penny from her. After all, she was her father's daughter. Maximus Dunroy wouldn't have sat back and allowed himself to be blackmailed, either.

So what could she do?

She walked to the window. Her bedroom overlooked the garden. It was just half past midnight. Most of the guests were still there. Those who had imbibed too much champagne laughed loudly on the back terrace.

No one gave a care for her.

Francesca sat on the window seat and pondered her problem. The one thing she could do to upset Penthorpe's plans was to steal the pearl back. He would lose all—no heiress, no one thousand pounds.

And that was exactly what Francesca knew she was going to do. Tonight, no less. After all, Penthorpe was out gaming. He wouldn't be home until dawn, or later if the rumors were true. If ever there was an opportunity to steal the pearl back, it was now.

It was a brazen move and one fraught with danger . . . but Francesca was not going to meekly accept his demands.

She rose from the window seat with renewed energy. In the bottom of her wardrobe was the boy's clothing she'd worn as a disguise to go to Penthorpe's apartments the other afternoon. Francesca picked up the leather breeches and rang for her maid, Rose. Rose's husband, Jeremy, a footman, had helped her sneak out of the house.

He could help her again.

Chapter 7

The Three Princes was a tavern located close to the docks. Torches by the front door provided the only light up and down the surprisingly busy and narrow street. A group of sailors with tarred pigtails stood out front involved in some boisterous, good-humored argument. From inside came the sound of male laughter and fiddle playing. It was a man's place and exactly what Justin needed to get pissing drunk. No one cared here if he was a duke or not.

He reached into his pocket. He carried two crowns. His estates might be cash-strapped, but he would spare this for a bottle and be bold enough to toss one of them to Clarens. "When you take the coach back for my brother and his wife, don't tell him where I am."

"Of course not, Your Grace."

Justin removed the gloves that had been annoying him all evening and tossed them and his neck cloth into the coach's cab. He motioned Clarens to leave and turned toward the tavern.

The sailors eyed him as he approached. They probably thought the soft leather dancing shoes he'd worn to the ball dandified. Justin would have agreed with them. He'd rather be wearing boots.

However, he was certain his height and strength would keep troublemakers at bay. He was right. The sailors stepped out of his way. He ducked under the low, narrow doorway.

Inside, the Three Princes was a rabbit warren of rooms. The ceiling was low, the lighting dim, and the tables and chairs full. Justin went from one room to the next until he found a place to stand by the tap.

The barman raised an eyebrow in his direction. Justin tossed the crown on the bar. The gold gleamed against the wood. "Whiskey."

The man nodded, scooped up the coin without offering change, and produced a pewter cup and a dirty bottle half full of the amber Scottish elixir of life. Justin wasn't usually a drinking man, but this was more than a wee nip. This was a link to his past. He uncorked the bottle, took a swig, and groaned his pleasure aloud as the smoky taste rolled over his tongue. It wasn't the best, but it wasn't the worst.

The whiskey slid down his throat, warming his body as it went.

How long had it been since he'd had a dram? How long since he'd been truly alone without servants or that annoying valet Biddle, or without feeling Phillip's disapproving stare? How long since he had felt free to be the man he once was? A man who knew nothing of titles, manners, or the chambers of Parliament—all information Phillip had been attempting to drill into Justin's head for weeks.

And perhaps because of all his twin's hard efforts, Justin toasted him by pouring another measure of whiskey into the cup. The barman started to take the bottle, but Justin stopped him with a hand around its neck. He'd paid enough for it and he'd not give it up.

The barman backed away.

A fight broke out between two men in the room by the door. Strong-armed barmen helped the lads out without fuss so they could settle their score out in the street.

Justin took his bottle and moved to the table they'd just vacated. It was close to the door. He threw himself down on the stool, leaned his back against the wall, and put his heels on the top of the stool across from him, a sign he wanted to be left alone. A lad or two eyed sitting at his table, took one look at him, and changed his mind.

The whiskey was starting to do the trick. Justin could feel his muscles relaxing. He was a man again. A grubby, hardworking, no-cologne-wearing man.

The sort of man who didn't care if he had offended Francesca or not.

If he wished, he could even return to being Tavis, the blacksmith. That had been the name he'd been given after the Lady Rowena had stolen him from his mother's breast. She'd pretended to be a midwife and had told his mother he'd died in childbirth.

Justin had known none of this or that he was a duke until close to two months ago when Phillip had risked his life to search for him.

Often, Justin wished Phillip hadn't found him.

Life was simpler as a blacksmith. His loyalties were clearer.

He shut his eyes, remembering the life he'd once had, torn between wanting to hold the memories close and yet keeping them at bay . . . and so he was a bit confused when he heard a familiar voice to his left, a voice he'd known for years, say in a rich Highland accent, "Hello, Tavis."

Justin opened his eyes.

Gordon Lachlan stood over his table.

Lachlan was two years younger than Justin's two and thirty. His family had lost all they owned to the Clearances, including the life of Gordon's father. Gordon had turned to his clansman Laird MacKenna for help and had quickly become MacKenna's right arm, rivaling Bruce in authority among the clan. Bruce had hated him, and for that reason alone, Justin gave Gordon allegiance . . . that, and the fact that Gordon was a warrior, the sort Justin had dreamed of being.

Almost as tall and muscular as Justin, Gordon had golden hair and green eyes so piercing, they might as well have been shards of glass. Several days' growth of beard covered his jaw.

"You appear well, Tavis," Gordon said, continuing to use Justin's Scots name. *Tavis . . . Gaelic for twin.* The name had been MacKenna's private jest.

"I've been better," Justin answered. "I've had a change of name. Or have you not heard?"

"I've heard."

Justin moved his feet, a signal for Lachlan to sit, and downed the rest of the whiskey in his mug in one burning swallow. It hit the pit of his stomach, filling him with a warm, reckless glow.

Gordon nodded to three men who flanked him. They were watchful men, wary ones. They moved away from Gordon to take positions in other sections of the room. Justin did not recognize them.

"Who are they?" he asked.

"Scots," Gordon answered, sitting on the stool across from Justin. He reached for the whiskey bottle and raised it to his lips, pausing to say, "They yearn for justice, the way you once did." He took a long drink.

"I'll have to ignore that barb," Justin said. "After all, I'm an English duke. One of *them*."

"Yes, and what shall you do about it, Tavis?"

Justin didn't want to think hard. He didn't want to recall his many failings. "I'm going to make changes," he said slowly, wanting Gordon to understand. "I've power now—" Or at least he would someday, as soon as he learned everything he needed to know, everything his brother already knew. "I'll see that there is justice."

"You? One man?" Gordon laughed his doubts.

"Yes, one man," Justin replied evenly, the whiskey making him believe. "I will speak out."

Gordon offered him the bottle. "It's not speaking we want, Tavis, and you know it. MacKenna has abandoned us. He ran."

This was news. Justin would never have thought the laird would leave his people. "Where did he run?"

"To Italy. The bastard took the money we raised. All of it. You know your brother alerted the garrison on us."

Justin straightened. "I do."

The corner of Gordon's mouth lifted into a sneer. "You let him."

"I knew nothing of it." Justin curled his hands into fists, experiencing again the frustration, the sense of betrayal. "My brother has only to say one word and they march at his command. I would have stopped him if I could."

"Oh, aye," Gordon agreed doubtfully.

Justin pounded his fist on the table. "I would have. That's why he kept it from me until after the garrison had left. It was reported back that the soldiers found Nathraichean deserted."

"Do you think we are such fools as to wait the pleasure of the king?"

"Is everyone safe?"

Gordon's gaze met his. "Do you mean Moira?" He shrugged. "You need never worry your head over her, Tavis. She's like a cat with a hundred and nine lives. Both she and Bruce are in Italy with the laird and Lady Rowena spending our money. It's left to the rest of us to pick up the pieces."

"I wasn't asking about Moira," Justin said, and there was a gram of truth to that statement. "I asked about the clan. I want to help. I don't want anyone to starve."

The question, of course, was what could he do? It took money to feed hungry bellies. Any income he had went to managing the ducal estates, all of which were entailed.

He reached for the bottle, and Lachlan grabbed his wrist, stopping him. "There is one thing you *can* do," he said. "You can give me the Sword of the MacKenna."

Justin's thirst for whiskey vanished. He'd known this day would come. "You can't have it. It's mine, remember? The laird gave it to me to use. He hoped I would kill my own brother, *my twin,* with it." The laird had wanted them to fight to the death. The horror of that night was still clear in Justin's mind. He could have run Phillip through and been left to live with the consequences. Charlotte and his own sense that something was not right had saved him. And Phillip.

"We have no feud with you or your brother," Gordon said. "It's the laird who is to blame." He leaned forward. "And either way, the sword does not belong to you."

"Or to you."

"Aye, it does," Gordon answered. "The man who holds that sword can pull Scotland together. *I'm* that man, Tavis. *I am the one.*"

Justin almost believed him. Gordon's was a rebel's soul. He would fight to his last breath . . . and for that reason alone, Justin could not give him the sword. "The English are too strong," he said quietly. "Can you not see that?" He pushed his whiskey away, his taste for it vanishing. "When I lived in Nathraichean, away from the world, I believed we could win freedom, too. But we can't, Gordon. The English can fight the French and us. Thousands will die if there is another rebellion."

Gordon sat back, his eyes alive with anger. "You don't have to fight, Your Grace. We know *you* can't. After all, you are just a puppet for your brother—"

"I'm no puppet," Justin answered.

"You aren't your own man, either. You were more one as a blacksmith than here as duke," Gordon taunted.

Justin's temper ignited, touched off by the truth in Gordon's words. He gripped the table lest he reach across it for Gordon's throat. "I hate the Clearances as much as any man. I've seen the aftermath, the families broken in spirit. However, I want to be a voice for change. I'll make our story heard."

"We don't have the time to wait," Gordon answered, coming to his feet. He leaned a hand on the table, his face inches from Justin's. "Give me the sword—or I'll make you sorry you ever laid eyes on it."

Justin didn't flinch from his gaze. "I already am sorry I ever saw the damn thing, but I'll not give it to you. I will not have the blood of the innocent on my hands."

Gordon brought his fist down on the table. The

bottle tipped over. Neither man made a move to right it. *"It's not yours."*

"But I have it." Justin rose to his feet. "War is not the way, Gordon." He spoke quietly, aware that they could be overheard.

But Lachlan would have none of it. He didn't attempt to lower his voice. "You are a traitor, Tavis. I once thought you had the makings of a warrior. Now I know you are a coward, and may God rest your soul in hell." With those words, he nodded to his clansmen and walked out the door.

For a long, long moment, Justin stood where he was, shaken by the vehemence in Gordon's voice. He had tried speaking reason and been branded a traitor.

He could tell himself that it was all MacKenna's fault. The tangled web of his life had been spun at birth with Lady Rowena's deception.

That still didn't mean that Gordon's words hadn't struck their mark—and he was suddenly tired, exhausted from the struggle. He was not Scot or Englishman. Neither blacksmith nor duke.

Was it the whiskey that sapped his energy? Or fear?

A group of men were moving closer, anxious to claim his table. Justin looked down at the overturned bottle. The last of the whiskey was still pooled inside it. He picked it up and drained it, wishing both Gordon and Phillip to the devil.

And those who believed he wasn't his own man were wrong. He had the Sword of the MacKenna, and no one would take it from him.

It was a good two hours before Justin finally found his way back to his apartments. His walk home had been a long one, and more than once he wished he'd had the foresight to order Clarens to return for him.

His building was located on a quiet side street not far from the fashionable shopping district. There were two apartments—his and Penthorpe's. Both apartments took up two floors. Servants' quarters and a cramped shared kitchen for the making of meals were on the ground floor, and the sitting room and bedrooms of each of the men's apartments were on the first.

As he climbed the stairs to his rooms, the whiskey still felt good in his veins . . . his bed was going to feel even better.

A candle burned on the hallway table. Penthorpe's was the first door and Justin's the second since his rooms were larger.

Justin didn't worry about keeping quiet. His neighbor was most likely out for the night. Penthorpe rarely returned home until well past dawn, and even if he was there, he was probably in the same shape Justin was.

For a moment Justin considered knocking on his neighbor's door and asking him over for a drink. Fortunately he dismissed the idea. He didn't like Penthorpe, and liked him even less imagining him with—

Justin came to a stop in front of his doorway, realizing he'd forgotten *her* name. *Her.* The woman whose lips and body knew how to melt into his.

Good. "I pray I never see her again," he muttered . . . even though he could recall the taste of her . . . the touch . . . the scent. In his mind's eye, he saw those vibrant red curls, that pert nose, generous mouth—

"No. I don't need another bloody woman," he spoke to the door. At least not one he could remember after a night of drinking—

Francesca.

Her name rang through his brain with the clearness of a bell.

He did remember. He *was* an idiot. With a groan, Justin leaned forward to bang sense into his head on the door, just as it opened.

His valet, Biddle, stood there. He was a morose-looking man with thinning hair and a fastidious nature.

"Good evening, Your Grace—" he started, but stopped, his jaw dropping. "Your Grace, what happened to you? Where is your neck cloth? And your gloves? Your shoes have lost all polish."

"They have," Justin agreed amiably. "I am unpolished."

Biddle blinked, as if overwhelmed by the whiskey fumes coming from Justin's mouth. Justin was tempted to open wide and just fume the man out. The thought made him laugh as he leaned against the door frame. "I'm tired, Biddle. I feel good, but tired."

"I can see that, Your Grace. Please come inside." He stepped back, holding the door open. A lamp on his desk cast a warm, golden glow around the room while a small fire burned the grate.

Justin bypassed the velvet settee before the hearth, moving toward his leather upholstered chair next to his desk, suddenly needing to sit down.

The chair was his favorite. It suited a man of his size. His apartments themselves were modern and very well appointed. Phillip had seen to that. The sitting room and bedroom were open to each other. Paneled doors could shut them off, but he liked them left open.

Off the bedroom was a bathing room. At first Justin had thought having a separate room for bathing a ridiculous luxury. After all, how much room did a man need to shave? Now he was quite fond of it. Another sign he was going English.

"Gordon would disapprove."

Kneeling on the carpet, Biddle stopped in the act of taking off Justin's shoes. "I beg your pardon, Your Grace?"

Justin waved him away. "You wouldn't know him, Biddle, and I doubt if you would like him." He frowned. He rarely overimbibed . . . but he knew he was reaching a point where half of him was sobering and the other remained drowsily intoxicated. "Go to bed. I'll undress myself."

"Let me prepare for you one of my special concoctions," Biddle offered. "It will, shall we say, take the edge off your mind in the morning?"

Stretching out in the chair, Justin laughed, the sound without mirth. "You can have my mind, Biddle. I don't want it. I don't want to think. Or to feel. I don't want . . ." He let his voice trail off with a frown. *To be here,* he'd almost said. To be in a world he didn't understand. "And yet, where else could I go?"

"Where do you wish to go, Your Grace?" Biddle asked.

That was the question.

"To bed," Justin said. He reached over to his desk beside the chair and picked up the top book, *Othello,* on a stack of books. Beneath it was one on the history of Ceylon.

Books were his indulgence. He'd only learned to read after Moira had left him. At that time, he'd taken in Father Nicholas, a renegade French

priest who had escaped the Terror in his home-
land by traveling to Scotland. The half-blind priest
had fallen out of favor with Lady Rowena and
would have had to sleep on the ground save for
Justin's charity.

The two of them had rubbed along well. Father
Nicholas had married Justin and Moira, as well as
all the couples in the clan, and had offered much-
needed sympathy at her defection. He'd also filled
the lonely hours by insisting on teaching Justin to
read.

That tutoring was now a godsend. Reading
filled the empty hours of his life as well as en-
abling him to learn on his own. He didn't need
Phillip for all his instruction.

But he wasn't in the mood to read tonight. He
placed the book back down and pushed up from
the chair. "Go on, Biddle. I don't need you further
tonight. You know I don't like the fuss."

"Let me make you a cup of special rhubarb tea.
You'll wake tomorrow with a mind as sharp as a
sword."

Justin shook his head. "I don't ever want to be
that sharp. Go to bed, Biddle. I'll be fine. I was
nursed on whiskey."

"I turned down the bedsheets," Biddle offered.

Justin glanced into the other room. "The bed
does look inviting."

"I can help you undress—"

"Leave," Justin said. "I'll bed myself down."

"Let me help with your coat—"

"Good night, Biddle."

The valet heard the finality in Justin's voice, and still he hesitated. "Lord Phillip will not be pleased with me."

"My brother is the first to know how difficult I am." He took Biddle's arm and escorted him to the door. "I'll see you in the morning. Blow out the candle in the hall. You know Penthorpe won't need it."

"Yes, Your Grace."

Justin shut the door and released his breath with a long sigh. The whiskey was wearing off. Picking up the lamp, he crossed his sitting room into the bedroom, heading for the water closet. Setting the lamp on a small table, he shrugged out of his evening jacket and hung it on a peg before using tooth powder to clean his teeth.

His shirt reeked of the streets. Justin pulled it off over his head and tossed it into a corner before splashing some water into his basin bowl. The lukewarm water felt good against his skin. He washed thoroughly, wishing now he hadn't ventured into the tavern. Wishing he hadn't had to confront Gordon, a man he'd always admired.

In the bedroom, he debated telling Phillip about what had happened at the tavern, and decided no. It would reopen the topic of the Sword of the

MacKenna and Phillip's expectations of loyalty. He offered it in return, but Justin wasn't ready. Everyone he had ever trusted had betrayed him. So why let another person close? Especially one whose very features mirrored his own?

He was tired. Exhausted beyond the night's exertions and the drink. He set the lamp on a bedside table and fell back on the bed, not bothering to remove his breeches or his socks.

For a long, silent moment, he stared at the ceiling, watching the shadows created by the lamplight.

It was then he heard the footfall out in the hall. He listened. Biddle should have gone to bed. Or was it Penthorpe? Had he returned early?

Or could it be Gordon, coming for the sword?

Suddenly sober, Justin rose from the bed. Turning down the lamp, he crossed to the hallway door on stockinged feet. He cracked the door open. Whoever was out there moved in darkness, and with stealth.

He waited.

Penthorpe's door creaked as it opened. Justin expected whoever went inside to light a candle.

No one did.

The door closed . . . and Justin had the eerie sense that someone was up to no good.

And because he needed to take his own restless mind off his troubles, Justin decided to investigate.

Chapter 8

Penthorpe was a terrible housekeeper.

The hallway had been dark, but the inside of his apartments was positively pitch black. Nor was Francesca prepared for what seemed to be a coat or breeches tossed on the floor right in front of the doorway.

She tripped but caught herself from falling by catching hold of a table edge. It had been closer to the door than she'd remembered. The sweet, rotting smell of orange peels wrinkled her nose, and her fingers pressed against what she suspected was dried wine. Pulling her hand away, she wiped it on her breeches.

Another cautious step warned her there was a pair of boots in her path. The apartment had been presentable when she'd visited two days ago, al-though now that she remembered, there had been a staleness in the air, the sort that comes with unwashed clothes. She'd ignored it because she'd been so shocked and excited by her own audacity that she hadn't paid attention to details. Her focus had been on him, more fool she.

Francesca had known not to expect Penthorpe's man waiting up for him. This building had servants' quarters on the ground floor, and no servant, not even a valet, spent the night up when he knew his employer would be out gambling all night.

However, she had thought there would be a fire in the grate, or some other form of light.

Trapped in the darkness, she stood a moment, attempting to remember the layout of the cold room. She rested her fingers on the edge of the table and reached out in search of the two chairs she recalled being close. She found one and inched her way to another, being careful of where she placed her feet. In this fashion, she made her way toward the open doorway between the sitting room and the bedroom.

She faltered over another pair of shoes, tried not to think of what personal articles of clothing she was kicking out of her way, and kept moving, placing a hand on the door frame. Penthorpe had attacked her in the sitting room and had dragged her into the bedroom toward a very large bed with carved scenes of nymphs and satyrs cavorting on the headboard and bedposts. She'd grabbed one of those bedposts, holding it so tight that the figures had pressed an imprint in her hands, but she had refused to let him throw her down upon the mattress.

Her toe now struck the bedpost, and she knew where she was.

A window was on the right side of the bed. She crossed to it and pulled back heavy velvet drapes to let what little moonlight there was into the room.

The bed was unmade, the sheets so rumpled they were twisted. Against the far wall, every drawer of the dresser was pulled out and clothes flung this way and that out of them.

If she'd ever been attracted to Penthorpe, this introduction to his slovenly personal habits would have ripped it to shreds.

And how was she going to find where he hid her pearl pendant and necklace in this mess—

She caught a gleam on the dresser. A reflection of moonlight in the black pearl's shell.

Francesca could not believe her good luck.

Jeremy waited outside the building to escort her home. She had hired a hack to arrive here and would hire another for the trip home. Time was of the essence, and to find the pearl just lying on Penthorpe's dresser was a blessing.

She was across the room in two steps and kissed the pendant's gold link chain, she was so happy. Never again would she let her mother's necklace out of her sight. She'd kill before she let that happen.

Francesca turned toward the front door, anxious to make her escape. The outer room was much darker than the moonlit bedroom but she managed to pick her way around the clutter on the floor more easily than when she'd first arrived.

She was almost to the hallway door when it opened. A dark shadow blocked her escape.

Francesca pulled up short, uncertain if her imagination was playing tricks. And then a large, strong body hit hers, grabbing her around the waist and knocking her to the floor.

Her first thought was, *Penthorpe has returned.*

The force of her fall made her hand open and sent the necklace flying into the darkness.

Personal fear evaporated. Francesca had to have that necklace. She attempted to turn over so she could crawl, if need be, in the direction the pearl had gone, but his weight was such that she couldn't move, and that was when she realized, *This isn't Penthorpe.*

He was too big, too heavy . . . *too* strong.

And he was half naked.

Francesca kicked out, trying to push him away by any means possible, and won her freedom enough to start scrambling away after the necklace.

A hand caught her ankle and pulled her back. "Give it up, damn you." The brogue was unmistakable—as were the fumes of spirits on his breath. "Quit your damn wiggling. You're caught and I've got you."

Francesca didn't know why Colster was here, but she wasn't about to let him catch *her* here.

Unfortunately it was already too late.

Arms like iron grabbed her around the chest and heaved her to her feet, but not before he received a surprise of his own. His hold loosened, but only to free one hand so that he could confirm his suspicions.

"Ah, damn, you are female. In *breeches.*" The Duke of Colster had the nerve to run his hand up her legs and over her bum as if confirming his words. He snorted his opinion. "Give me your name, girl, and tell me why you're here. Is it robbery, or are you and Penthorpe playing games?" He didn't wait for an answer but raised his voice. "Penny, are you here? Have I spoiled your fun?"

Of course there was no answer, and Francesca wasn't about to speak and reveal who she was. She was going to escape. Her necklace was lost in the darkness, and there it would have to stay.

Without hesitation, she doubled her fist and punched upward, aiming for his nose.

Unfortunately he turned at the wrong moment, and her fist went into his jaw. Pain shot down her arm.

But he didn't seem to feel a thing. She'd done better when she'd slapped him earlier.

"You are irritating me, lass," he grumbled. "Come along. You and I are going to wait for Penny together." He took her wrist in a grip as tight as a vise and walked out of the room, dragging her after him as if she were a disobedient child and he a schoolmaster.

However, out in the hallway, she had another chance to escape. There was the sound of booted steps on the stairs. Someone carried a candle, and in a second, her footman Jeremy's head came into view. Francesca threw all caution to the wind in a desperate effort to win her freedom. "Jeremy, help me," she ordered.

"Miss Dunroy, what has happened?" her footman said in alarm, his face pale in the candlelight.

Colster whirled around. "Miss *Dunroy*?" He snatched off her cap. Her hair came tumbling down in a mass of irrepressible curls.

For a moment the three of them stood in a stunned tableau—and then the duke expressed his opinion in a succinct "Damn." He let go of her arm as if he'd been scalded.

Surprisingly, Francesca hadn't been ready for such an easy release. All her weight had been resisting him, and she now fell backward onto her bum.

Here was her chance to escape, if Jeremy had proved to be a braver soul. However, instead of helping her up and away, he took off down the stairs, taking the candle with him.

"Wait," Colster called. "You forgot her." He started toward the stairs, going down them and shouting at Jeremy, "Come back here and take her."

A door slammed.

It was opened.

It slammed again.

Francesca heard muffled shouting and realized Colster was outside with Jeremy. The fear that he would murder her footman paralyzed her.

But then Colster came back into the house with a roar of anger. *"Can't one thing go right this night?"*

He started up the stairs, just as Francesca's wits returned. She scrambled to her feet with one overriding thought—*hide.*

She knew he'd look in Penthorpe's rooms so she ran to the only other door in the hall. It was unlocked and proved to be, inside, a mirror image of Penthorpe's apartments although better furnished and infinitely tidier. A fire burned in the grate and an oil-burning lamp sitting on a plain utilitarian desk stacked with books sent out a warm, welcoming glow.

No one seemed at home, although Francesca was not in a situation to be choosy. She'd throw herself on the mercy of whoever lived here. It was either a stranger or Colster and she'd take the stranger.

Francesca shut the door, hearing him reach the top of the stairs.

There was no key to turn in the lock so she searched for something to put before the door. A settee with velvet cushions had been placed before the hearth, but the desk appeared more substantial. She shoved the stacks of books on it to the floor, being careful to place the lamp in a safe place out of the way, and started dragging the desk toward the door. She almost had it in place when Colster started to turn the handle.

Pushing the door shut with one hip, she tried to block the door with the desk but she was too late. Muttering dark Scottish curses, Colster shoved the door open enough to get an arm and a shoulder through.

Francesca picked up a book, noticing it an account of the Seven Years' War, and whacked his hand.

He drew it back with a snarl, but before he could do more, a man's polite voice asked from the stairway, "Is something the matter, Your Grace?"

Colster turned, and Francesca was able to close the door. She heard him answer, "Nothing's wrong that setting Penthorpe's place on fire couldn't cure. Return to bed, Biddle."

Francesca used the momentary diversion to push the desk in place, realizing as she did so that she had foolishly run into Colster's apartments. She'd been so focused on the pearl and her anger with Penthorpe that she'd put out of her mind overhearing the rake tell Lord Phillip that Colster was his neighbor. *He lived here.* She was hiding in his private quarters.

What ill fate had conspired against her to have both her enemies living under the same roof? If she'd known Colster lived here, she would have never set foot outside her bedroom door.

The servant protested. "If I can be of help—? Perhaps that tea I offered to brew."

"Go to bed," Colster commanded.

Francesca sat on the desk, adding her own weight to the task of keeping him out. It was the best she could do. She dug her booted heels into the carpeting on the floor and searched the area for a weapon of sorts. All she had immediately at hand were books. Beyond the sitting room was the bedroom and a four-poster bed, albeit one far less ornate than Penthorpe's. More books were piled on a bedside table. It was clear to see what each man valued—Penthorpe, his hideously carved bed; Colster, books.

She debated calling to the servant for help. Then

again, where would Biddle's loyalties lie? In aiding her or obeying his master?

Colster shoved on the door, but he was stopped once again by the obsequious Biddle. "Is someone in your room?"

"It's nothing, Biddle," Colster said, irritation making him impatient. "Just a prowler I caught in Penthorpe's room and one I'm going to hang out the window by the heels." He obviously said this last for Francesca's benefit.

"A prowler?" Biddle repeated. "Shall I call the watch?"

No, don't call the watch, Francesca wanted to shout.

"Don't call the watch," Colster snapped.

"I believe I *should* call the watch," Biddle answered, his voice fading as if he were going down the stairs.

Colster followed him, the stomping of his angry footsteps echoing in the hallway. "Call the watch and you'll be searching for new employ, Biddle."

There was a moment of silence . . . and then a greatly affronted Biddle said, "Then what shall I do, Your Grace?"

"Get your arse back to bed," Colster answered, completely ungracious. "And don't you breathe one word of this to any person. Including my brother."

A second later, there was a slam from one of the downstairs doors. Biddle obviously didn't appreciate Colster's plain speaking, but Francesca was too busy pulling the settee over to shove against the desk to give a worry for an arguing servant.

Now, securely trapped in his rooms, she realized she had to think of a way out. And once she did, she was going to see that Jeremy regretted deserting her—

The door started to open.

Francesca sat on the settee, leaning her shoulder against the back to help bolster the barricade she'd created between herself and Colster.

"Give it up, Miss Dunroy," he warned. "Or should I call you just plain Dunroy, since you are passing yourself off as a lad. Did no one mention there is a difference between men and women? Or is that part of the game you and Penthorpe are playing?"

Heat rushed to her cheeks. She combed her hair back with her fingers, wishing she were a man. Then she'd run him through just for the sport of it and enjoy the shock on his stubborn face. Here was one man who needed his comeuppance.

But for now, she needed to escape. She started moving toward the window in the bedroom, praying her barricade would hold him long enough for her to find a way out. Perhaps there was a back servants' entrance?

"Very well," came his curt response to her silence. "We shall do this your way."

Before she could blink, he rammed the door with such force, the desk began moving as if it weighed nothing. The settee started to tip, the front legs catching on the carpet. The Duke of Colster's head, then his shirtless body started coming through the door. An angry muscle worked in his jaw, and his eyes were hard and bright.

Francesca ran to the bedroom window. They were some twelve, fifteen feet above the street. She'd jump if she had to. Anything to save herself from this madman.

Tossing back the curtains, she attempted to open the window, but the sash was locked tight. She heard him shut the hallway door, heard footsteps behind her, knew he was close.

Spinning to face him, she reached for the first weapon she could find, a book. Its weight felt good in her hand. She threw it at him as hard as she could and reached for another.

Her first aim was true. A corner of the book struck him in the temple.

Colster stopped and raised a hand to his forehead, just as she heaved the other, a heavier volume, at him. The book tore from its binding in the air before catching him square in the chest.

He grabbed for the book as if upset it had torn. "Would you be more careful?" he ordered.

That's when Francesca realized her efforts were not having the desired effect. He was too big, too strong for her to beat him back. She then saw the door to another room. She ran for it, her hair flowing wildly around her shoulders.

Just as she placed her hands on the door frame, his arm caught her around the waist. He whirled her around and down onto the bed.

Panic shot through her. This was almost what it had been like with Penthorpe, only Colster was angry.

Cornered, she fought back. Unfortunately her blows and kicks seemed to do little more than make him more irate.

"Stop it," he ordered.

But she couldn't. She acted on instinct, her goal freedom. The way to the door was clear now that he wasn't guarding it. She could escape.

He used the weight of his arms to hold hers down. "Miss Dunroy, you are trying my patience," he warned.

Francesca knew she must be wiser. She pretended to swoon. He relaxed his hold—and that was when she raised her knee.

It had worked on Penthorpe . . . but it didn't work on Colster.

He moved in time to save himself but he was not pleased by what she'd intended. Men seemed to be humorless about that particular part of their anatomy.

"You she-devil." He raised her up on the bed,

lifting her as if she were nothing more than a doll.

Francesca stared into his eyes and knew fear. His face was livid with rage. She'd made many men angry in her life, but none as furious as she'd made Colster.

For a second, she thought he was going to throw her across the room. In a tight voice, he said, "I don't like having my books thrown."

Of all the things he could have accused her of, that was not the one she'd expected . . . anymore than she could have anticipated what he would do next.

He kissed her.

This was not a welcoming kiss like the ones on the terrace. This kiss was clearly a punishment. She sensed that if he didn't kiss her, he would throttle her . . . and it was still taking all his control to keep him from doing that.

His kiss was bruising and hard and angry. She pressed her lips tight, wanting him to know she was angry, too. She'd not give him any satisfaction. She'd fight him tooth and nail, and if he thought she was done . . .

Her outrage faded as she became aware that he wasn't being so forceful.

The tension with which he held her arms lessened. His lips softened.

Without being conscious of it, the tension in her lips eased, too.

The kiss changed.

It didn't lose the anger. Colster was furious with her . . . and perhaps rightfully so. He hadn't asked her to make a shambles of his apartment.

But the kiss ceased to be about punishment and became more about communicating his frustration.

Through this kiss, she could say what her pride would never let her admit—she'd made a mess of the evening. She was alone and scared and didn't know how it would all turn out.

And the most amazing thing was, he understood.

That's when the kiss really became important.

That's when she realized what had happened between them on the library terrace had been no accident. There was something between them . . . and it started with this kiss.

Chapter 9

This was madness.

And yet Justin couldn't have pulled back if a garrison of soldiers led by his brother had marched through the door and ordered him to do so.

Not after Francesca settled her body against his as sweet and loving as you please, her soft curves melding with his hard planes in all the right places.

Anger still drove him. She had no business being out in the night disguised as a boy. She was a fool to chase after a rake like Penthorpe. Her father probably assumed she was snug in her bed instead of here in Justin's arms. He thought his daughter a precious virgin.

Justin now knew better, and it didn't make a

farthing's difference. Francesca Dunroy was headstrong and alarmingly independent, and Justin wanted to plow into her with a need so primal, it threatened to turn him inside out.

It was the breeches. She filled them nicely. *Too* nicely. He couldn't take his hands off her. He cupped her buttocks and pulled her against his erection. She practically melted against him—and Justin knew he was cursed.

He'd not felt this driving hunger for a woman since Moira, another who had played hot and cold. It was his curse, he realized. He always wanted the wrong women.

However, right now, he was powerless to prevent this from going toward its logical conclusion.

And he wouldn't stop it if he could.

Francesca felt possessed. The world, her obligations, her mother's necklace . . . all faded in the onslaught of his kisses, of his touch.

She should push away. She should stop him. This was not right . . . but it felt so good.

His tongue caught and held hers.

Startled, she attempted to pull back. He wouldn't let her. Instead he pressed deeper until she had no choice but to accept him . . . and she did.

He kissed her as if he would swallow her very breath.

Her breasts grew full and tight. It was as if they

reached for him, ached for his touch, yearned for what only he could give.

His hand moved down between them, his fingers catching on the waist of her breeches. His touch felt warm against her skin. He unbuttoned the top button, then a second. His fingers slipped between leather and skin.

Francesca drew in a sharp breath, tightening her abdomen even as she rose on her toes, anxious to meet him. His fist clutched her leather breeches, holding her. His kiss was greedy, even more demanding. She held on by wrapping her arms around his neck and curling her fingers in his hair.

He released her breeches but brought his hand up under her shirt and the lace and cotton camisole she wore for decency to cover her breasts.

Her knees threatened to buckle at the pleasure of his touch.

Justin broke the kiss. He leaned his head against hers.

"No," she protested, her voice as breathless as if she'd run a very long race.

He hesitated. She sensed him readying to pull back. She didn't know if she could stand it. Every inch of her body yearned. She'd never experienced this driving desire, this anxious need for—what? She had no words to describe it, no experience with which to compare it.

Desperate, aching for what she didn't yet understand, Francesca covered his hand beneath her shirt with her own. Her nipples were tight and hard. The pressure of his palm eased some of the tension while rousing a moist, anxious wanting deep within her.

His lips returned to hers. His knee came up between her legs as he gently lowered her onto the bed behind them.

He was right. This was easier. More comfortable.

And she was glad he wasn't wearing a shirt now. The play of muscles beneath his warm skin felt good under her hands.

Justin joined her on the bed. He breathed into her neck before kissing a line up toward her ear. Francesca tensed, waiting for that sensation of his breath against this very sensitive spot.

He wrapped his hand in her hair as if to hold her. He didn't need to do so. She wasn't going anywhere. He nipped her neck and then pressed a hot kiss over the bite, his arms tight bonds around her.

Francesca heard herself whimper. She couldn't help herself. This man's touch was magic. He knew what she'd like before she did.

His hand slid up her shirt, and she realized he was pulling it off her. For a second, she hung on shyly. Undeterred, he surprised her by covering her nipple with his mouth.

A shaft of pure, molten heat shot through her.

The will to resist vanished. Her shirt and camisole were pulled over her head without further protest. She dug her fingers into his hair and let him have his way.

This was desire. *This* was why men and women came together. It wasn't for mere kisses. They wanted something else. Here was the mystery revealed, the unknown discovered. He was strong and handsome and powerful. His kisses, his touch made her want to weep from the sheer pleasure of them.

Francesca didn't know if she could take more. Certainly she would burst into flames like a Chinese rocket if she didn't find a release. She was helpless to stop him.

Instead she pulled his head up to hers and kissed him with every fiber of her being. To her joy, her touch and her scent seemed as potent to him as his were to her.

It was as if he would gobble her up with his desire—and she would happily let him.

"You're beautiful," he whispered between gobbles—and she believed him. His kisses made her feel beautiful.

His hand smoothed over the flatness of her belly, slipping beneath her half-unbuttoned breeches, pushing them over her hips and down her thighs as he unerringly went toward the center of her.

At his first touch, reason reasserted its ugly head.

She must not let him do this. They were going too far.

But then he circled the nub of her femininity with his fingertip, and panic melted into desire.

Her body wept for his touch. She ran her palms over the smooth strength of his shoulders, drowning in the spiraling sensations he created as he explored and touched her, unable to do anything but gasp his name.

He reached for her hand, lowering it, and she found herself twisting and unfastening the buttons of his breeches. His mouth returned to her breasts. It was too much, all that he was doing. She could barely breathe, let alone think—and then she discovered the length of him. His arousal pushed its way forward as if with a mind of its own.

Francesca ran an experimental hand down him. She had seen the male anatomy in art and occasionally on the street on a pauper's baby. She'd never imagined it this smooth and velvety soft.

Justin lifted his head to nuzzle her neck while he covered her hand with his, showing her what he wanted.

So this was how it was. This was how men and women pleasured each other.

It wasn't scary at all. In fact, it was overwhelmingly pleasant. Brilliant even.

He struggled out of his breeches, not bothering with his socks. He rolled on his back, bringing her to lie across him. A portion of her mind, the part that was still rational, warned her to be careful, but when his hand pushed her breeches farther down to free one leg that he rested across his, she made no protest.

The lamp was still burning in the other room. His lips curved into a lazy, certain smile. His eyes were dark with desire—desire for her. He pushed her unruly hair back from her face and lightly bit her neck.

Francesca loved it. His skin smelled of the very essence of him, and she was as pliant in his hands as warm wax. He was still aroused, but his erection no longer intimidated her. She was too busy feasting on his kisses, eagerly yearning toward something she didn't quite understand. She was hot and tense and needy and—

Justin half rose from the bed. He lifted her up, his hands at her waist. She smiled down at him, wondering what marvelous trick he had next for her.

She found out when he placed her over his hips and then brought her down, impaling her on his proud hardness.

And Francesca felt as if she were being ripped in two.

Chapter 10

*C*onsidering all that had happened between them that evening, considering her response to him, her eagerness, her *willingness*, the last thing Justin had anticipated was Francesca being an innocent.

She certainly hadn't kissed like a novice—or had she?

In truth, he'd been so attracted to her, he hadn't really noticed. And after all, how long did it take to teach someone to kiss? Especially when he really wanted to kiss her?

Now she stared down at him, her eyes wide and filled with horror. He'd felt the rip. The thin barrier had been as if nothing against his lust, and he felt the warmth of blood.

Slowly, their bodies still joined, he lowered her to the bed. He reached out, brushed her hair at the temple. "It's all right," he whispered. "The pain will be gone if it isn't already."

She was in shock. Moira had been the same way on their wedding night, although, back then, Justin had been equally naïve.

But matters were different now. He knew how to pleasure a woman. He knew he couldn't leave Francesca this way.

Nor did he want to. Her leg rested on his hip. He was buried to the hilt, and there was only one thing to do to make amends for both of them.

Francesca came to her senses with a cry of realization. She started to push away. He caught her wrists and leaned over her, resting his weight on his arms as he placed her beneath him. He didn't pull out. She needed to become accustomed to the feel of him—even though it was taking an incredible amount of willpower on his own part.

"Don't be afraid," he whispered. "It won't hurt. Not anymore."

Her eyes, which moments ago had trusted him implicitly, now darkened with accusation and the pain of unshed tears. "I shouldn't be here." Her voice shuddered as she spoke.

"Aye, but you are," he said.

"I want to go home."

"You can't," he said quietly. He could feel the racing of her heart, knew her fear. "Not right now. I can't let it end this way. I owe you that much, lass."

Tension stretched between them. Neither moved. Justin was afraid even to breathe, lest she bolt.

Slowly her breathing settled. She didn't relax, but the panic lost its edge.

He knew what he must do. "Forgive me," he whispered. " 'Tis not what you want, but it is what must be done." He moved his hands up to clasp hers, pressing them down into the mattress. He covered her lips with his own. The kiss surprised her. He took full advantage, moving his hips.

Francesca bucked, ready to toss him off, but Justin held fast. He kissed her temple, her ear. "Easy, lass, don't be afraid. Give it a chance. Just a wee chance."

He thrust deep and hard. She fit him like a glove, and it was all he could do to hold himself at bay, giving her this opportunity to understand. "God made you for this, lass," he crooned. "You're fashioned for me. And I for you. Can you not feel it, lass? Do you understand how well we mold together?"

She'd closed her eyes against him, but her resistance faded.

Justin released a sigh of relief at finally clearing this first hurdle. It was a gift she was giving him.

Not her body, but her trust. That trust was worth more than gold or her maidenhead.

Francesca might have been raised in a life of wealth and luxury . . . but, like him, she kept her own counsel. She depended on herself.

No wonder the two of them were attracted to each other. They were kindred spirits. Rebels caught in a world that wasn't of their own making.

But tonight would be different. Tonight would be about the moment. For this small span of time, he was going to let the future take care of itself.

He began moving, taking his time, working to see that she enjoyed it. He never wanted her to look back on this moment with regret.

Her eyes opened. She met his gaze, a furrow of concern between her brows. Justin kissed her, tasting her. The line of worry eased and her body began meeting his thrusts, cautiously at first and then with a growing awareness of what he could offer.

They worked together now like dancers learning the steps. Justin kissed her, and she had enough presence of mind to kiss him back. He released his hold on her wrists and her arms came around his neck. Her legs widened, the better able to cradle him.

Justin was only too happy to please her. It had been a long time since he'd felt this connection with a woman. A long time since sex had meant something other than a release. It now became a gift, a lesson, a prayer—

Francesca raised her hips, allowing him to thrust deeper, harder, and he lost control. A portion of him knew he should hold back, but he couldn't. It was she. There was something about her that had slipped past his guard from the very beginning.

Nor was she helping his control with her soft gasps of wonder.

Yes, *wonder.*

He truly was joining with this woman, his body melding with hers into one. There was a miracle in this moment. Years spent with someone who'd lost all caring, years spent alone fell away. Francesca was making him believe again. She was awakening the magic—

He felt deep muscles clench, felt her contraction. Watched her eyes widen in surprise as she whispered his name.

And then wave after endless, blessed wave flowed from her through him.

Justin could hold back no longer. She was taking him. He thrust deep. Once, twice, a third time before losing himself completely in her arms.

For a long time, they held each other. Neither seemed able to move.

Slowly, awareness returned—and with it, the ugliness of reality.

It was Francesca who realized it first. "I'm ruined." Her pronouncement brought him to his senses, but not before she shoved him off her. As agile as a cat, she came to her feet beside the bed. Her breeches were still on one leg. Her hair was a tangled mass around her shoulders, her nipples red and tight.

Seeing the direction of his gaze, she covered her breasts with one arm. "How could you do that to me?" she demanded, reaching for her breeches to awkwardly put her other leg in them and pull them up with her free hand.

"Why didn't you tell me you were a virgin?" he wondered. "Then I wouldn't have." He was feeling a bit silly himself lying there stark naked save for a pair of socks on his feet.

"You didn't ask," she snapped, reaching down to the floor and throwing his breeches in his face.

Justin grabbed his breeches in his fist. This was not the way he would have chosen to cap off such intense lovemaking. However, she was setting the tone. He was merely reacting to her tantrum.

Her father might indulge her spoiled snippiness but Justin wouldn't.

He tossed his breeches aside and stood up. Her gaze went straight to his spent manhood. She blushed so furiously that her face blended with her hair, and Justin had the irrational urge to cover himself up. But he wouldn't do that. He was a man. He'd done nothing wrong other than to be true to his nature.

She looked away. "I have to find my clothes. I have to leave."

"You have to do nothing of the sort," he answered.

"What do you mean?"

He made an impatient sound. "Don't be naïve. You know what price has to be paid for this night's work. You know the cost."

Francesca crossed her arms against her breasts. "Do you mean marriage? To *you*?"

"There's no one else in the room with us," he said, enunciating each word, a warning she'd be wise to heed. "I'm not pleased at the prospect, either, lass, but the least you could do is pretend some appreciation."

"Why? All you want is my money."

Justin's blood started to boil. He was tired. Spent. He had no desire to marry *or argue* with her. In truth, all he really wanted right now was to climb into his bed and, surprisingly, cuddle her up and sleep until noon. His favorite part of sex was the aftermath. He enjoyed the closeness.

Then again, considering the chaos she'd now brought into his already complicated life, right now he'd rather hug a thorny hawthorne bush than the spoiled and headstrong Miss Dunroy.

"We'll discuss this in the morning," he replied.

"That room is the bathing room for private needs. There's water and a towel. Take a moment to yourself and try and relax. What's done is done." He knew he sounded hard. She'd asked for it.

Her frown deepened. He braced himself, expecting further argument. But then she leaned to sweep her shirt up off the floor and marched into the bathing room, holding her head high, one arm still across her breasts. She slammed the door behind her.

She already had a duchess's arrogance. "She must have been bred for the part," he muttered to himself.

With her out of the room, and as a concession to her, *and* because he really did feel silly standing there with nothing but socks on, he picked up his breeches and put them on. He shucked off the socks at the same time. He walked into the sitting room and picked the lamp up from the floor. The room was a bloody shambles. He carried the lamp to set in the bedroom, turned to pick up the books she'd thrown on the floor—but stopped before he'd taken more than a step.

The lamp's soft light fell on a smear of blood on the counterpane. Her blood.

His temper evaporated.

This was his fault. He'd allowed lust and anger to overcome his sense of decency. Looking back, reviewing the sequence of events, he could see now how he must have frightened her.

The one thing he didn't understand was why she was in Penny's apartments. She'd had an assignation with the rake earlier. Could it be her heart was set on Penthorpe?

If it was, then of course the prospect of having to marry Justin would be upsetting. Just as it was upsetting to him that in doing the right thing, he'd be marrying a woman who cared for another. He'd already done that once.

Justin crossed to the closed bathroom door. Leaning a shoulder against it, he asked the question he had to know, "What were you doing in Penthorpe's apartments?"

He could hear her moving in there. He knew she could hear him . . . but she didn't answer.

She must truly be heartbroken.

"Francesca, do you love him? Is that why you were there?"

Justin was uncertain whether he wanted to know the answer. Theirs had been no ordinary coupling. In spite of everything, there was true passion between them. He found he didn't like the idea of letting her go to another man—

The bathing room window creaked as it was pushed open.

She was attempting to escape.

They were two floors up, and there was no way to go out the window other than to jump or perhaps walk the ledge to the drainpipe. Only a fool would try such a thing.

Then again, Francesca hadn't done anything sensible all evening.

Justin threw open the door and caught her with one foot on the windowsill. In two strides he was across the room. He grabbed her by the nape of the neck, burying his hands in her glorious hair. She mule-kicked out with her bare feet, but he caught her around the waist and carried her flailing body back into the bedroom. He threw her down on the bed.

"What is the matter with you?" he demanded. "You could have broken your neck climbing out of that window."

Her green eyes were bright with defiance. "I must return home. I must be there before I'm missed."

"And I can't let you run around London's streets dressed as you are. You've not even shoes on your feet." He picked up a pillow and threw it down on the bed in frustration, before saying, "Besides, you can't go. Not after what happened between us. You're ruined, lass. Done. Tomorrow we'll have to talk to your father—"

"No." She came up on her knees before him.

"He doesn't need to know about this. No one needs to know. Take me back tonight. Please."

It was tempting . . . But it wouldn't be honorable.

"I can't," he said. "I may have been raised a lowly blacksmith, but I am a man of honor. It wouldn't be right to let you face this alone. You could be having my bairn."

Her hand flew to her belly. She studied him a moment, regret clear in her eyes. "I couldn't be."

"You could."

"This isn't your fault," she said softly. "I don't blame you. It was my rashness—" She shook her head. "Everything used to be so clear. I don't even know myself anymore." She bowed her head in a long moment of silence before releasing her breath like a soldier determined to carry on. "Whatever happens, you are not accountable. Take me home, and I'll not speak a word of it to anyone."

He could have cursed her stubbornness. He recognized it for what it was: She stood alone. She made her own choices, and she was too independent to ask for help or advice from another— failings he understood all too well from personal experience.

He also knew fighting with her wouldn't help. He was tired. Exhausted. And he suspected she was also.

"We'll discuss this in the morning," he said.

"I need to return *now*," she insisted. "I'll be missed. I absolve you of all responsibility."

"Thank you very much, *Princess* Francesca. However, I decide what is and is not my responsibility."

A mutinous gleam lit her eye, and he knew that if he wanted her to obey, he would need extreme measures.

He crossed to his dresser and pulled out one of his starched neck cloths. "Sit back on the bed," he instructed.

Her response was to stand.

Justin was done with arguing. With his fingertips, he pushed her in the chest with enough force to land her bum on the bed. Without wasting a second, he grabbed her wrists and, using the neck cloth, bound them together before she could blink.

"What are you doing?" Francesca demanded, struggling to free her hands.

"Ensuring you are here in the morning." He tied her hands to the bedpost. She could lie with her head on the pillow, but that was all she could do.

"You can't tie me up. This is unheard of. It's outrageous."

"It's done," he replied.

Her eyes widened. "You mustn't do this, Colster. It's not wise."

"We're talking to your father in the morning. It's done."

"Please, Your Grace, reconsider—"

"Your Grace? Now I'm receiving a bit of respect?" He grunted his opinion.

Her response was to attempt to kick out at him. She almost threw herself off the bed. He lifted her back up and pulled the bedclothes over her shoulders. "Sweet dreams," he said and left the room, taking a feather pillow with him.

He'd not share the bed with her. In spite of being spitting mad, she looked too tempting with her boy's breeches and curling mass of hair. He even found the snap in her eyes attractive. If he lay beside her, he'd have her again, and he'd already done enough damage for one night.

"You can't tie me up," she shouted.

Justin walked toward his settee and pulled it over close to his chair. "I already have."

She bucked and kicked the mattress. "I'll carry on all night until someone hears me."

"You are welcome to do so." He threw his pillow to one end of the settee and reached down to pick up three of the books she'd dumped off the desk earlier. "But there is no one on this floor besides myself. Biddle is downstairs, but he sleeps like the dead. It's too bad Penthorpe didn't pay his man his wages so there would be another servant for you to disturb. As for Penny, he won't be back until midmorning, if you can shout that long—"

He broke off, struck by a sudden suspicion.

"You knew Penthorpe *wouldn't* be home. You weren't there *for* him . . . but for another reason."

Her anger vanished, replaced by an immediate about-face. "I'm tired," she complained. "I don't want to talk any longer." She slid down onto the mattress, having to wiggle a bit to find comfort.

But Justin wasn't done with her. He marched into the bedroom to stand over her. "You didn't want Penthorpe there, so you could do what? Burglarize him? No, wait, Penthorpe doesn't own anything worth burglarizing, at least not from someone like yourself."

She closed her eyes so she wouldn't have to look at him and feigned a yawn. "The lamp is bothering me. Would you turn the wick down?"

"What were you doing there?" Justin asked. "Why did you risk so much?"

But she didn't answer. Instead she pretended to be asleep.

He stood over her for a long moment, waiting for her to give up the game and answer his questions. It was a war of wills . . . or so he thought until, to his surprise, she did fall asleep. Her features softened, and he realized she'd been as exhausted as he.

Justin shook his head. "You are a bold one, lass," he told her sleeping form. "But if you think you can hide from me, you're wrong. I'll have your story in the morning."

For once she didn't snap back at him.

In fact she appeared as peaceful and loving as an angel. He had to protect her from herself. She didn't understand the world. She'd been sheltered and cosseted. It was up to him to see this matter set to rights.

Although his motives weren't completely pure. He wanted nothing more right now than to climb into bed and bury himself in her.

No matter what Justin thought of Miss Dunroy, another part of him lusted for her.

Justin put out the lamp and made himself walk into the other room. The fire was dying. He didn't bother to add more fuel. He needed the room cold. The colder the better.

With that thought, he stretched out again between settee and chair. He wasn't comfortable, which was good. He needed a bit of spartan treatment. He closed his eyes, his body so tense, he doubted if sleep would come.

He surprised himself.

In less than a minute, he was lost to the world.

Justin heard the knocking on his door, but he didn't want to wake up. His lashes felt glued shut, and he was having the best dream. It was one about sex. He was making love to a vibrant redhead on the edge of a rock cliff. Beyond them was the North Sea, as swirling and tumultuous as the joining of their bodies. His mission was to keep her safe from falling over that cliff, but first *he* needed some satisfaction. He was hard as an iron rod and there would be no peace—

"I know you are at home." Phillip's voice injected itself in the dream just when it was becoming interesting. "Open the door. We need to talk."

Sod off, Justin wanted to say but couldn't . . . anymore than he could recapture his dream. The redhead, Francesca—he recognized her now— had vanished. Disappeared from his arms, leaving him edgy and dissatisfied . . . and sleeping sprawled out between the settee and a chair in the most uncomfortable position possible.

Justin opened an eye. He was in his sitting room. *And why was that?*

Out in the hall, Phillip said, "Wake up, Justin." He pounded the door so hard, it shook on its hinges.

"Enough!" Justin barked. "I'll open the damn bloody door." He rolled off the settee. Nothing in this room was where it should be.

The moment he stood, he wished he hadn't, remembering the whiskey and Gordon. He reached over and tossed back the bolt on the door, just as another memory hit him.

It hadn't been a dream. He had made love to Francesca Dunroy.

He looked toward his bedroom. There was a movement under a bump of covers. *She was here.*

Phillip turned the handle, the door started to open, and Justin did what he must. He slammed that door shut, right in his twin's face, and threw the bolt.

Chapter 11

*T*he slamming of a door woke Francesca. She opened her eyes, her head still groggy from sleep, uncertain whether she imagined the man's protest of *"Hey"* or dreamed it.

She started to stretch but found her way hampered because her hands were bound with a white neck cloth to the bed's headboard. The knots didn't hurt but she was bound securely.

For a long second, Francesca stared at her bindings and then, to her horror, she remembered *everything*.

She'd let the Duke of Colster have his way with her.

And the duke, wearing nothing other than a pair of black evening breeches, was leaning on his front door, attempting to keep someone out of his rooms.

"What game are you playing?" the voice in the hallway demanded.

"Is that Penthorpe?" she asked in a hushed, panicked whisper.

Colster shook his head. "My brother."

Francesca thought her heart would stop. His brother, an acquaintance of her father's, and the model of respectability. *This was worse than Penthorpe.*

She should have left last night.

He wouldn't let her leave last night.

She should have left anyway. She should have jumped out of that window. Her nerve had failed her when she'd tried. She'd realized how far the drop was to the ground and had hesitated. That hesitation had been all the time Colster had needed to pull her back. But now it would be better to be dead on the pavement than discovered in the duke's bed by the most respectable man in London.

"Who are you talking to?" Lord Phillip asked from his side of the door.

In a hushed, confidential tone, the duke said, "I've got company, brother. Met a lass last night, and we've been a wee bit busy. Leave me to my sport and come back later."

Francesca frowned at him, even while memories of what had happened between them brought heat to her cheeks. She'd been a far too willing accomplice in her own ruin. Still . . . *How could he be bragging about bedding her?*

He correctly interpreted the glare in her eyes and gave her a *keep quiet* scowl of his own.

"You are in trouble," Lord Phillip said. "I can tell."

Colster rolled his eyes heavenward. "Stop pretending to read my mind. You can't do it. It's all wives' tales and twin nonsense."

"I'm not reading your mind," came the answer through the door. "Your brogue is always stronger when you are lying."

"My brogue is what it always is," the duke practically growled, his accent indeed sounding more pronounced.

"Justin, let me in. I woke last night with the strangest feeling you were in danger."

"The only danger I'm in now is of my temper exploding," the duke answered.

"It's a feeling I have," Lord Phillip insisted against the door.

"*I knew it.* I knew that was the direction you were heading. I am bloody tired of your 'feelings.' You can't feel what I'm feeling, Phillip. Because if you could, you'd know I'd had a jolly good time rogering a sweet young thing who right now is looking daggers at me because she wasn't ready to wake this early. Now go away. Be gone."

There was a long silence out in the hallway. Francesca could sense Phillip right there on the other side of the door. A piece of wood might be physically separating the twin brothers, but something more kept them apart.

When he answered, Lord Phillip's voice was so quiet, she needed to strain to hear it. "I worry about you."

"Don't." Colster's sharp reply held no pretense, and Francesca felt sorry for Lord Phillip. The man truly longed for a closeness with his brother, a closeness Colster appeared to resent.

Her suspicions were confirmed when Lord Phillip conceded, "You are right. I can be over-bearing."

"Can you?" Sarcasm laced Colster's words.

It was a jab that hit its mark.

"I am," Lord Phillip admitted. "Sorry. I just—" He stopped, and Francesca wished he'd finish. He shouldn't give up, even though it was obvious there was no reasoning with the duke at this point. For whatever reason, he was dead set against his twin . . . in much the same way she felt bitter about her father's marriage.

Her reasoning shocked her.

It seemed to have come out of nowhere and its truth made her uncomfortable. She scooted to sit taller in the bed, denying this errant thought. After all, all of London agreed with her.

Well, not *all* of London. A good portion of the *ton* had shown up under her father's roof to sip his champagne last night. Yes, they'd been there for the gossip, but they'd compromised their earlier outrage. Only her mother's great friend Lady Bastone had the courage and sense of propriety to refuse the invitation.

"I'll see you at dinner," Lord Phillip said.

"Dinner?" Colster asked.

"Remember? You promised to join us this evening before we leave for the opera. Come at half past seven."

Colster's response was to form his hand into a fist and pretend he was hitting the door with a mallet. "I'll be there," he answered with little enthusiasm.

Lord Phillip didn't respond. Colster waited, listening. A moment later he pushed away from the door. "He's gone."

Francesca was uncertain. She'd been too lost in her own problems to pick out the undercurrents between the twins. "Are you certain?" she asked.

He walked into the bedroom. "Yes, and not because I can read his mind," he said. "I heard him go down the stairs and the door close. Let me untie your hands."

But Francesca didn't move. She was angry on Lord Phillip's behalf. It kept a barrier between her and Colster. "You were rude to him."

"I wanted to send him away," he answered.

"But you weren't nice about it."

Colster pulled at the knot in her bindings. He looked scruffy in the morning . . . and perhaps even more handsome than he did clean-shaven.

Francesca edged away from him as far as she could. She didn't want to notice these things about him. She didn't want to be so aware of him . . . or aware of what they'd done last night.

He pulled on the knot. "You can't be nice with Phillip. He's too persistent, and it's either his way or none." He seemed very intent on the knot, or was he refusing to look at her?

"He's attempting to help you, to guide you."

Colster gave up loosening the knot. He faced her. "Miss Dunroy, my relationship with my brother isn't any of your business."

"You are just fortunate you have a brother to bicker with. If my brother was still alive, I'd be blessed to eat dinner with him every night." Her response surprised her, because it was true. She did envy him his sibling. And then to her horror, she burst into tears.

Colster stood abruptly as if her tears had stung him. That was fine. She wanted him to keep his distance, especially as she found herself crying harder. It wasn't that she hadn't cried when David died. Or for her mother.

Now she cried because everything seemed to have changed since that day her brother had drowned. Her life had lost its moorings. Her mother, always fragile, had given herself over to the weaknesses of her body and spirit. Her father had seemed to push all of them away. And Francesca's attempts to make everything right had failed.

It had been a disgrace, really, the way her family had fallen apart. Francesca had hidden her fears and worries in her mourning—and in disapproving of her father's behavior.

Now who was the sinner? What would everyone think once they knew that Francesca had been running around London in boy's clothes? Or had reacted with such wanton abandon to Colster's kisses?

She'd disgraced not only her brother and her mother's memories, but her father and Regina as well.

Colster lingered a moment in uncertainty and then walked to the dresser, pulled out a clean kerchief, and brought it over to her. "Here," he said, holding it out at arm's length, almost as if he feared coming closer.

Francesca hated having a witness to her tears.

Someone had once told her a good cry was good for the soul, but she didn't believe it. Nothing good had ever come to her through tears. They'd never solved one thing.

Nor could she take the kerchief from him with her hands tied.

She lifted them to let him see just how ridiculous his offer was. She wanted to stay angry with him. Anger would stem the flow of tears.

But it didn't. Now that she'd started, she was powerless to stop.

And then he did the worst thing he could. He untied her bonds, but instead of leaving her, he sat on the edge of the bed beside her and gathered her in his arms.

Her first instinct was to push him away, but her resistance was momentary. He had only to croon, "Come now," for her to bury her head against his shoulder and give in to the flood of emotion.

Ironically, once she'd given herself permission to cry, it was easier to stop the tears.

Spent, she couldn't have moved from his shoulder if she'd wanted to.

He placed the kerchief in her hand and she noisily wiped her nose, not moving from her resting place against his chest. He'd placed his arms around her, creating a protective, safe haven for her tears.

For a long moment, Francesca let him hold her.

And then he said, "I wasn't that mean to Phillip. All right, perhaps I was a bit spiteful." He was attempting humor, and it worked. His admission startled a laugh out of her, one that twisted into another sob.

"Stop," he ordered gently. "Men aren't good with tears, or at least I never am. I hate seeing women cry."

She couldn't look at him as she said, "I usually don't cry."

"I didn't think you did. That's why these are so alarming."

Francesca went still, her cheek against his chest. "Why didn't you think I'd cry?"

"Because you didn't last night," he said.

Shame threatened to consume her. His arms around her tightened, preventing her from pushing him away. "I'm sorry, Francesca. I should have stopped."

He'd given her the kerchief that she now balled up in her hand before asking, "Why didn't you?"

There was a beat of silence. She couldn't see his face but watched the movement of his throat as he answered, "You know why."

She did. They'd *both* gone too far. "I didn't want you to stop."

He tilted his head to rest it against hers. "Only because you haven't had the opportunity to consider the consequences. Trust me, Miss Dunroy, once you do, you will hate me. Perhaps forever."

Francesca doubted that. Wrapped in the comforting warmth of his arms, she knew he was the last person she could hate. She closed her eyes a moment and felt the pulse of his heart beating through his veins. "Like you want your brother to hate you?" The words just rolled out of her mouth, but once spoken, they made perfect sense.

And they caught him off guard. He pulled back to look down at her. Their eyes met, his so brown they could be black. The corners of his mouth tightened. "You don't know anything about it."

"I understand being angry all the time and knowing there is nothing you can do to stop. That anger you have . . . it's not at him. Not really."

Colster might have been raised a blacksmith but he had the pride of a duke. His arms opened and he stood, his manner suddenly cold. "I'll let you have a moment alone first," he said, nodding toward the bathroom.

She resented his abrupt change. A moment ago they'd been so close, her skin had seemed to meld with his. Now he acted as if they were strangers, and she didn't like it.

"I beg your pardon, Your Grace. I didn't mean to overstep my bounds." She started to rise and would have swept into the bathroom except he placed himself in her path.

"You are right. I am angry." He shook his head, a muscle tightening in his whisker-scruffy jaw. "Where did you come from, Francesca? You are not like anyone else I've met here. You see too much, and you think about it. You are like a thorn in my conscience."

"Does your conscience need a good jabbing?" she asked, uncaring if she offended him or not.

"No," he answered. "I was fine until I met you. I'll be fine after."

"And what does that mean?" she challenged.

"It means you don't know anything, lass. Your life has been perfect." He would have turned and walked away, but the last accusation had aroused Francesca's temper.

She caught him by the crook of the arm. "My life is far from perfect. And I know a thing or two about how unsettling it is to lose what you had once known. There was a time when my father and I were close. That was a long time ago, when my brother was alive. Everything went wrong after his death, so don't believe you are the only one who is at odds with his family."

"Your brother died?" Colster repeated. "How?"

"He drowned. He was out sailing with friends and a storm came up. They were all lost."

"I'm sorry."

I'm sorry. How many times had she heard those meaningless words after David's death? After her mother's?

"It was years ago," she answered with a shrug. She rarely said more . . . except this time, she found herself adding, "Mother had never been strong, but after his death, she just stopped trying. And then Father found Regina, and all that was left of what we once were was me."

"And you believe I'm harsh on Phillip."

"I thought you brutal to him."

Colster's gaze narrowed. "Would you rather I had invited him in?"

He had a point. She wouldn't. At the same time, she sensed there was more. "Don't use me as an excuse. Last night, when I met you on the library terrace, you were avoiding him."

"And you would, too," Colster answered as if throwing down a gauntlet. "Phillip's perfect. He knows how to be a duke. He's never muddled or blundered his way through anything. When he walks into a room, everyone bows and scrapes—and do you know why? Because they respect him. When I walk into a room, they gawk like a gaggle of geese and then talk past me to my brother."

"They are curious. They don't know you," she answered.

"They don't want to know me."

He was right.

"They enjoy the drama," the duke assured her, and she had to nod.

At the same time, she needed to say, "If you don't want them to enjoy it so much, then you shouldn't give it to them."

"Is this advice from the woman who slapped me in front of everyone last night?"

He had her. "I was provoked."

Colster smirked his response. "Your father gives you your lead far more than is good for you. If you were my daughter, I would have you tied to my side where you couldn't find trouble with the likes of Penthorpe."

"Or yourself," she answered with a false sweetness, bristling at the notion that she needed watching. "Oh, wait, you are the one who tied me to the bedpost."

The lines of his mouth flattened. "Oh, that you had been better guarded last night," Colster agreed. "Then we wouldn't be in the devil of a fix we are this morning."

Francesca's guard came up. She knew where he was going. " 'We' are in no difficulty. I don't hold you accountable, Your Grace. Help me return to my house unseen and your responsibility to me is done." She would have punctuated her words by walking right past him—except for his arm coming out to bar her way.

There was an unholy gleam in his eye as he said, "Do you expect me to turn my back on my obligations as a gentleman, lass?"

She used all her courage to meet his eye. "What I'm saying is that I won't marry for anything but love, Your Grace. Now, if you will excuse me——?" She started toward the door to the bathing room.

He moved out of her way.

However, once alone with the bathing room's door shut, she almost collapsed. Matching wits with him was dangerous. She was relieved that he'd finally let her go.

"There's tooth powder on the shelf," he called to her through the door. "And the soap is my scent but I don't think you'll mind it much. I have nothing else."

Francesca walked toward the washbasin, reaching for the tooth powder as if her body moved by pulleys and levers. A glance in the mirror told her she had never looked worse. Her hair was every which way and hopelessly tangled, and her eyes were still swollen from crying. She felt soiled, dirty . . . but not used.

What had happened last night couldn't be undone. There was no denying it, but she knew she could overcome the consequences of her own decisions.

"After all, you are an heiress," she reminded

her reflection. "You have money. Someone will marry you." It's just that she'd never know what it was like to be loved.

And maybe she'd been foolish to dream of such a thing. She'd fancied herself in love with Penthorpe and look how he'd betrayed her. Even her father hadn't loved her mother, not truly. He'd married too soon after her death. If he had loved her, he would have waited . . . maybe even forever.

She leaned forward, resting her head against the glass, wondering if she was foolish to believe such a love as the one conjured from her imagination and wistfulness could exist—

"The water in the pitcher is probably cold," Colster's voice said from the other side of the door, intruding on her thoughts. "It will have to do. I've no desire to call my valet for fresh or he'll wonder what's come over me. I usually don't trouble him in the mornings."

Francesca poured water into the basin bowl and reached for a towel to wet and press against her skin. "The water is fine," she said.

"I'm not ruined," she vowed to her reflection. "I will survive." She'd already survived so much, she would not be defeated yet—

"Francesca, you sound a bit strained."

"I'm not going to cry again," she assured him, splashing some more water on her face. "I'm strong.

This will all work out," she tried to say, but the words came out a whisper.

The door handle turned. Before she could stop him, Colster entered. He'd put on a shirt, clean breeches, and boots. He appeared gallant, noble.

For a second he stood there. "I'm not much. I know that. But I will make it all right."

He sounded humble, earnest—and it made her feel vile. This was her fault. But she had her pride. She'd not trick a man into marrying her.

Francesca ran a hand through her wayward hair. "Didn't you hear me a few moments ago? I won't marry someone I don't love."

She expected him to be relieved. Instead the lines on his face deepened. "What does love have to do with bloody marriage? Besides, you don't have a choice, lass." He paused as if struck by a new thought. "Think of your mother. Would you disgrace her memory?"

"You—" She broke off, unable to think of a word ugly enough to describe him. "How dare you bring up my mother's name?"

"I dare because that is what she would want me to do."

She sliced the air with an angry hand. "You know nothing about her, *or me*. And if you think to blackmail me into marriage, then let me inform you, it won't work. *I* will decide whom I marry."

Colster leaned back against the door frame, studying her for a moment, the expression in his eyes unreadable. "And what do we say about last night? Do you really believe we pretend it didn't happen?"

Something in his voice caught her. She wasn't certain what he was saying. She assumed he didn't truly want to marry her any more than she wanted to marry him. And yet was there a wistfulness in his speech . . . or was it her imagination?

To discover the answer, she would have to reveal something of herself.

Francesca could not allow herself to be that vulnerable. "We must."

"Is it Penthorpe then?" he asked. "Do you love him?"

She was so startled by the question, she almost laughed. "No."

Colster's scrutiny seared her. She met his gaze, her head high, but it took courage.

At last he straightened. "Very well, we shall do this your way, Miss Dunroy. But understand, if you are with child, all games are over."

Francesca hadn't thought about pregnancy. She placed a hand on her abdomen. She'd hardly ever thought about becoming a mother. "I understand."

"You'd come to me." It wasn't a question but a statement.

He was willing to take care of her, to do what

was noble. It was the price they'd both pay for last night. "I would."

He released his breath as if he'd been uncertain. "Good. We'll have to do something with your hair if you are to continue this charade. I'll fetch a hat."

"I had one I wore over here."

"It's gone now."

He was right. A moment later, he handed her a floppy brimmed hat that had seen better days. "It's the sort of hat one wears doing hard work in the sun," he explained, seeing the question in her eyes.

"Was it yours?"

A dull red crept up his neck. "No," he said curtly. "I bought it from a man."

"Why?" she wondered.

"It reminded me of one I once had." He acted dismissive . . . but Francesca sensed there was more.

"It's a reminder of who you were?" she suggested.

Colster took a step back, and she knew she'd been right. However, instead of answering, he started out the door. "Take your time," he said. "I'll order Biddle to hire a hack. If we are to sneak you back into your father's house, a ducal coach would not be wise."

"No," she agreed.

Their gazes met again briefly. They both looked away at the same time. He shut the door. A few minutes later, she heard the hallway door open and close.

Francesca sat on the edge of the plunge tub, realizing that here was a man she could admire. There was a kindness to Colster she'd not seen in others. And he meant his words. He would help her. He didn't agree with what she wanted to do, but he meant those words.

She wondered if it would be possible for them to put this behind them. She knew she would never forget what had happened between them.

But no good came of regrets.

Besides, Colster was a man, and she'd be naïve to think he wasn't like all the others. No matter what he said now, he probably was secretly relieved he'd have her off his hands.

She forced herself to think about the tasks at hand. Use of the tooth powder made her feel better, as did taming her hair by braiding it the best she could. She tucked it under the hat that was far too large for her head. However, it accommodated all her hair very well.

Colster had returned while she'd repaired her appearance. He'd put on a coat of marine blue superfine and a fresh, starched neck cloth and was tidying the sitting room when she made her presence known by saying, "Most people have servants for that."

He acknowledged her with a smile. "Poor Biddle only irritates me most the time. I've already spent years taking care of myself and am a bit set in my ways."

"There was no one in your life before coming to London?" She knew he would think she was asking about servants, but she wasn't.

She *was* curious if there had been a woman. There had to have been. He was too much of a man, too strong, too masculine—too experienced a lover—to have been alone.

For a second, she sensed he knew her true question. His gaze shifted away from hers. "I was a blacksmith, Miss Dunroy. No one cared about me." He changed the subject, the tone in his voice lighter, "That hat doesn't suit you, lass."

"I wanted it to make me ugly."

"It doesn't do that, any more than your disguise hides you are a woman. It's the breeches, you know. Men don't wear breeches the same as women. And we must do something about your breasts."

Heat flooded her cheeks. She had to resist crossing her arms as he went into the bedroom and came out with the neck cloth he'd used to tie her up. "You'd best flatten yourself, lass."

Francesca took the neck cloth and practically ran into the privacy of the bathing room. When she came out, he embarrassed her with a grunt of approval. He put on his hat and picked up a stack of books.

"You carry this," he ordered, plopping the heavy books into her hands. For the briefest second, they touched, and she realized how conscious she was of every nuance about him. "Our ruse is that you are some boy I've hired to do an errand."

She nodded, just as a knock sounded on the door. "Your Grace, the hack has arrived."

"Thank you, Biddle," Colster answered. He rubbed his cheek where the scar was. "Do you have a way back into your house without being detected?" he asked.

"Yes, I'm going to climb the brick wall."

"Climb a wall? In daylight?"

She ignored his doubts. "That part of the garden is hidden by trees. I shall manage if you can help me reach the back alleyway."

He frowned.

"I'm a good climber," she assured him. "My brother and I climbed over those walls many times. We used to drive our father mad with that game."

"He'd be really irritated now."

"He's not going to catch me," she vowed.

"We can hope," Colster murmured and placed a hand on the door. However, before he opened it, he said quietly, "And you are right, Francesca. No good comes of marrying a man if you can't love him fully and completely. Being trapped in a loveless marriage makes life a private hell."

There had been someone in his life before. The bite of jealousy was staggering. She'd not known him long enough to feel anything, let alone territorial.

He didn't seem to notice her reaction to his inadvertent confession. Instead he squared his shoulders, the role of bored aristocrat settling around him with ease. "Come along, boy. We have books to deliver."

He opened the door and started through without waiting for her. It was assumed Francesca would accept her role and follow like a dutiful lackey.

And she did. She had no choice except to lower her head like any good servant, the floppy brim of her hat covering her eyes, and follow. For now she was completely dependent upon Colster's whims and wishes and word as a gentleman.

The worst of this whole escapade was that it had been for naught, because she didn't have the pearl. There had been a few sweet seconds when she'd held it in her hand. However, after the force of Colster's tackle, it was probably lost forever in Penthorpe's untidy clutter.

Indeed, in the light of day, last night's bold plan seemed remarkably foolish. She should have paid off Penthorpe and been done with it. That was what comes from too much pride—

Francesca walked into Colster's back. She hadn't even noticed he'd stopped—and then realized that they weren't alone. Penthorpe was in front of his door, leaning against it as if his head hurt. He was having difficulty finding the handle.

Colster's hand came back and gave her arm a reassuring squeeze before he stepped forward. "Good morning, Penny," he said as if he'd said it a hundred times. "A winning night?"

"If it had been, I would feel better," came the guttural reply. Penthorpe released his breath and the liquor fumes rolled through the air, reaching even as far as where Francesca stood. "I say, Your Grace, can you help me find a way into my rooms?"

"Down a bundle, hmmm?" Colster asked as he reached over and opened the door.

Penthorpe practically rolled into his room. "My luck will return."

The duke didn't say anything. He merely smiled, and Francesca suspected he was pleased she had the opportunity to see this dark side to Penthorpe.

Little did he know, she'd already witnessed it.

With a tilt of his head, Colster motioned her forward as he started down the stairs.

Francesca gave one last tug of her hat over her eyes and followed. Penthorpe shut the door without a second glance at her, and Francesca released the breath she was holding.

At the bottom of the stairs, in front of the door, where they were alone, Colster stopped. Without looking back at her, his hand on the door, he said, "I don't regret what happened last night."

She didn't, either. But she couldn't confess that. The habit of keeping her emotions to herself was too strong.

"If you need me, Francesca, send word and I will come to your side. You aren't alone."

His promise touched her deeply. It had been so long since anyone had cared about her welfare, her needs. "I will."

"I'll hold you to that promise, lass." He opened the door.

The hack waited outside, as did Colster's valet. "I could have sent for the ducal coach, Your Grace," Biddle said anxiously. He reached to open the door. The hack's driver sat in the box with his hat in his hand out of respect for the status of his passenger.

Colster scowled. Francesca knew he didn't want a fuss made. "I didn't want the ducal coach," he answered Biddle, and motioned for Francesca to climb in, no small feat with her load of books.

She could feel the valet's inquisitive gaze upon her. Personal servants always wanted to know their master's business, and a "boy" hired without his knowledge would inspire curiosity. Consequently she ducked her head and obeyed Colster, but was brought up short when she realized the coach wasn't empty.

Lord Phillip sat inside the hack's close confines, waiting for them.

Chapter 12

*T*he moment Francesca hesitated, half in and half out of the hack, Justin knew something was wrong.

He was not surprised to see the "problem" was his brother.

A cold rage stole over him.

"Climb in," he instructed Francesca in a voice that brooked no argument.

She did as ordered.

Justin swung himself into the hack and took his seat. He and his twin took up most of the space inside the cab. Miss Dunroy was squeezed between them, the stack of books on her lap.

It was a good thing she was there. Otherwise Justin would not have been able to control the impulse to throttle Phillip. Did his twin believe that he had the right to force himself into every nook and cranny of his life?

Shutting the door, Justin leaned out the window to say to Biddle, "Pack your bags. You're no longer under my employ."

The valet's face paled.

Phillip quickly interjected, "My being here isn't his fault. I took it upon myself."

"Then take it upon yourself to employ him," Justin countered. "I'll not pay wages to a man who isn't loyal to me."

Phillip didn't miss a beat. Leaning across Francesca, he said out the window, "Present yourself to my household, Biddle."

"Yes, my lord," the chastened valet answered, backing away from the hack.

"And you can climb right out of this hack," Justin said to his brother. "I'm not riding with you. Not when I'm so bloody angry."

Phillip leaned back in his corner to look down his nose at Francesca. "What are you up to, Justin? You told me you were lazing in bed with a lass. Boys are not your style—"

His voice broke off. He then blinked in surprise. "What the devil—?" He pulled Francesca's hat off her head. Her braid came tumbling down while the curls around her face sprang to life. "Miss Dunroy?"

"Since you know who she is," Justin drawled, "why don't you give the driver her address."

"You spent the night with Francesca Dunroy?" Phillip turned to Francesca. "The two of you were together?"

"Don't answer him," Justin ordered. "I would, but any answer *I* give, he won't believe."

"Justin, what the blazes have you done?" Phillip said but Francesca was quick to jump in.

"It's not his fault. It's mine. I went to him."

"You went to my brother's apartments?" Phillip shook his head. "I'm sorry, but I find that difficult to believe—"

"Absolutely," Justin agreed, interrupting. "After all, I am the wayward twin. I lured you there and ravished you."

"Justin, you aren't making this better," Phillip said.

"Give the driver her address," Justin flashed back.

But it was Francesca who took the books off her lap, placing half on Phillip's and half on Justin's. She had to rise to uncap and use the speaking tube. She gave the driver the instructions and sat back down between the glowering brothers. The hack started forward. She didn't bother to take the books back but crossed her arms, looking as if she felt decidedly uncomfortable.

Justin didn't bother to hide all the distrust and

resentment he was feeling. He'd had every intention of speaking to Phillip today about Gordon's accusations last night. He would have done so in private but he was so angry at his twin's constant interference in his life, he could not hold back.

"You sent troops back to Nathraichean," he lashed out. "After what you and I discussed in Edinburgh, that we would leave the people alone, you betrayed your word. The garrison returned and set fire to cottages, tents, and fields."

Phillip's jaw tightened. "We *were* talking about you having the daughter of a respectable family in your bed. He was our host last night, Justin. What do you think you are doing?"

Francesca opened her mouth as if to speak, but Justin silenced her by dumping the books back in her lap. He leaned across her to say to his brother, "You lied to me."

Phillip moved back in his corner of the hack, but this time, he addressed the subject. "Nathraichean was built to be a militant stronghold," he answered. "After our return to London, higher authorities felt we should investigate further. We couldn't allow Laird MacKenna, Bruce, and Gordon free rein. They were rebels."

"You burned the fields, Phillip. MacKenna wasn't out in the fields. Those were for food for women and children. You left them nothing."

"I didn't order anything burned," his twin

countered. "But I have a responsibility to the Crown—"

"Yes," Justin agreed. "The same one I'm expected to have." And *couldn't*. Gordon was right. He would have to take sides. "At the very least, why didn't you tell me what had happened at Nathraichean, Phillip? You obviously didn't want me to know. You knew I'd be angry, didn't you? You wanted me so busy learning how to use the right fork, I'd not think of my clansmen."

"No," Phillip said, "I thought family, your *true* family was more important . . . even though since we arrived in London you've done everything to tell me different."

Here was the gist of it. The question was one of loyalty.

"I can't change years of what I was taught in a few weeks," Justin said.

"You aren't even trying," his brother countered. "You have shut me out. And who have you been talking to? How did you know about Nathraichean?"

"Why?" Justin wanted to know. "Was its fate a secret?"

Phillip's gaze narrowed. "Are you going to give *them* the sword?"

Justin didn't answer.

Phillip eyed him warily. "Don't. You could set the Highlands on fire. So many lives would be lost—and we'd win, Justin. They can't defeat the Crown."

"I know that."

His twin waited, expecting something more. The silence stretched between them. Francesca stared straight ahead as if wishing she were someplace else. Justin wondered if she understood what was being discussed, and assumed she had pieced it together. She was no fool.

Finally Phillip asked the question Justin knew he'd wanted to all along. "Where is the sword?"

"Safe."

"How can you be certain?"

Justin smiled grimly. "Oh, I'm certain. But your true question is how can *you* be certain? You'll have to trust me."

An angry muscle ticked in his brother's jaw. "And will I have to trust you about Miss Dunroy, too?"

"Yes, but not for my sake. For hers."

"None of this is his fault," Francesca said quickly.

Phillip sat back in his corner. "What? Are you going to tell me you took yourself over to his apartments . . ." His voice trailed off as he looked her up and down, truly taking notice beyond her face for the first time. "You're wearing breeches."

Francesca, God bless her darling soul, didn't even flinch. "I am. Do you believe I'll set a new style?"

"I pray not," came the dampening reply. "And I believe you are flirting with disaster."

"I have been," Francesca admitted. "But it's my fault. His Grace is blameless."

Justin could argue that point with her. He sat beside her, his hands resting on the book she'd shoved into his lap, careful not to touch her in any way, and completely conscious of her every movement, even to the very breath she drew.

She was his. Last night he'd claimed her, and if Phillip said anything rude, if he insulted her in any way, Justin was ready to rip out his twin's tongue, if need be.

And, yet, at the same time, Justin was conscious that he didn't really want to be at odds with his brother. He'd put distance between them for Phillip's protection as well as his own. He'd feared what those who wanted the sword would do . . . although he did trust Gordon to be honorable.

Phillip's gaze met his, and Justin knew his brother understood that on the topic of Francesca, there would be no compromise. He either accepted the circumstances or there *would* be an irreconcilable difference between them.

"So," Phillip said at last, "we are taking you home."

He spoke to Francesca, but Justin answered. "We are."

"Are we speaking to her father?" Phillip asked.

"*No*," Francesca said.

Phillip frowned. "I'm sorry, but this goes against my sense of right and wrong, Miss Dunroy. You know, my brother really isn't such a bad sort. I'll grant you that he is grumpy and often ill-mannered, but he does have an occasional charm. You could do worse for a husband."

"Thank you, Phillip," Justin said. "I love you, too."

The hint of a smile came to his brother's lips. "I only live to serve," he murmured.

However, Francesca answered him seriously. "I agree with you," she said baldly. "And I'd add the word 'overbearing' to your list. But this matter is between *us*." She said this last sweetly, but firmly.

"I'm not the overbearing one," Justin couldn't help muttering.

"The two of you are more alike than you wish," Francesca informed him complacently.

Phillip's face split into a huge grin. Justin glanced at him. "What?" he demanded.

His twin shrugged. "Did I speak a word?"

"You don't have to," Justin informed him. He knew Phillip liked Francesca's outspokenness. And well he should. His wife, Charlotte, never held back her opinion, either.

Francesca placed herself between the brothers by commenting on how pleased she was that autumn had at last arrived, a polite but firm changing from more volatile subjects. Phillip picked up her cue and commented that he actually enjoyed summer. He liked the heat. The two proceeded to discuss the vagaries of the weather as if it were the most fascinating of subjects.

Justin was left to his own thoughts.

A part of him was actually relieved Francesca wasn't insisting on marriage.

Another was disappointed, and more than slightly offended. He'd had the impression that debutantes were like hothouse flowers and had to be handled carefully.

Francesca was the opposite. He'd frightened her last night. She had not expected sex. Had not truly known what it was. But she had adapted to circumstances. Hers was the sort of courage that would see her through anything. The sort of courage he admired. And he was still strongly attracted to her. Perhaps even more so than when they'd first met.

He reminded himself that at one time, he'd admired and been attracted to Moira, too. Early on, when they'd first married and before Bruce laid eyes on her, they'd been happy. Then came the day when she'd informed him she'd never loved him and had left him for Bruce. It was like having a knife put through his heart. He'd been raised an orphan, and Moira's love had been all he'd wanted.

Just a little over a month ago, she'd physically

attempted to stab him in an effort to claim the Sword of the MacKenna from him.

Francesca was right to insist upon love in a marriage.

Justin glanced at her. She talked to Phillip about strawberries in June, completely at ease with the small talk that was so much a part of their set . . . of their upbringing.

If she had doubts or fears, she had the courage to keep them to herself.

And he found himself wondering what it would take for a man to claim the love of such a woman.

Then he thought of Penthorpe. Francesca didn't act as if she admired or even liked the rake . . . still, she had to have a reason for risking all to go to his rooms . . . and it was easier, and wiser, for him to focus on her inconsistencies instead of her attractions.

The hack slowed to a halt by Miss Dunroy's front door. With an impatient sound, Justin ordered the driver to keep moving and go around back.

They were all quiet as the vehicle made its way to the coach alley behind the row of houses on the street. Both Phillip and Justin placed the books on the floor.

"What is the plan?" Phillip asked, ready to take part in whatever.

"I don't have a plan," Justin answered, "other than to see her over that wall safe."

"You don't need to stay with me," she quickly informed him. "I don't want you caught up in my foolishness."

"I'll see you over the wall," Justin insisted, and this time she didn't protest.

"Take the hack a block away to the north," he informed Phillip. "I'll meet up with you there after I know she is safely home."

Phillip didn't argue, either.

Justin got out on his side of the hack and held the door open for the disguised Francesca before motioning the driver to go on. At this time of the morning, between early chores and luncheon, the alley was deserted.

The hack moved on and Justin found himself in front of a ten-foot-high brick wall. "I used a gate to leave last night," he said, remembering. He nodded to the arched door built into the wall. "You can just go in."

"It's locked," she answered, staring at the wall with a furrow of concern between her brows. "It's always locked from the outside. I'm not such a ninny I wouldn't have thought of using it if I could. After all, it's how I left last night. However, there used to be ivy covering this wall. Father has had it cut away. You can see it was done recently. Perhaps for last night's party." She released a heavy sigh. "I'll have to walk in the front door."

"There is no servants' entrance?"

"It leads right into the kitchen. I'll certainly be caught that way. However, if I time my entrance right, this time of day, when the servants take their meal, the front door is often unguarded."

"Didn't you have one of your footmen with you last night?" Justin asked.

"Yes, Jeremy. His wife is my maid, Rose. They should be watching for me." She squared her shoulders and gave him a brave smile. "You go on, Your Grace . . . and thank you. I'm sorry I've been so foolish."

She meant those words and he wasn't leaving.

"You'll be caught," he said. "Dressed in lad's clothing, there is no fib you can tell to cover yourself."

"It's the risk I'll take."

"No, you wait here." He removed his hat and looked up at the wall.

"What are you going to do?"

"Scale it." It was a high wall, but he might be able to do it. He shrugged out of his coat. "Hold this, please." He handed both coat and hat to her and then stepped back. If he could jump high enough to reach the top, he could pull himself over. Farther down the alley, he noticed a wooden water trough. It would give him the leverage he needed to reach the top. "I'll climb the wall and let you in through the gate. Your father doesn't have any dogs, does he?"

"None you need to worry over—but why are you doing this? Your Grace?" she called as he went after the water trough. She followed him. "What excuse will *you* give if you are caught?"

Justin stopped. "What were *you* going to say?"

"I wasn't planning to be caught," she informed him.

"I'm not, either." The water trough was practically empty. Justin lifted it with muscles honed through years spent over a forge, dumped what little water was in it, and carried it to the wall.

Francesca followed with a worried expression on her face. "I don't want you involved. The risk is too great."

"I already am involved," he said, setting the trough against the wall. He stepped on it. It held his weight easily. He smiled down at her. "See? We won't be caught because everything is going our way."

Her answer was to grip his coat tighter. "Don't hurt yourself then," she whispered.

"I won't."

It had been years since he'd scrambled up a wall. He was a man now and not a boy—but he still managed.

For a moment he sat on top of the wall, enjoying

the view of Dunroy's garden. "You were wise not to attempt this," he informed Francesca. "The vines on the other side have been cut away, too."

As he said the last, he looked down at her—and his heart made the funniest little skip.

She held his coat close in her arms. Red curls had escaped from her cap, and no one seeing her would believe she was a male. Her figure might be hidden but there was too much femininity in her eyes. Even her nose had the sweetest feminine tilt. But what really caught him was the implicit trust in her eyes.

This was what it felt like to be a hero.

Her trust made him believe he could slay the demons of society by jumping over walls and protecting stubborn redheads from themselves.

She was the one who brought reality to the moment. "You'd best hurry," she urged. "Someone could come out of the house at any moment."

He threw his other leg over the wall and jumped to the ground, with bone-jarring force. He waited a moment, listening. No alarm sounded, so he crossed over to the door, lifted the latch, and let her in.

Safely inside the garden, she was so relieved and so happy, she came up on her toes and threw her arms around him, crushing both his coat and his hat. "Thank you," she whispered into his neck. "Thank you, *thank you.*"

And that was how it started.

Justin hadn't meant to kiss her. He should have taken his jacket and hat from her and moved on.

But he couldn't. His arms went around her waist. Their lips found each other.

One last kiss, he told himself. One taste of her before their lives moved on in different directions.

She didn't fight him. Instead she, too, understood this would be the last between them. With a soft sigh that sounded very much like contentment, she opened to him.

The sunshine, the greenness of the garden, the air against his cheek, the busy hum of bees—all faded. And just as it had happened the night before, the world centered on their kiss.

Her head tilted back and that silly hat fell off and onto the ground. Her vibrant braid tumbled free. It was coming loose from its plaiting and he was tempted to spread it loose around her shoulders. Hair like hers tempted a man. It was her halo, her crowning glory—

All was rudely cut short by Maximus Dunroy's stern, deep voice saying, "Take your hands off my daughter."

Chapter 13

Francesca turned, startled by the interruption, and stared at her father, needing a moment after that kiss to even recognize him—and the trouble she was in.

Her first thought was to protect Justin. "It's not what you think, Father—"

"Go to your room," he cut in, not sparing her so much as a glance.

"But—" she started.

"To your room, Francesca." He spoke to her as if she were a child. To Justin, he said, "Your Grace, I believe we have something to discuss."

"At your pleasure, sir," Justin answered. He dropped his hands from her waist.

"My pleasure is *now*."

Justin bowed his agreement, before saying quietly to her, "Go. It will be all right."

No, it wouldn't. "Father, if you would please let me have a moment to explain—"

Her father whirled on her, his eyes ablaze with fury. "Did I not send you to your room? Or are you going to continue to parade yourself around in indecent clothing?"

"It's not what it seems," she answered, needing for him to understand.

"It doesn't matter 'what it seems,'" her father answered, mocking her. "'Tis what it *is* that has importance."

Justin's hands came down upon her shoulders. "Do as he says, lass. Go change."

She turned to him. "I want him to listen to me."

Her father made a rude, impatient noise. "I've had enough of this. Your Grace, follow me." He didn't wait but went marching toward the house.

The duke said to her, "This is a matter between men, Francesca."

"It concerns me, too," she said. She wanted a voice. She wanted to be heard . . . but then she saw Regina standing on the terrace where only last night the party had been held.

She came down the stairs into the garden, walking toward them. "Francesca, your father wants me to take you upstairs."

Francesca's response was to stand in front of

Justin, her hands on her hips as if she'd protect him from all of them.

But he didn't want protection. "Go on," he told her. "I can tend for myself."

He was right. Still . . . "Why do men believe they can run roughshod over women?"

"Because, in this case," Justin said, "the man is your father and he does have your best interests at heart. Go on, love."

The word "love" caught her. His use of it meant that he saw the two of them as a pair. A team.

Her feet started moving in the direction he wanted her to go. He followed her a step or two before splitting off, heading in the direction of the library terrace on the other side of the house.

Francesca stopped, wanting to ask him if he'd really said what she thought he'd said. *Love.* It had fallen so easily from his lips.

Or had she imagined it?

"Francesca," Regina prompted. "The servants are watching."

It wasn't Regina's reminder to good behavior that gave Francesca's feet wings. It was the need to see Justin as quickly as possible. She wanted to know if he would use that word again.

She was so anxious, she practically raced Regina inside the house and up the back stairs to her bedroom.

"Francesca, stop," Regina complained.

"I can't. I must change so I can talk to Father." She went into her room calling for her maid.

But Rose didn't appear as summoned. Usually Rose was always present when Francesca needed her. Francesca took a step toward the dressing room, only to have Regina's voice at the doorway stop her cold with the words, "Rose is no longer with us."

Uncertain she'd heard correctly, Francesca turned. "Excuse me? Rose has been my maid for ten years and more. What has happened to her?"

"She's been sacked." Regina signaled to someone down the hall to come before entering the bedroom. A step later, Regina's maid, Kathleen, came in carrying Francesca's green muslin day dress, freshly pressed, over her arm. The soft muslin was trimmed in apricot ribbons and was one of her most demure dresses and her father's favorite.

Francesca didn't move. "Father would not have let Rose go."

"He did when we discovered you missing. Jeremy is no longer in our employ, either."

The air suddenly seemed to be sucked from the room. Francesca struggled to breathe. "When did Father know I was gone?"

"Jeremy told him," Regina said, sitting on the dainty chair beside Francesca's writing table. "He was a very loyal servant. He was worried for you—although he said he didn't know who had taken you and refused to divulge where you'd gone. Your father was so angry, he had him tossed out of the house."

Poor Jeremy. He'd been caught between loyalty to her and fear of what had happened.

"Your father was organizing a search party to go through every building in London, if necessary, when we saw the Duke of Colster come over the wall." She frowned, her expression petulant. "Francesca, what were you thinking, leaving like that? And how did you end up with Colster? Did he rescue you in some way?"

Francesca ignored her questions. She was still too stunned about the fate of her most trusted servants. "Rose was with me when they gave me the news my brother drowned. She sat beside me through countless nights as I nursed Mother. She was like a member of the family."

"She helped you leave the house last night. Such a transgression cannot be overlooked," Regina replied.

Francesca stifled the urge to scream her anger. Instead she moved toward action. The sooner she changed, the sooner she could confront her father. Everything must be set to rights. She turned to Regina's stern-faced lady's maid. "Follow me." She marched into her dressing room, Kathleen on her heels. Regina followed uninvited.

Kicking the breeches off onto the floor and tearing

the shirt up over her head, Francesca made quick work of undressing, mentally rehearsing what she would say to her father. She would confess all, even to the clandestine meeting with Penthorpe and losing the necklace, if her father would let Rose and Jeremy stay.

Kathleen's fingers were nimble and she had Francesca laced into petticoats and dressed in a heartbeat. While she'd dressed, Regina had been twirling and arranging her own blond curls. Francesca had caught her admiring herself before. It was all part of her stepmother's silliness. She was like a child.

Francesca walked right over to the vanity, picked up the brush, and shouldered Regina out of the way of the mirror.

For once her stepmother didn't take offense. Instead she suggested, "Why don't you sit and let Kathleen do your hair? She's very good. And quick."

It was the quickness that caused Francesca to sit. Kathleen hurried over to take the brush. With efficient movements she began styling Francesca's hair on top of her head, allowing the curls to fall in a riot of bright color around her shoulders. No amount of time under a cap or braiding could tame them.

However, allowing Kathleen to style her hair gave Francesca time to think. Her temper cooled, but not her resolve. She shoved aside all pretenses she'd once had. Her role in this household was as a guest.

Her stepmother came to stand beside her. "Oleander was the one who informed your father and me you were missing." Oleander was the Dunroy family butler. "Poor Max couldn't relax until you returned. Of course, I was the same way—"

Francesca doubted that.

"—but in my condition, I must be very careful."

Her condition?

Francesca motioned to Kathleen to pause. "Your condition?"

Regina smiled and placed her palm against her belly. "Your father and I are to have a baby."

If the hand of God had come down from the heavens and knocked Francesca off the stool in front of the vanity, she could not have been more shocked. She hadn't ever thought about her father and Regina breeding—

"Your father hopes for a son," Regina continued, sounding actually happy and not at all as if she'd just thrown Francesca's world off its axis. "He wants one to replace your brother."

Francesca balled her hands into fists, hurt by such callous words. "My brother can't be replaced." She had to force the words out of her throat.

Regina's lips parted in genuine surprise. "I didn't mean it to sound that way."

Yes, you did. But Francesca bit the words back.

Instead she murmured, "I need to see my father." She came to her feet. Kathleen was still fussing with her hair but Francesca waved her away. "It's fine. Thank you."

Regina followed her out. "Francesca, please. I didn't mean to say something to upset you. It's just that we are so happy."

Francesca whirled on her. "Of course you are—" She stopped, not trusting herself to say more. Nor did she pause until she reached the top of the stairs. There she doubled over, giving way to the almost overwhelming pain of betrayal.

How could her father start another family? He'd replaced his wife, and now he would replace his son. He didn't even want his daughter.

And he was probably downstairs now, carrying on to Justin about how precious she was to him. Anything to marry Francesca off to a duke.

Unshed tears burned her eyes, begging for release. But she wouldn't give in. Not yet. She had to reach the library.

Francesca hurried down the stairs and through the hallway to the library door. She slowed her step when she saw Oleander standing guard. He saw her coming and drew himself up, ready to block her entry. He was a compact, trim man with gray, closely cropped hair. He'd once told her his hairstyle came from years of wearing a wig, something he abhorred to do now.

Francesca stopped. Oleander eyed her warily. He'd been in charge of the Dunroy household since she was born. She'd spent many afternoons following him around and teasing him with questions.

Now he blocked her way.

She moved toward him. "You, too, Oleander? You would turn against me? You, who came to this house with my mother upon her marriage. You would defend him?" She referred to her father.

"The master insists you wait in the sitting room."

Sent away to wait like a child. The old rules, the relationships she had once counted on, no longer existed. They'd died when she'd continued to mourn and her father had taken a new wife.

Penthorpe had been an act of rebellion, a temper tantrum, a way of making her father notice her. Unfortunately the whole bit of nonsense had cost her, and those close to her, dearly.

Well, no more. She was taking control of her fate.

"Oleander, I will go in." Her voice was steady. It reminded her of her mother's, a woman whose strength of will had been broken only by the death of her son.

The butler studied her a moment, and then stepped out of the way.

"You were called to another area of the house," she advised him quietly. She'd not have another servant bear the brunt of her father's temper. He nodded and moved down the hall. She turned the door handle and let herself in, not knowing what to expect . . . but certainly not the picture that greeted her.

Her father sat behind his large, carved mahogany desk located by the window overlooking the garden. The duke sat in a chair before the desk, his long legs stretched out. They appeared completely relaxed with each other. At her entrance, His Grace came to his feet and her father said warmly, "Daughter, I was just preparing to send for you. His Grace has asked for your hand in marriage, and I've agreed."

Thoughts of defending the servants fled her mind. "*No.* I don't love him."

"And he doesn't love you but he's willing to do the right thing," her father answered as if all problems were solved.

Her father's response didn't set well. Not since the duke had referred to her as "love." She'd known he hadn't meant the endearment. It had been a slip of the tongue.

But her father didn't need to be so joyful about it.

"Am I to have no say?" she asked, her voice embarrassing her with a slight tremble. She was aware of Colster standing there, a tall, silent presence.

"No," her father said happily. "The matter has been discussed. It's done."

Francesca moved to the edge of his desk so that

she could speak to him with some form of privacy. "So I have no choice in the matter?"

Her father's conviviality vanished. "You made the choice when you left the protection of my house last night."

"The duke is an innocent bystander."

Her admission hung in the air a moment before her father said, "He said you left to meet him. Are you saying the Duke of Colster is a liar?"

She glanced at Colster in surprise. Had he not told her father what had happened? Why would he take the blame upon himself?

"I didn't leave to meet anyone," she answered, the words somewhat truthful. "The duke saved me from my own foolishness. If it hadn't been for him, I could have come to great harm."

"Perhaps that would have been better," her father answered.

His bluntness robbed her of speech.

He realized what he'd said, what he'd implied, and made an impatient gesture. "I didn't wish harm on you."

"Yes, you did," she answered.

"It's not what I meant." He nodded toward the duke. "Let's not discuss this now."

But it was too late. Francesca's temper had ignited. She didn't care who was present. She would have it out. All of it.

"Regina tells me you both have happy news."

Immediately the peevishness left her father's face. "My wife is expecting," he announced to Colster. "Naughty puss, she didn't tell me until this morning. She knew if she had, I would have canceled the whole affair last night. I can't have her taxing herself worrying over details. We will leave for our Sussex estates as soon as this matter is settled. I believe the country air will be good for her."

" 'This matter,' Father? Are you speaking about my marriage or sending one of the servants to the market for that jam you like so well?"

Her father's smile turned into a frown. "Don't be dramatic, daughter."

"How hasty will this marriage be?" Francesca asked, already hating the answer. "After all, we don't want Regina lingering in the city air."

"No, we don't," her father agreed. "You'll marry a week from today by special license. His Grace and I believe there is no purpose to delay this wedding. We were just finalizing the details."

So it was done. Without her desires, wishes, wants being given any consideration.

"I never thought I would say this"—she leaned toward him, her words for his ears alone—"but I could turn my back and walk out of this room and never give another thought to you."

Her father didn't even flinch. "You could. Go on. I have Regina to worry about now. I have a son on the way."

Francesca almost staggered back as if he'd given her a physical blow—but she caught herself in time.

Pride masked the hurt. In that moment, she would have married the devil himself if it meant escaping another moment under her father's roof.

And the horrible thing was, her father didn't realize how deeply he hurt her.

It was Justin who knew.

He placed a hand on her arm. "Francesca—"

She shook him off, warning him back. Composing herself, she turned to face him. "Father told you about my inheritance?"

"I was coming to that point," her father said.

"Fifty thousand a year," she said as if he hadn't spoken. "In funds. There is another seventy-five thousand in land. It's all in trust and only goes to my husband upon marriage."

"Fifty thousand pounds?" Justin repeated, incredulous.

"A year," she confirmed. "Be certain you collect it. It was my mother who had the fortune, and now it shall belong to my husband." She said this last for her father.

"You believe you are bothering me, girl? I made my own fortune."

"With the help of my mother's."

"She never minded."

"Because she wanted you to love her," Francesca said, and would have accused him of never having such a feeling, but Justin placed his hands on her arms.

He gave her a warning squeeze before saying, "May I have a moment to speak to your daughter alone?"

Her father didn't hesitate. "Please do. And talk sense into her. I fear I've spoiled her. She doesn't understand her obligations or that her wishes mean little under this roof. My wife is the mistress here." With that pronouncement, he rose and left the room, closing the door behind him.

What followed was silence.

A part of Francesca was too wounded to speak. Another, too angry.

She stared at the garden beyond the library window. A sparrow splashed playfully in one of the many birdbaths on the property. Her mother had enjoyed watching birds. She focused on that memory. It was easier to think of her mother than of her future.

The sparrow flew away, going only a few feet to the lower branches of the pear tree, and then she saw the cat creeping through the bushes. The sparrow had noticed it long before Francesca had been aware.

But she *was* very aware of Colster. Of his height, his presence, the scent of his skin . . . his slightest movement.

And she didn't want to feel this way.

She didn't want to need anyone. Not right now.

Francesca moved to the other side of her father's desk, Colster's hands dropping away. She lightly touched her fingertips to the ledger books her father had stacked there before admitting, "I've been stupid. But it isn't right that you pay a price. Unless it is the money? Do you need it?" She found the courage to raise her gaze to meet his.

The lines of his mouth flattened. "You have a way of emasculating a man, Francesca."

"So you *do* need the money?"

The sunlight from the window caught his eyes, bringing out a tawny gold in their darkness. "Sometimes choices are taken from us," he said. "Sometimes circumstances make it obvious what our stubborn natures refuse to see."

"You are calling me stubborn?"

"Aye, and too proud for sense."

Francesca pressed her lips together, biting back all the anger and resentment she felt. She'd not unleash it on him. He was blameless.

Justin raised an eyebrow. She knew she frustrated him. "Come here," he ordered.

She didn't want to obey. She wanted to stand her ground, but her feet moved around the desk until she stood before him.

Standing before him, she was almost overwhelmed by his presence . . . by the scent of him . . . and by the memory of him lying naked beside her, being inside her.

"Miss Dunroy, would you do me the honor of marrying me?"

Francesca couldn't look at him. This wasn't the way she had wanted it done. She'd dreamed of being swept off her feet. She'd dreamed of—

His mouth came down on hers.

Protest vanished.

He kissed her long and hard, and, heaven help her, she kissed him back.

As the kiss ended, Justin said, "There, that's answer enough for both of us for now." He turned and walked to the door. "I'll see what I must do for the license." He placed his hand on the door before saying, "You're mine, Francesca. It's not what we both might want, but it is our only choice."

He left.

Francesca started to take a step after him, but then stopped. He was right. She had no choice. Not now that the servants knew she'd been missing.

She also realized that the Duke of Colster was an honorable man. He didn't keep secrets, not the way she had.

Her father entered the library, rubbing his hands together. "So it is settled," he said, pleased.

"Yes," she answered, without elaborating.

"Good, this is *good*."

"But there is one condition," she was bold enough to say.

"From him, or you?"

Francesca smiled. "Both of us." Chances were the duke would never know her request. "I want Rose and Jeremy brought back into our service. They will go with me when I leave."

Her father frowned. "They betrayed me."

"*I* betrayed you. I would have slipped out of the house without them. I was determined to go. They were the only protection I had. I will not have them suffer for my foolishness."

"All right. Done." He paused a moment. "When did you turn so willful?" he demanded, as if truly seeing her for the first time.

When you dishonored my mother by marrying Regina. But she kept her silence. He was her father, after all . . . and their time together was growing shorter. She had no pretense. Once Regina had her baby, he'd not remember he had a daughter.

Then again, as a duchess, Francesca could *make* him remember.

He consented with a curt gesture, and she felt powerful as she moved past him toward the door.

But then he stopped her. "One more thing, daughter. The necklace I gave your mother, the black pearl pendant."

So much had happened over the past several hours, Francesca had almost forgotten about it. Now her heart filled her throat. "Yes?"

"I want Regina to have it," he said.

"But you gave it to my mother. She handed it to me." She could still feel the weight of the necklace as it had slipped from her mother's weak fingers into the palm of her hand.

"Yes, but it *is* mine," her father insisted. "I haven't said anything because I knew you were still mourning, but the time has come, Francesca. It's been two years. We must move on. That pendant was the beginning of my fortune. I want Regina to know how pleased I am over the baby."

Francesca's mind worked furiously. "Of course I'll be happy to return it. But may I wear it for my wedding? It will be a symbol of Mother's presence."

He immediately turned solicitous. "Of course." He took a step closer, suddenly shy. "To be honest, Regina doesn't feel as if you like her overmuch. She doesn't believe you've accepted her as a stepmother."

"She is a year younger than I am," Francesca reminded him.

"But she's mature beyond her years."

That hadn't been Francesca's observation. "Has she mentioned the pearl, Papa? Has she asked for it?"

"No. She's not that way, Francesca. I know you think the worst of her, but she truly is a kind and gentle person."

Francesca was absolutely certain Regina wanted the pearl, and her father either couldn't or wouldn't see his new wife's greed. But then understanding struck: *What her father saw in Regina didn't matter.* The truth was, he no longer had a place for Francesca in his life. Marriage to Colster would not give her love, but she would have power. The sort of power both her father and Regina would have to respect.

Something inside her hardened.

Regina had best beware. Francesca had nothing to lose.

But the one person innocent in all this was Justin. He deserved the full story, including her foolishness over Penthorpe. It would be her act of faith. She wanted no secrets between them. She trusted him. At the first opportunity, she would tell him the truth.

She'd also have to pay Penthorpe's price, but now she saw a way clear to do so. She'd heard that women had a way of collecting money in spite of their husbands' and fathers' watchful eyes. They used their dressmakers, who would advance funds and pad their bills with the money owed. It was said that, as of yet, no man had caught on to the game.

The method had struck Francesca as dishonest, but she knew there was no other way to receive money from her father.

"I need to go shopping," she told her father. "For my wedding clothes." Madame Simone was her favorite dressmaker, and her shop was not far from Penthorpe's, and Colster's, residence. If she was quick and lucky, she could have the necklace matter resolved before tomorrow evening.

"Of course, my daughter. Spare no expense," her father said, his willingness to let her shop a sign of how pleased he was with this marriage. "Regina will go with you."

That was not going to happen. Francesca pretended to be pleased, but then paused as if struck by a disturbing thought. "Is she not newly with child? I understand expecting women need to nap, and the shopping trip I'm planning will be very taxing. After all, I have so little time to prepare, and she is so frail, we don't want anything to happen to her baby."

"Absolutely not," her father agreed, his brows coming together in concern.

Noting Oleander hovering out in the hallway, Francesca said, "I'll take Oleander, and a maid, of course."

"Not Rose," her father answered, a sign he had decided to take the maid and footman back. "She'll not be your personal servant."

"She will when I leave this house."

Her father's gaze met hers. For a second he appeared ready to argue, but then he nodded a curt assent. "And yes, you should take Oleander. I trust him."

Oleander had overheard his name mentioned and had moved to the door. Francesca sensed he knew she was up to something. She attempted to send him a reassuring smile. She'd protect him. He'd not be treated as Rose and Jeremy had been.

"Oleander, order the coach for my daughter on the morrow," her father said expansively, his good humor returning. "She's on the hunt for wedding wear."

Oleander had no choice but to agree.

Francesca started out the door, but her father caught her arm. "And the necklace?" he prompted.

She glanced down at his hand. He released his hold, and she smiled, already feeling this new, heady power. She'd never give up the necklace. *It was hers.* "Don't worry," she answered, her calm voice that of a duchess. "I will find a suitable time to honor Regina with the pearl."

Chapter 14

Justin had taken only a few steps away from Dunroy's front door when the reality of what he'd just committed to fully hit him. He was going to remarry, the one thing he'd sworn not to do.

And to a woman he'd already caught in another man's room. A woman he couldn't seem to keep his hands off.

Memories of the humiliation he'd suffered through Moira rammed him.

What the devil was he doing?

Before he could fully digest the question, let alone consider the answer, the hired hack pulled up alongside him. The driver tipped his hat as Phillip threw open the door.

"Get in," his brother said, sliding across the hard leather seat to make room.

For once, Justin obeyed his twin's order without argument.

Phillip gave the driver the address to his home and pulled the canvas flaps over the windows before asking, "What happened? Why were you in the house?"

"She was caught going through the gate," Justin said.

"With you."

"Yes."

"Yes, *and*—?" Phillip prodded.

Justin glared at his brother, realizing he suspected what had happened, and wasn't upset at all. He muttered, "You are a bleeding bastard."

Phillip crowed his delight that he was right. "You couldn't keep your hands off her." He gave Justin a playful punch in the arm. "Come on, don't be so surly. I saw how you were looking at her. You *like* her."

"No, I don't." But then Justin's honesty came out and he amended his words. "Well, she is a fetching thing."

His brother enjoyed his discomfort. "Did Dunroy rake you over the coals?"

"And then some." Justin took a breath and released it before saying, "Congratulate me. I'm about to be married."

Instead of the pleased I-told-you-so reaction Justin anticipated, Phillip startled him by saying, "No." He sat upright. "He can't make you marry his daughter. This is absolute nonsense. The girl was running around in breeches. Was this some sort of scheme to trap you?"

"I thought you said you believed she'd be a good match," Justin replied.

"She's wealthy beyond anyone's imagination, and you could use her money. However," Phillip continued, "that doesn't mean I'm going to sit idly by and allow my brother to be trapped into marriage. Ever since Dunroy married Regina Rumford, he's been anxious to rid himself of his daughter. Everyone in London knows that. But she refused to go out until a decent mourning period for her mother had passed. This past season, Dunroy has brought her out but supposedly she hasn't taken."

"Francesca?" Justin was surprised. "I would have imagined every man in London would be lined up for her. She's a spirited, handsome lass with a fortune."

"And very strong opinions," Phillip pointed out. "She was the one who refused all suitors. On the other hand, because of her father's transgressions, she wasn't truly considered good *ton*."

Justin frowned. "What does that mean?"

"It means that the ladies of the *ton*, those who

are high sticklers like Lady Bastone, were angry with her father and had set about showing their displeasure by snubbing him . . . and consequently his daughter."

"What were they so upset over?"

"Francesca's mother, Grace, was one of them. They felt Max Dunroy hadn't done enough for his wife during her illness. Women can close ranks around each other with remarkable effectiveness. Then, when he remarried the second after Grace drew her last breath, it earned him all of their animosity. I suppose they could see the same fate befalling themselves if they didn't put a stop to it."

"And did they? Dunroy's married."

Phillip leaned back in the seat. "Aye, but his young wife is shut out of any meaningful society gathering. I'd heard his daughter was included, but only under the most guarded circumstances. And let us not forget, she is older than the usual debutante."

"The ball last night appeared very well attended to me."

"Yes. I was surprised, too. I had chosen Dunroy's ball as your first time out in society because I had assumed it would *not* be well attended. You were the draw. Everyone was there for you."

Justin didn't like to be reminded. He'd felt damn uncomfortable.

"Dunroy was hoping to buy his wife a place in the social world by flashing his wealth. And he wanted Francesca to have another opportunity to meet a husband, something she didn't do during her season." Phillip shrugged. "Dunroy's plan worked. She found one."

"She didn't lay a trap for me, if that is what you are implying," Justin answered.

"How can you be certain?"

"Because I am." Justin wasn't going to tell Phillip the tale of last night. That would only heighten his brother's suspicions . . . and Justin had enough doubts for both of them. He didn't understand where Penthorpe fit into the story. "Phillip, Francesca didn't want to marry me. Her father and I forced the issue."

His brother's brows rose. "She refused you?"

"Several times, in fact. And let us not forget, you were promoting a match. Only hours ago, if I recall correctly."

Phillip was silent a moment, thinking, and then he asked, "Is she really worth what they rumor she is?"

"And how much is that?"

"Thirty-five thousand a year."

"She's worth more," Justin assured him, and he wasn't just discussing her monetary value.

Phillip surprised him by releasing his breath in a low whistle. "This is good for you. Very, very good. But how did the two of you come to be together last night?"

"Mistaken identities," Justin answered. He could feel Phillip waiting for more, but he wasn't going to hear the rest. Francesca Dunroy brought out a protective instinct in him . . . much as Moira had, he reminded himself.

"When will the wedding be?" Phillip asked.

"Five days. I need a special license. Will you help me with that?"

Now Phillip sat up. "Why the haste?"

Justin told him of Dunroy's wife's pregnancy.

"I told you he was anxious," Phillip said.

"He all but packed Francesca's bags," Justin agreed.

"What are the terms of the marriage settlement?" His twin's mind had turned to practical matters. "Or do I need to pay a call later this day and work out the arrangements? It's usually done by the groom's representative," he added, as if wanting Justin to know that this wasn't another case of him being domineering.

Justin appreciated it. "Aye, that would be best."

They rode in silence a moment. Justin opened and closed his gloved hand resting on his leg. *He was to remarry.* He still hadn't fully grasped all that it would mean. Not in this new world where he found himself.

"What about the Sword of the MacKenna?"

Phillip asked as if broaching the subject carefully. "You won't want to keep it now—"

"Of course I'll keep it."

"Justin, I wish you would trust me—"

"I can't, Phillip. If they thought you knew, they would use you against me. Gordon wants the sword." He let the import of that information sink in. "And there will be others," he predicted.

"I am your brother, Justin. I would give my life for you—"

"I'm not asking that, but I am asking for your trust." He faced his twin. "Can you give me that, Phillip?"

For a long moment, his brother frowned, and then he said, "You've always had my trust, Justin. How many times in Scotland were you willing to lay down your own life for mine? Even before you realized we were related or that we were nothing more than pawns in a larger game. Do you believe my loyalty is based on nothing more than an accident of birth? How little you know me."

He was right.

"I'm attempting to earn your respect, Justin," Phillip said. "You've earned mine. I knew that telling you what had happened at Nathraichean would anger you, but you must understand that just as you have loyalties, so do I. If that keeps us apart, so be it."

Justin didn't know what to say. His brother, the great diplomat, spoke to him as an equal.

And Justin realized that he'd been the outsider for so long, he didn't know if he *could* trust.

He dropped his gaze to his hands. He ran a thumb over the soft kid leather of his other hand. When he spoke, his voice was thoughtful. "You made me purchase these. Before, my gloves were heavy and made to protect my hands from the sparks off the forge. These dainty things"—he frowned at the gloves on his hands—"would not protect even a goat's hide." He raised his eyes to his brother's. "Not only that, you taught me there was a *proper* way for a man to wear his gloves. And even though I can count the weeks I've been in London on my two hands, I now carry these gloves and put them on without a second's thought." He was quiet a moment before asserting, "There are differences between us."

"There always will be," Phillip agreed. "The question is—do we let Laird MacKenna and his sister win? Will they have created such distrust in us that we can never take true joy in the fact we are family?"

"What you really are asking is, can we set our differences aside?"

With a wave of his hand, Phillip conceded the point. "Can *you*? I've already made my decision.

You are the duke, the head of the family. My loyalty is to you."

For a long moment there was only the sound of the hack's iron wheels over cobbles. "I must," Justin answered. "I'm remarrying. Francesca and I could have a child." That he and Moira had not had children had been a disappointment at one time. Now he saw it as a blessing. "I don't want any child of mine to not have a place in this world. To be as lost as I've been." He looked to Phillip. "It's not easy, but you are my brother. If something happened to you, I would take care of your family."

"As I would yours." Phillip shook his head as if he couldn't believe what he was hearing. "It's finally happening."

"What?"

"*Us.*"

Justin leaned back. "You aren't going to start on that twin superstitious nonsense again?" he asked, but his question lacked the heat of anger.

"No, this is about respect and earning it from each other."

His reply deeply touched Justin. He realized that many of the disagreements the two of them had been having were of his making. He was grateful Phillip didn't bear grudges. Still, the habit of trust was new to Justin. "I'm not always going to agree with you."

"I would be surprised if you did," Phillip assured him. "After all, Charlotte rarely does."

His candid comment about the wife he loved so much made Justin smile. He held out a hand. His brother took it, and for a moment, yes, there was a connection—one born of blood, but also of understanding . . . and respect.

The hack rolled to a stop. Phillip lifted the shade. They were in front of the family's London house. "I wish you would move back here," he told Justin.

"You and Charlotte need time alone. After all, you've not been married long."

"Actually, what we need is a place of our own."

This information was news to Justin. Phillip grinned as if pleased he'd surprised his brother. "You and Francesca will need time alone," he said. "And I have longed to build a house. Charlotte agrees it would be fun. So don't stay in your apartments because you don't wish to disturb us. After all, within the week, you will have a wife."

Yes, he would. Justin fell back against the seat, too aware of all that now rested on his shoulders. "You know, since I met you, my life has been one enormous change after another."

Phillip's teeth flashed white in his smile. "I won't take credit for this last change. You performed that one all by yourself." Laughing at his own humor, he let himself out of the hack. "Don't forget dinner this evening. I shall have some points to discuss on the marriage settlement."

Justin nodded. Being married as a duke carried more weight than being married as a blacksmith. He was relieved that the negotiations with Dunroy would be in his brother's capable hands.

It felt good to trust someone.

He gave the driver his address and waved at his twin as the vehicle pulled away.

Phillip watched his brother leave . . . and then turned toward the house where Thomas, his secretary, waited with the door open.

"Lord Hawkesbury is waiting for you in your study," Thomas said in a low, urgent voice.

"Thank you." Of course Hawkesbury would appear just when he and Justin were reaching a consensus.

As Phillip entered his panel-lined study, Hawkesbury set aside the drink Thomas had offered him and came to his feet. "I see you are having some work done to the house," he said pleasantly. "I like the marble hearth in this room. I've been thinking of doing some improvements to my own place. Did you find that here?" He motioned to the carved mantel.

"Yes, it's from Italy. This fireplace is so large, it was hard to find a suitable piece that would fit."

"Handsome." Having dispensed with niceties, Hawkesbury asked, "Has he given you the sword yet?" He didn't even mention Justin by name.

Phillip poured himself a drink from a crystal decanter on the serving table. "We don't even know if my brother has it," he lied.

"He has it," Hawkesbury answered.

"I've not seen it in his possession. It would be like Justin to destroy it."

Hawkesbury shook his head. "Lachlan is in London. He met your brother last night at a tavern by the wharves called the Three Princes."

Justin hadn't said a word. No, that wasn't entirely true. He had mentioned Gordon.

"How are you certain?" Phillip asked.

"The way we are always certain, Your Grace. We find our man and we follow him."

"I no longer have the title," Phillip answered, correcting him. "My brother is the duke. I would expect you to treat him as you would me."

A smile spread across Hawkesbury's face. "We do . . . provided he is loyal to the Crown. But I would be remiss if I didn't assure you there are those who would like to see the title returned to you, Lord Phillip. You deserve the dukedom, not this Scots interloper."

With a flash of anger and not a small amount of alarm, Phillip said, "My *twin* is not Scots. And I don't want the title, Hawkesbury. Nor do I want any harm to come to my brother, especially in my name."

"Then tell him to give us the sword," Hawkesbury said. "Or Lachlan."

"You had Lachlan last night and you didn't take him."

"We will, eventually, but we prefer to have the sword." Hawkesbury lowered his voice to confide, "We know they spoke of it."

"But Justin didn't give it to him, did he?" Phillip drained his glass, thankful that Hawkesbury didn't tell him differently. He set his glass on the new mantel. "No one cares about Lachlan. Catch him and string him up."

"It's not as easy as it once was," Hawkesbury confessed. "There was a day, my father's day, when we could string a passel of Highlanders up and no one would give a care. That's all changed. We must go through the courts. But there is an easier way to handle this matter. Whoever has the sword has the power. England wants that sword."

Phillip shook his head. "This is all superstition. The sword has meant nothing for decades."

"It means something now," Hawkesbury said. "If it didn't, Lachlan wouldn't want it. And think of this, Lord Phillip, all the Highlands need is a leader with enough power to organize them. The Crown will not tolerate another rebellion like '43."

"It won't come to that. I promise you," Phillip said.

"With all due respect, Your Grace"—he stopped and smiled, then corrected himself—"Lord Phillip. You didn't even know your brother was in contact with Lachlan."

"I shall discuss the matter with him."

Hawkesbury's jaw tightened. "I want more than discussion. I want the sword. Remember, England is not above hanging a duke, especially for treason." He bowed and started to leave the room, but Phillip stopped him.

"I won't betray my brother, Hawkesbury," he said, the words sounding right to his ears. "I would fight to the death for him."

"Let us hope it doesn't come to that." He let himself out of the study.

Chapter 15

*J*ustin sat in the hack, his mind assailed by one overriding thought.

He was marrying. Again.

His and Moira's marriage had been a country affair with everyone in Nathraichean attending. He'd purchased a keg of hard cider and a barrel of whiskey, and the dancing had gone on all night . . . as had the loving. He and Moira had been young and vital and ready for each other.

But that flush of passion, that heady desire had died, and he'd never seen it coming. She'd changed, or so he had told himself.

Although now, sitting in a hack and watching the passing scenery, he considered at last that perhaps she hadn't ever loved him as he'd loved her.

Her father had wanted the marriage, and Moira had had very little say.

Perhaps Bruce *was* the first man she'd loved—

The idea stopped Justin cold. He had never allowed himself to think that way before. He'd always preferred believing she'd been stolen from him, seduced by Bruce's power.

But what if she had loved Bruce . . . even loved him more than Justin?

Or was this ability to see the past objectively a sign he was finally falling out of love with her?

Even in close confines of the hack, Justin could transport himself back to that time and place. He could smell the salt of Nathraichean and remember the first market day after Moira had left. The gossips had had a busy morning and the clan had quickly taken sides. Being the center of all the talk and speculation hadn't been easy on him. He had closed himself off and become aloof.

Then again, in many ways his wife's rejection had prepared him for what was to come. After all, the clan probably thought she'd chosen rightly now that he was aligned with the English.

They thought, as Gordon had said, that he'd forgotten that their cause was just.

He would never forget.

If there was a way he could give them back what they'd lost, he would do so—and then he realized he could.

Through marriage to Francesca, he would inherit not only more land to go with what he already owned as duke, but also money.

What if he invited his clansmen to live on his property? What if he took on the role of chieftain and provided for them? What if he attempted to do right where there had once been wrong?

His mind began whirling with ideas.

Father Nicholas had always said matters happened for a purpose. His life had taken many confusing twists, but in this moment, finally, it started to take on meaning. Suddenly being a duke seemed a perfect purpose.

He would become laird of his clan. He would protect the women and children and give the men good, honest work. Phillip would help. He'd show Justin how to use the money to good advantage.

And he wouldn't use Francesca only for her money. He would be a good husband to her. Yes, he'd played bedroom games with lonely widows since he'd left Scotland, but that had grown tiring. The truth was, he was a man who liked to be married. He liked the companionship of a woman. And he liked Francesca.

Certainly he liked bedding her.

There was a rare and strong attraction between them. Stronger even than what he'd felt for Moira.

In fact, the more Justin thought about it, the happier he was with this marriage.

That evening he dined with Phillip and Charlotte. After the meal, he and Phillip discussed the terms in the marriage contract. Phillip would be meeting with Dunroy in the morning.

And that night, Justin stayed up late, making plans for what his "Nathraichean," the one he would build in England, would look like. When he did retire to his bed, he slept with a peacefulness he'd not known in years, and the next morning was up early.

He breakfasted with Phillip and Charlotte. The twins discussed last-minute thoughts on the marriage settlement, and then Phillip was on his way. Two hours later he returned with a contract for Justin's signature.

"Dunroy didn't quibble over a thing," he told Justin. "It's as if he is happy to be rid of his daughter."

"That is sad," Charlotte noted.

"She is going to be a duchess," Phillip said. "That would make any father agreeable to whatever terms we requested." He offered Justin a pen.

Justin looked down at the contract and noticed Francesca hadn't signed it. Her father had signed it for her.

He didn't know her well, but had an inkling she would not be pleased. "It's odd," he said to Phillip and Charlotte. "In a country marriage, a woman has more say about what happens to her than if she marries in the *ton*."

"And especially if she is an heiress," Phillip assured him. "Miss Dunroy has very little say."

"Did you see her at the house?" Justin asked.

"Yes," Phillip answered. "She passed me in the hallway."

"That was all, she just passed you?" It seemed to him that, knowing Francesca what little he did, she would take more of an interest in the terms of her marriage settlement.

"Her father didn't allow her to say much," Phillip said. "He did tell me she was going shopping for her wedding clothes, so I assume she is happy."

"What is it, Justin?" Charlotte asked. "Does something concern you?"

Justin looked back down at the marriage contract and realized his concern was that Francesca might not truly want this marriage. That he would find himself in another faithless match.

And surprisingly, a part of him wanted more from Francesca.

Then again, this marriage served a purpose. He would have money to help his clan. Money to right wrongs. Money to be a hero.

He signed.

Phillip insisted upon a toast and his staying for

lunch but Justin left shortly afterward. Clarens drove him to his building in the ducal coach.

It was well after two in the afternoon.

Justin removed his hat as he entered the building, taking the steps up to his apartments two at a time. The hallway was quiet. He assumed Penthorpe was asleep. The man usually snoozed until early evening. However, as Justin passed, Penthorpe's door came open.

The rake stood there in a velvet dressing gown that had seen better days, his breeches, and his boots. His red-rimmed eyes were framed by deep, dark circles. His hair went every which way over a face that was sickly pale and much worse-looking than usual. He seemed distraught.

"Your Grace, I beg your pardon, but do you have a moment?"

"Is something the matter?"

"Did you hear anything or see anyone unusual around my door last night?" Penthorpe asked. "Or even the night before?"

"In what way?" Justin wondered, *very* curious about the answer.

"I believe I've been burglarized. Something valuable was taken from me."

"What?" Justin asked.

"Something," Penthorpe answered, being as evasive as Francesca had been.

"I didn't see anyone," Justin said and then tried a different tack. "What ails you, man? You appear near collapse." His skin even appeared clammy. "Why don't you come into my rooms and I'll pour a whiskey."

Penthorpe shook his head. "No, it's fine." His hand trembled slightly. He forced a smile. "Have you ever thought you had something that would make everything right and discovered you'd lost it?"

"Aye, I have." Justin thought of the sword, of his failed marriage . . . of his impending marriage. "Perhaps you just misplaced it," he suggested.

"I've looked everywhere it could be. It's my damnable luck, that's what it is." Penthorpe backed into his room, closing the door as if fearing he'd said too much. "Thank you, Your Grace." He shut the door.

Justin studied the closed door, wishing he could read minds. Whatever it was that Penthorpe was missing, Francesca had it. He was absolutely certain—

His thoughts broke off when he realized the door to his apartments was cracked open.

Justin rarely locked it, leaving the matter for Biddle. But he had let Biddle go . . . something he was starting to regret now that he was in a better frame of mind. Still, he was certain he had closed the door. He pushed the door open, listening carefully for movement inside. There was nothing.

He pushed the door wider and then stared in surprise.

Someone had ransacked his rooms. His books were thrown everywhere. Drawers had been pulled open, and he could see into the bedroom that the mattress had been yanked off the bed and cut clean open. The cotton stuffing had been tossed every which way . . . but the chest on his dresser that held his money was untouched.

Gordon had come here looking for the sword.

He hadn't found it, but he wouldn't give up.

Justin turned and walked to Penthorpe's door. At his pounding, the rake opened it, a drink in his hand this time. If all else failed, a man could always drown his sorrows. "Yes, Your Grace?"

Glancing into Penthorpe's rooms, Justin thought for a second that Gordon had searched in here, too—but then realized that the mess came from Penthorpe's slovenly habits. He invited himself in, not wanting to have this conversation out in the hallway.

"Someone broke into my apartments, Penny. Did you hear anything?"

"Absolutely nothing, Your Grace," Penthorpe answered, rousing himself. "Why this is infamous!" He marched around his room, waving his drink with furious movements. "It's as if a man can't go from his home without thieves attacking. First me, then you. Did they take anything?"

"Nothing of importance," Justin answered, and realized here was an opportunity. "What of you? What was the item they took from you?"

But Penthorpe wasn't listening. Instead he frowned at a far corner of the room before crossing over and picking up what appeared to be a gold chain with a very large black pearl pendant swinging from it.

"I'll be damned," he said to himself as if forgetting Justin was in the room.

"What is it?" Justin asked.

Penny turned as if just remembering he wasn't alone. He took care to stuff the chain and pendant into the pocket of his breeches, and Justin knew in a flash of insight that the necklace had been what Francesca had come for the other night. She must have had it in her hands when he'd tackled her. That was the moment when she'd started fighting back the hardest.

"Nothing," Penthorpe said. The color had returned to his face. He broke out into silent laughter, sitting down at the table.

"What is so funny?" Justin pressed, wanting answers.

Penthorpe shook his head and then, as if he couldn't contain himself, said, "Do you know Maximus Dunroy?"

Justin went still. "I've heard of him."

"I've had his daughter," Penthorpe leaned forward to confide. "Had her right here under this roof, in fact. On that bed in there. And on this table." He slapped the table with the flat of his fingers to show exactly where he'd "had" her. "On the floor, too."

Justin knew the man was lying. After all, *he'd* been the one to have her first . . . but the knowledge didn't stop the surge of jealousy that reared its ugly head inside him.

And he wondered what the truth was.

"She came dressed in boy's clothes. Only way she could sneak out of her house. She couldn't wait to have me." He leaned back in his chair and closed his eyes as if in ecstasy at the memory.

"How did you lure her to your rooms?" Justin demanded, having to keep his closed fists at his sides lest he go for the man's lying throat.

"It was easy. Women really should be married by one and twenty. Beyond that age, they develop this curiosity for the unknown, and we all know what curiosity does. She was bored." He opened his eyes. "And I provided her with entertainment. Several times, in fact. I couldn't keep her from my door."

Justin was ready to do more than call Penthorpe a liar—he was ready to pull the teeth out of the man's head—except at that moment, one of the stairs out in the hallway creaked. Someone was coming up them.

Both men went still. Justin's first thought was that Gordon or his men had returned. On silent feet, he moved to the door and pressed his ear there.

Whoever was in the hall was being very quiet.

Penthorpe came up behind him to listen.

There was a tapping on Justin's apartment door.

When there was no answer, his visitor walked on catlike feet toward Penthorpe's door.

Penny caught Justin's gaze with a wide one of his own. He had not anticipated a visitor.

There was a tap at the door. "Penthorpe?" came the whispered question—and Justin immediately recognized the voice.

Francesca was tapping on Penthorpe's door.

Chapter 16

*F*rancesca had wanted to speak to Justin first. Her need for honesty had weighed heavy on her conscience all night. Seeing his brother after his meeting with her father had added a sense of urgency to her confession.

However, he wasn't at home.

She just prayed that Penthorpe was in or her risk in leaving Madame Simone's would be for naught.

Madame had been a willing accomplice. Obviously she'd helped many of her clients make assignations in what was an apparently lucrative side to her business. She certainly charged enough for it.

Smoothly, Madame had ordered Oleander to cool his heels out in the entrance to her shop. No men were allowed past the velvet curtain leading to the fitting rooms. Regina had sent Kathleen, her maid, to chaperone. Commenting on how tedious the choosing of fabrics and styles and making quick mockups of the gowns would be because of the short time period before the wedding, Madame had invited Kathleen to relax in a room with tea and biscuits set aside for servants. The overtaxed maid had been only too happy to take advantage of the hospitality. Madame reported to Francesca that the maid had closed her eyes and nodded off for a nap.

For once, Francesca was pleased her stepmother was so demanding. Poor Kathleen had her hands full taking care of both her and Regina.

Madame estimated Francesca had approximately a good hour, maybe two, before Oleander or Kathleen would ask questions. Francesca had wasted no time in leaving. Her poke bonnet with its wide brim had shielded her face from curious passersby. She wore a creamy muslin dress trimmed in ribbons the color of robin's eggs, and a yellow and green patterned shawl she'd kept pulled close around her as if it could hide her identity.

On one arm, she carried her reticule with a note for one thousand pounds Penthorpe could claim from Madame Simone in Francesca's name.

Madame had been shocked by the amount, but had made the loan with a lucrative interest. Francesca knew she was being fleeced, but she was an heiress. She was about to marry a duke. And she did want the necklace back.

Now Francesca tapped on Penthorpe's door again, anxious to see this matter through.

What she *didn't* want, when Penthorpe's door opened, was to find herself staring into the angry expression of her future husband.

Justin didn't waste time with greetings. "What are you doing here?"

For a second, Francesca couldn't speak. She couldn't move.

That gave Penthorpe enough time to sidle up beside Justin to say with lewd delight, "We're friends. I told you as much. Come in, Francesca, and, Your Grace, you don't mind giving us a moment alone?"

Justin's response was to throw aside his hat and grab Penthorpe by the scruff of the neck. He lifted the startled rake up in the air as if he weighed nothing and carried him to the window. With one hand, Justin opened it. Before Francesca could blink, he dumped Penthorpe over the ledge, grabbing him by his ankles and dangling him over the ground. Penthorpe's dressing gown fell over his head. His arms flailed the air as he appeared too shocked to speak.

Francesca gasped her horror and started for the window, but Justin warned her back with a curt nod of his head. He leaned against the window ledge, completely at ease, as if he could hold Penthorpe in this manner all day, and perhaps he could. He certainly was strong enough to do so.

"Y-y-your Grace," Penthorpe stuttered, his voice rising a pitch with each gulp of air. "Why are you doing this? H-h-help."

"Penny," Justin said conversationally, "did you know I am to be married to Miss Dunroy?"

The rake waved his arms in the air so that he could look to see if Justin was serious. His eyes widened. "You are? I wish you'd told me earlier."

"Such as before you were bragging about making love to her?" Justin suggested.

Francesca's sympathy for Penthorpe vanished. "He *didn't.*" She turned to Justin. "There is nothing he can say."

"Oh, he said plenty," Justin assured her. "Let me see if I remember, and correct me if I am wrong, Penny. You said you made love on the bed, on the table, on—"

"*I was jesting,*" Penthorpe confessed. "It was a small joke."

"I see no humor in it at all," Francesca informed him, her own fists doubling. To Justin, she declared, "He didn't touch me. He wanted to but I stopped him."

Justin straightened, stretching his arms holding Penthorpe as he did so. The scoundrel sobbed for mercy. Justin gave him a dismissive look. "How did you stop him?" he asked Francesca.

"I kicked him," she answered.

"Neutered me, she did," Penthorpe agreed. His face was turning red from being upside down. "I haven't touched a woman since. My balls still hurt."

Francesca wrinkled her nose at his crudeness, but Justin had more questions in mind . . . questions she knew she had to answer whether he held Penthorpe out a window or not.

"What were you doing with him in his rooms?" Justin asked.

She pulled her shawl closer around her. Her reticule seemed to weigh a hundred pounds between the note she carried and her guilt. "I came here to see him," she admitted.

"Why?" Justin asked.

"We were going to do charity work together," Penthorpe said.

"*Please*, Penthorpe," Francesca said. "His Grace is no fool." She leaned her shoulder against the window frame, facing Justin. "I thought him attractive and a bit dangerous."

"Go on," Justin said. His gaze had gone hard, unrelenting. Perhaps she *should* have claimed a charity mission.

Instead she told the truth and prayed he took pity on her. "He paid attention to me."

It had been that simple.

"Everyone else gossiped or whispered," she explained. "They went on about my inheritance and my father disgracing my mother's memory and how *old* I was to be making my first season. Penthorpe came right up to me at Lord and Lady Dearling's reception and introduced himself to me. He was witty and handsome and helped make me feel as if I fit in."

"It was gallantry, Your Grace," Penthorpe declared. "I was being gallant."

"A gallant doesn't invite a lady to his private rooms," Justin corrected him. Penthorpe closed his mouth with a snap.

Francesca set the record straight. "A true lady doesn't accept." It embarrassed her to make that admission.

"Then why did you do it?" Justin asked. There was real anger in his eyes. Her behavior had upset him.

"The adventure," she admitted, realizing how silly she sounded. "I've lived a sheltered life. Most women my age are married, and many have children and freedom. I've spent years either in mourning or nursing my mother . . . and while I don't begrudge her the time, I feel as if I've missed most of life."

"And you thought to find it with Penthorpe?"

Justin asked, his brogue stressing how preposterous he found the idea.

"When he's dressed, he's quite handsome," Francesca answered, defending herself.

"Thank you," Penthorpe said, but pressed his lips closed at the scowl Justin gave him.

"Bring him in," Francesca pleaded quietly. "I'm the one you should be angry with, not him."

Justin glanced at Penthorpe as if he agreed, but he didn't do as she suggested. He seemed to know that as long as he had Penthorpe like this, she would answer any question.

"You don't trust me," she noted.

The corners of Justin's mouth tightened. It was all the answer she needed.

"I don't blame you. I was foolish. People warned me about Penthorpe. I knew my father would never approve of him. But I didn't want to listen. Perhaps because he was the worst possible suitor for me. I had to learn the hard way for myself."

"He didn't hurt you, did he?" Justin asked, his voice low.

Out the window, Penthorpe held his breath, realizing his fate truly was in her hands.

"No," Francesca said. "If anything, he wanted to marry me. He knew he would never receive my father's permission to marry me. I refused to elope—"

"And he attempted rape," Justin finished. He looked at Penthorpe. "You figured Dunroy would have no choice but to let you have his daughter and her fortune if she was defiled."

For once Penthorpe had the intelligence to keep his mouth shut.

But then Justin turned his dark gaze on Francesca. "So why are you here now?"

Francesca drew in a deep breath. "Two reasons. The first is that I came to tell you this story."

"And for that, you needed to knock on Penthorpe's door? I don't see an escort. I assume your father doesn't know you are here—*again*."

He wasn't going to make this easy for her at all.

"You are right. My father believes I am at Madame Simone's, the dressmaker. There are servants waiting for me there. They don't even know I'm gone," she hurried to add, lest Oleander and Kathleen be blamed.

Justin hummed his opinion before repeating, "Why were you knocking on Penthorpe's door?"

"I've always worn a necklace my mother gave me the night she died. I've never taken it off since she handed it to me. The pearl had been a gift to her from my father. My mother's fortune helped him start his shipping empire, but, in his mind, it was the discovery of that pearl that told him he would succeed. He found it on his first trip to the

Orient and had it made into a pendant for her. It's brought good fortune to my family ever since."

"What does the necklace have to do with Penthorpe?" Justin asked . . . and Penthorpe sighed, because he knew she was going to tell the duke.

"If you do decide to drop me," he said to Justin, "then don't give a warning. I don't want one. I'll settle for the splat of my head hitting the cobbles. In fact, I'll close my eyes just to be certain I don't see what is to happen."

Justin turned to Francesca. "I'm not going to like this," he predicted.

"Please bring him in. It truly isn't his fault."

"Tell me the tale, lass, and I'll be the decider of that."

She crossed her arms and said, "When I was fighting Penthorpe off, I lost the necklace. I noticed it missing as soon as I reached the hack I'd hired but was afraid to go back because he was so angry—"

"I was in pain," Penthorpe corrected.

"At the ball, I'd asked him to meet me privately so I could ask for the necklace," she continued. "He told me I could have it, and his silence, for a thousand pounds."

"I'm doomed," Penthorpe muttered and brought his arms protectively around his head.

But Justin wasn't thinking about Penthorpe. His

agile mind had pieced together the rest of the story. "You came here the night before last to search his rooms for it."

"You were here last night?" Penthorpe said in surprise. He lowered his arms from his head. "I *knew* it. I knew something was wrong. The necklace was missing from my dresser."

"And then I caught you," Justin continued as if he hadn't heard the man.

"And then what happened?" Penthorpe wondered, his eyes going round.

"I sent her home," was the answer.

Penthorpe looked between Justin and Francesca. "I don't believe so," he said slowly, his own mind working furiously. "Did you not say, Your Grace, that you are *marrying* Miss Dunroy?"

Justin's response was to let go of one of Penthorpe's ankles.

The rake cried out. Justin held him as securely with one hand as he had with two.

Alarmed, Francesca begged, "Please, Justin, bring him in." Below, someone on the street must have heard Penthorpe's cry and there were shouts.

Unmoved by either Francesca's entreaty or the risk of discovery, Justin said to Penthorpe, "What did you just imply?"

"*Nothing,*" Penthorpe answered. "I implied *nothing.*"

"And what are you going to tell people when they mention Miss Dunroy's name in the future?" Justin said.

"Nothing," the rake squeaked out.

"And what are you going to do with the necklace?" Justin said. "Because you did find it. Right here in this room in front of me."

"I'm going to give it back."

"Thank you," Justin said and reached to grab Penthorpe by his waistband and haul him back into the room. Penthorpe collapsed on the floor as if his legs had gone to jelly.

Merciless, Justin held out his hand. "The necklace?"

Penthorpe pushed aside the folds of his robe, reached inside his pocket, and pulled out the pearl and chain. His gaze on the ground, he offered it to Justin, who handed it to Francesca.

As he placed the broken chain in her palm, that little jolt of current always present between them went straight up her arm and came perilously close to her heart.

Here was an honorable man.

She closed her fingers around the necklace, feeling as if he'd just slain a dragon . . . for her. "Thank you," she whispered.

"Shall we leave?" he asked. He didn't wait for her response but took her elbow and guided her toward the door, picking his hat up from the floor as they left. Penthorpe rose to his feet. Even Francesca could see the anger seething from him, but Justin stopped him from retaliating with one look.

"Don't cross me, Penthorpe. Let it be." His brogue made the implied threat all the more menacing.

The rake kept silent.

Justin guided Francesca out into the hallway, shut the door, and marched her down the stairs. Outside, on the quiet street, Justin stopped and looked around. "Where's your coach?" he asked.

"I don't have one," she admitted.

"You walked here?"

She nodded.

Justin raised his eyes heavenward. "You take too many risks," he said.

"I won't ever again," she vowed. She raised her hand holding the necklace. "But I had no choice. My father wants this necklace back. I was desperate." She decided not to tell him about the loan from Madame Simone. Some information should not be volunteered.

"When we marry, lass," he said, giving her a stern look in the eye, "I don't ever want you to lie to me again. Ever."

"I borrowed a thousand pounds from Madame Simone to pay off Penthorpe." The words just popped out of her mouth.

He said something in Gaelic under his breath,

forcibly struggling with his temper before saying, "You should have gone to your father."

"I would have if I'd thought I could."

Justin frowned his doubts. "Come along. I'll walk you back to the dress shop. There's nothing worse that can happen between us now."

Heat rose to her cheeks. She had been called to account for bad behavior. Before she'd met Penthorpe, she'd never done anything out of step.

He realized how he'd made her feel. "*Och*, listen to me, lass. I sound like a preacher, and I've made my mistakes. I'm sorry for being such an illtempered boor."

It took a moment for Francesca to understand what he'd said. "You are apologizing?"

"To you. I'm not going up those stairs to apologize to Penny. He deserved a foot hanging."

Francesca rocked back slightly, stunned. "I've never heard a man apologize for anything."

Justin's brows came together. "He should if he is wrong. It's just—" He placed his hand on her arm above the elbow, rubbing the spot slowly before admitting, "It's just that *trust* is important. Honesty also has to matter. Especially between a man and woman who are going to marry." He raised a hand to his head as if he'd said too much and didn't know what to make of it.

"What is it?" she asked.

"Nothing." He paused, frowned at her, and then

added, "I just heard myself saying something I should practice. Something I hadn't realized was so vital until this moment. It's humbling." He changed the subject by glancing down the road. "Which way is it to this dressmaker?"

She nodded to her right, uncertain how to interpret his last statement. He placed her hand on his arm as they started walking. "I suppose we will be traveling through an alley?" he asked, his voice sounding deliberately light.

"Yes, and it isn't as tidy as the one behind my father's house," she answered, her mind not on where they were going.

"You should pick your alleys better," he observed dryly, but Francesca didn't laugh. She didn't even smile. Her mind was still caught by what he'd said, still wondering what he'd meant.

"I didn't want to lie to you. Not even the other night when you found me in Penthorpe's rooms."

"The other night, if you'd told me the truth, you could have saved both of us some trouble. I would have seen you home safe without—" He shrugged, knowing she would understand what he meant. He meant without their making love.

Her stomach went hollow. She didn't like the idea that he regretted that night. She knew she should, but she didn't.

In one afternoon, Justin had gone from an ordinary man to an extraordinary one. He'd defended her when, in truth, she had behaved poorly. No one had ever done that for her before.

And a little voice whispered inside her, *This is what love is like.*

Francesca pulled up short, frightened by the direction of her thoughts. For a second, she found it hard to breathe. She didn't like being vulnerable. It led to hurt, and she'd had enough pain in her life. She'd lost too many people she loved.

"Perhaps we should call this marriage off." She spoke without thinking, almost surprised herself that she'd said the words aloud.

The easiness left his being. "I believed this was settled?"

Francesca felt his tension and confusion as if it were her own. Something connected them. Something she didn't understand . . . or was afraid to.

"I know the marriage contract is signed, but if you wish, I would understand if you cried off." Her words sounded stilted even to her own ears. "I don't want you to sacrifice your happiness for the sake of my reputation."

He studied her a moment. "I'm doing what is right."

"Not for my sake," she answered, the words coming out more defiant than she had intended, and she wished she could call them back.

If there were passersby on the street, she didn't register them. Everything about her was focused on him.

But then, that had been the way it was since they'd first met.

"Why are you doing this?" he said.

His stark honesty cut through her defenses. "Because I am ashamed of my behavior. Because I'm sorry I've dragged you into this."

"You are worried about me?" He shook his head. "I'm no more than a country blacksmith, but even I know a man is only as good as his word. If I cry off, I'll be shaming myself and my family."

He was right.

Francesca clasped her arms against her middle. "You are right. I didn't mean offense."

Justin tilted her chin up so that she had no choice but to look into his eyes. "If I hadn't wanted this marriage, I would not have offered."

The tightness in her eased.

He took her arm and they continued down the street, walking in an amiable silence. Cynics would claim he was marrying her for her money, but Francesca knew differently. There was a connection between them. She realized he was right; trust was everything and she trusted him.

At the back door of Madame Simone's shop, he said, "The announcement will be in the paper in the morning. Phillip has helped me arrange for the license."

Francesca kept her hand on his arm as she turned to him. "My stepmother is busy planning our ceremony and wedding breakfast."

His brows came together. "Will you have no say?"

She looked down at her gloved hand resting on his arm, and then shook her head. "I don't care about the festivities. My concern is for the man." She raised her gaze to his. "Thank you, Your Grace, thank you for doing me the honor of rescuing me from my own foolishness."

To her surprise, he actually blushed. "You are hard to rescue, lass." And then he lifted her hand to his lips and kissed her fingertips.

"You did that very well for a blacksmith," she answered, and he rewarded her with a grin that made her knees go weak.

But before they could say more, the back door opened and Oleander poked his head out. Seeing her, he gave an audible sigh of relief.

Francesca squeezed Justin's hand holding hers, released it, and hurried inside, going toward the dressing room Madame had originally chosen for her.

Oleander closed the door behind her without saying a word. He didn't have to. She could feel his disapproval. He went back through the velvet curtains separating the dressmaker's to resume his place waiting out there.

Inside her dressing room, Francesca found Kathleen huddled over and sniveling in a chair.

"What is the matter?" Francesca asked.

Kathleen looked up with a gasp of relief. "I thought you were gone, miss, and I'd be let go."

"I won't let anything happen to you," Francesca promised.

The maid nodded, her doubt clear in her eyes. "I'm sorry for saying something to Mr. Oleander."

Before she could say more, Madame Simone sailed into the room followed by three assistants, one carrying a tray with sherry and glasses; another, pattern books; and a third, bolts of fabric. The last put the fabric down and left to fetch more.

"I told your maid not to worry," Madame said in a clipped French accent that was too pronounced to be real. "Here, have a glass of sherry, mademoiselle. We have much work to do. I've hired seven more assistances to help with your sewing."

"Thank you, Madame," Francesca said, taking the wine. "Kathleen, wait for me in the other room."

Once the maid had left, Francesca took the note out of her reticule. "This was not needed, Madame. However, I appreciate your service and will not forget your kindness."

Madame smiled. "I am more than happy to

be of service. I appreciate the patronage of a duchess."

A duchess.

The title held import. But what Francesca thought of was not rank and privilege but a man. A good man. An honorable man.

A man who would soon be her husband.

She didn't know what the future would hold, but she was not displeased.

And what did she bring to this marriage, besides money?

He spoke of trust. She longed for love.

Francesca placed her glass on the table, daring to believe he could love her. "Let us find the most perfect dress, Madame. One that will make me beautiful for my wedding day."

Justin liked Francesca Dunroy, but he didn't know if he could trust her.

Granted she had spirit and honesty and spoke what she truly felt. She was the sort of woman a man could build a life with.

She was also proud and independent.

Still, in spite of his doubts and her flaws, the sense of being alone that had dogged him from his earliest memories, a sense that niggled him even after meeting his twin and learning his background, started to recede.

He didn't know what special magic Francesca

possessed, but he no longer felt alone. He hadn't, he realized, since the moment he'd kissed her on the terrace. Looking back to the unintended passion of that moment, it seemed now that, of course, it was only natural that they would have made love.

She was the sort of woman who would stand beside her husband. She knew her duty. That's why her conscience had bothered her so much over the necklace.

Nor was she the only one by his side. Phillip had been repeatedly attempting to prove his loyalty. Unfortunately Justin had been a loner for so long, he'd been unable to accept his twin's open arms. He hadn't trusted him.

He wanted to now. He wanted to believe that both of them—Phillip and Francesca—were worthy of his trust.

A few moments later, he arrived at his building just as Biddle was approaching the door. At the sight of Justin, Biddle's step slowed to a stop. He ducked his head and studied the ground, waiting for Justin to enter the building first.

Justin approached him. "Biddle, I'm sorry."

If he had pushed the servant over, the man couldn't have appeared more surprised. "I beg your pardon, Your Grace?"

"I said I was sorry, man. I lost my temper yesterday. The truth is, I can't tie a proper knot in my neck cloth without you or make it to appointments on time or hire a hack or summon the coach. I know I was rude but I shouldn't mind if we could forget all that happened yesterday and start again."

He expected the valet to accept his apology. He was a duke, after all, and starting to learn that people toadied up to dukes.

Instead Biddle drew himself up to his tall, skinny height. "I'm sorry, Your Grace, but I have accepted another position. After all, I am a valet of the first stare. Look at what miracles I have wrought with you."

Justin swallowed back a sharp bark of laughing surprise. He knew pride when he saw it. After all, he had an excess of his own to contend with. So he lowered his head and frowned. "What shall I do then?" he wondered aloud. "I've had the best valet in London. How can I settle for another?"

"Well, you could," Biddle suggested, "offer me *more* than what my new employer is considering."

Justin wondered if there indeed was a new employer. Still, paying the man a higher wage to atone for his earlier rudeness seemed fair. Justin didn't even pretend to mull over his decision. "Name your price."

"One hundred and fifty pounds."

"Why, you rogue," Justin said. "That's double what I'm paying you now." And money, at the time, he could ill afford.

Biddle's eyebrows rose, a silent way to say, *That's my price.*

"All right then," Justin answered. "One hundred and fifty it is, but you'll have your hands full. I'm to be married. You shall be responsible for seeing me turned out right and proper for my wedding."

"My hands have been full since we first met, Your Grace," Biddle remarked without hesitation or any remorse. "May I inquire, who are you marrying?"

"That lad you saw me climb in the coach with," Justin said, unable to help himself. It was a good moment. Poor Biddle began choking with what appeared to be an apoplectic fit.

Justin clapped a hand on his back. "I'm teasing you, man. I'm to marry Miss Francesca Dunroy, the prettiest lass in all London." He'd not tell Biddle that the "lad" had actually been Francesca.

Biddle's eyes rounded. "You'll be marrying the heiress? Maximus Dunroy's only child?"

So even the servants of London knew of Francesca's fortune. "I shall." The words filled him with a good feeling. He was meeting the responsibilities of his title.

"Congratulations, Your Grace. *Congratulations,*" Biddle repeated with growing enthusiasm. "No wonder you could pay my price."

"I do have some bad news," Justin said. "My

apartments were burglarized." That explanation seemed the easiest.

"When, Your Grace?" Biddle asked, scandalized.

"At some point during the day. Someone must have frightened the thieves off because they ran away without taking anything. Still, my rooms are ransacked."

"I'm sorry, Your Grace, I have been in and out moving personal items but I didn't hear a noise upstairs or I would have investigated."

"Penthorpe didn't hear anything, either," Justin answered, knowing that Highlanders were wily enough to be silent when they needed to be. "Thieves are clever. They waited for the right moment. However, I didn't want you to be shocked when you saw the state of my rooms. And it doesn't need to be attended to right this minute. Collect your things from my brother's home and settle in first. Oh, yes," Justin said, remembering one other item of business for Biddle. "Dunroy sacked a footman and a maid. I believe their names are Jeremy and Rose. Hire them for me. After all, I shall need staff. But keep your eye on them and let me know your opinion."

Hiring Francesca's servants would be an act of good faith and an easy way to win her approval, something Justin was discovering he wanted.

"Yes, Your Grace. I will, Your Grace. Thank you, Your Grace." The servant hurried back the way he had come, moving with a new sense of importance.

Justin went inside, took off his hat, and climbed the stairs. He dreaded going into his apartments. He walked past Penthorpe's closed door—

He stopped. His door was slightly open again—only this time, the person or persons were still in his rooms. He heard the sound of his chair being moved and then a sigh of discontent.

A *feminine* sigh.

She couldn't be Francesca. There was no way Francesca could have returned in the short time since he'd left her at the dressmaker's. She couldn't have slipped by him.

Justin walked to the door and pushed it open with one finger.

He knew, before he saw her, exactly who his uninvited visitor was. He knew the scent of her skin better than any perfume—*Moira*.

The wife he'd divorced stood by his desk, one of his books open in front of her. She was dressed in the very height of fashion, pearls at her ears and neck, and wearing a dress of muslin so fine, it was almost transparent. She even had dampened her petticoats so that the fabric followed her every curve.

At his entrance, she looked up from the book and smiled as if it was right and natural for her to be under his roof. "Hello, Tavis."

Chapter 17

 ustin shut the door. He'd dreamed of this scene before. It was a dream he'd had ever since she'd left him. He'd always thought it signified he missed her . . . Now he wasn't so certain.

"I'm no longer called Tavis. Turns out it wasn't my name."

A dimple appeared in Moira's cheek as if she held back a secret only she knew. "I've heard . . . but you will always be 'Tavis' to me, Your Grace."

She was so perfectly beautiful—raven black hair, blue eyes, and skin as smooth as cream. She was accustomed to having her way around men and rarely, even when she was as young as ten, appeared flustered or at a disadvantage.

He had a history with this woman. She knew his weaknesses. The best moments of his life, and the worst, had been spent with her.

"What do you want, Moira?"

She smirked. "Why must you think I want something, Tavis?"

"Because you always do."

He walked into the room and placed his hat on the desk before taking off his gloves. For once he didn't peel them off but pulled each finger, the way Biddle and Phillip had insisted he do it. He tossed the gloves into his hat. "Where's your husband?"

Delicately raised eyebrows indicated Moira had noticed the changes in him. "You appear well, and prosperous. Who would have thought the blacksmith could be turned out into such a handsome and noble duke? Especially in such a short amount of time? I know I could never do anything with you."

"What do you want?" he repeated.

"And you've grown hard." She made a pout. "I suppose dukes no longer have to be polite to those of us who are underlings." She started to move around the desk toward him, her manner kittenish and cajoling.

"Stay where you are, Moira. The last time we met, you put a knife between my shoulder blades. I'll not give you a second chance. I can still feel the blade going in, and the shame of knowing it came from a woman I once called wife."

Her eyes met his briefly and then she looked away. No apology. No regret. Not even a hint of pleasure out of baiting him. But then she had always been a cold one. He couldn't help himself from contrasting her coldness to Francesca's vibrant red hair and open honesty.

Looking around the room, Moira declared, "Your housekeeping leaves a great deal to be desired."

"The maid had the day off," he said dryly.

"You must be very rough on beds." She nodded toward his mattress in the other room, half tossed off the bed and with stuffing pulled out.

He tired of playing her game. "Did you have a hand in tearing this place apart?"

"If I had, it wouldn't be such a mess. You know I don't like clutter."

"But you do want the sword, don't you?" he answered.

"Yes, if you have it."

"I don't."

Small, perfect teeth flashed in her smile. "You are lying. You know how valuable that sword is, my love. You would never let it go."

My love. How easily she used the endearment . . . and how completely devoid of any true feeling or affection.

"I'm sorry, Moira, but you'll have to return to the laird and tell him you've failed—again. I don't have the sword. I can't give what I don't have."

Her gaze narrowed. Her smile no longer reached her eyes. "Obviously someone besides myself believes that you do," she answered, a hint of steel in her voice. "Is it Gordon?"

"You don't know?" he asked, already knowing the answer. Her response confirmed what Gordon had said about severing his ties with Laird MacKenna and Bruce. "The laird should not have left his people and run. Especially since he took what money the clan had, didn't he, Moira?"

She lifted her chin. "It was his to take."

"It came to him by right of the chieftain. There was a responsibility that went with that money."

"You were always so simple, Tavis."

"Yes, it is clear to me," he agreed. "It's black and white. To be laird, a man must take care of his own. And MacKenna has made a grave mistake. He and Gordon were stronger as a team. I don't even count Bruce as a threat," he continued. "Any real man would not have sent his woman to do his dirty work."

Lightning lit Moira's eyes at the insult to her husband. "He does as the laird bids," she answered. "As do I. Give us the sword, Tavis, or you shall be sorry."

Her threat made him laugh. "What more can

you do to me, Moira, than what you've already done? You no longer have a hold on me." To his surprise, those last words were true. He'd always blamed himself for his failed marriage—but now he no longer felt guilt. And it wasn't just because of learning of his past. In a way he'd not anticipated, Francesca had made the difference.

She'd forced him to realize not all women were cut from the same cloth.

Out of his hurt and anger, he'd wanted to believe that. Since leaving Nathraichean, he'd gone from his monkish mourning for Moira to satisfying himself with other women who meant nothing to him.

But, whether by design or chance, Francesca had broken him from the pattern. Her intrusion in his life had made him face some stark realities, one being that he wasn't a bystander in his life. He could make decisions.

He might have once been a blacksmith, but now he was something even more powerful than a duke. He was a warrior.

"Tell MacKenna the sword is mine, and what I own, I keep. Its fate is in my hands, and if he dares to carry out any threat against me or mine, I shall use what power I hold against him."

Moira jerked her head back as if shocked he would dare make such a statement. "Do you really think you are stronger than the MacKenna?"

she challenged. "Do you place yourself higher than the chieftain?"

"The chieftain is gone, Moira. He's in Italy, enjoying the sun, while those who followed him starve. What sort of leader is that?"

"The one who will someday lead Scotland against the English," she declared.

"Or is he one who wants the sword to sell to the highest bidder?"

She pulled back as if seeing him with new eyes. "You would criticize the MacKenna?"

"Aye, and about time I did." He shook his head. "You truly believe in him. There was a time I was willing, biddable, and loyal. How blind I was."

She shook her head. "They've changed you. The laird said they would, but *I* said no. I thought I knew you better."

"You were wrong, but it wasn't Phillip who changed me. I changed myself once I started seeing the truth."

"We'll pay for it," Moira said, changing her tactics. "Name your price. After all, if you no longer feel loyalty to those that raised you and treated you like one of their own—"

"They *kidnapped* me, Moira, with the purpose of *destroying* my family. They made me into the bastard. You know that. There was no warm love and milk at mother's knee."

Guile and pretense disappeared from her face.

"There was from my father. He cared for you, Tavis."

Justin took a step away from her. "Aye, he was a good man." Her father had taught him his trade. Angus had encouraged him to live like a man, assuring him that sooner or later, the others would notice. He'd made Justin believe anything was possible.

When Angus died, it had only seemed right that Justin marry Moira, who was all of sixteen at the time. Justin hadn't been much older. And those years had been very good . . . or at least for him they had. He no longer knew what she thought.

A clever gleam appeared in Moira's eyes, as if she thought she knew what he was thinking. "*We were a family once*. That's what you always wanted, wasn't it, Tavis? A family? That's why you were loyal to the clan. You were one of us until your brother came and filled you with lies."

"Phillip has never lied to me." Justin crossed to the door and opened it. "Go, Moira. You won't find what you are looking for here."

She shook her head. "You are being a fool. Look at what has happened here. Do you not realize exactly how far any of us will go for that sword?"

"It's a stick of metal, Moira. Nothing more."

"It is so *much* more." She came around the desk, her steps measured and deliberate. "Mark my words, husband—"

"I'm not your husband."

"You could be again . . . for the sword." She shut the door and reached up to pull the sleeve of her dress down over one shoulder. It slid to reveal the curve of her breast. Her nipples were hard. "We were good together," she said, her voice low. "You were always good at loving, Tavis. Bruce has never been the fine, lusty man you were. You knew how to give me pleasure." She slid her hands beneath his coat, her eyes promising. "I miss that between us. And I know you must miss me, too." She started to slip her fingers under his waistband.

Justin caught her hands before they wandered too far. "Stop," he ordered, feeling pity, not lust. "It's over between us, Moira. Your betrayal killed anything I once felt for you."

"That is not true." She frowned at him. "I know you, Tavis. You longed for me. You *wanted* me."

"I wanted my *wife*," he answered. "I meant those vows I made years ago in front of Father Nicholas. But you left me. You told the laird you wanted me to divorce you so you could have Bruce. I didn't want to, Moira, but the laird insisted, and I, being the good, loyal follower, did as I was told, especially since my wife treated me worse than a dog."

"But you knew divorce was wrong," she wheedled, coming back toward him. "You knew you couldn't leave me—"

"I *have* left you," he said, pushing her away. "We are done. I'm to be married, Moira, to a good woman. One who understands honor."

Her jaw dropped open, her eyes widening. "You are marrying——?" Her puzzled voice broke off. "Who are you marrying?"

Justin grinned, enjoying the moment. "You sound jealous, Moira."

She yanked up her sleeve. "They have you marrying some Englishwoman, don't they?" She reached for the purse and gloves she'd placed on the desk, her temper roiling inside her until she exploded, "You are such a fool. Do you know why I left you? Because you couldn't understand anything. You had no ambition. No desire to be better than what you were."

"I was a good blacksmith."

His calm response almost set her whirling with outrage. "A blacksmith." She practically spit the words out. "I was worth so much more. I deserved more."

"You have what you deserved," he agreed, and opened the door.

This time she went out it but stopped in the threshold. "I will have that sword, Tavis, and if you don't give it to me—or if you hand it over to Gordon—I shall destroy you."

"Take your threats and return to Italy, Moira. Return to your husband and your precious, traitorous laird. Report to them that you've failed in gaining the sword." He slammed the door in her face, barely able to stand the sight of her.

What had happened to the lass he'd married? What power did MacKenna wield to have turned her so completely?

Justin stopped, a new suspicion rising in his mind.

He and everyone else had accused Bruce of being the one to turn her head. For the first time, Justin realized it was MacKenna who ordered her. MacKenna who had kept her close by having her serve his sister, the Lady Rowena. MacKenna whom Moira obeyed the way a woman should obey her husband.

Suddenly so many odd bits of happenings in his married life made sense. Moira and the laird. He just hadn't been able to see what was right beneath his nose because he'd been so upset over losing her.

Poor bloody Bruce. He was probably experiencing the same hell Justin had after she'd left him, and he deserved it.

They'd all been nothing but pawns in the laird's machinations.

Could it be that Laird MacKenna was as demented as his sister? Was there a strain of madness in his line? After all, he had been English educated. He should have known what Justin understood—that the English were too powerful for a clan of angry Scotsmen to overthrow.

And why did he want the Sword of the Mac-Kenna? Gordon wanted it for the fight. Gordon would never give up. However, the laird was a different man, an older one who had liked having his clan serve him. Justin didn't see him returning to live the life of a soldier. Not at his age.

He could want the sword because it was his birthright . . . or he could want it because there were those, Gordon among them, who would pay all they had for that sword.

Then again, what did it matter? Justin alone knew where the Sword of the MacKenna was, and if it hadn't been discovered yet, he knew it wouldn't be.

Standing in the center of his ravaged rooms, Justin also came to a momentous realization: He alone could decide his future. He could spend his time lamenting the wrongs that had been done to him and noticing his shortcomings and comparing himself to his brother the way he had done for the last several weeks, or he could step into the role of duke. Not just the donning of clothes and the knowledge of table manners—but becoming a man who held power.

Perhaps Phillip *was* more suited to be a duke.

He'd had a lifetime of training. But Justin held the title.

The time for waiting was done. It was time for action. Besides taking over the role of chieftain to his clan, he could speak out against injustice. When he, Phillip, and Charlotte had been in Edinburgh, Lord Monarch had encouraged him to do so. Lord Monarch often championed Scottish questions in the House of Lords. At the time, being a duke was too new to Justin. He couldn't see himself making a speech in a taproom let alone before important men.

But now he knew he would do it because it was right. His cause in life would be to speak for justice.

In that way, he would become the warrior he'd always wanted to be, but instead of wielding a sword, he'd learn diplomacy. Phillip would teach him what he'd need to know, and he'd study his twin with the same intensity he had studied his letters when Father Nicholas had taught him to read last year.

Looking around at the damage Gordon and his men had done to his rooms, Justin realized they might have done him a favor. It was time to leave this place.

He thought he'd left his ancestral home to protect his brother. Now he faced the fact that he'd left because he was afraid. He would be afraid no longer. He could not accomplish his purpose by being at odds with his brother, and he did need a suitable home for his wife.

Francesca. His glance turned to the bed. He remembered being inside her, feeling her move with him, closing around him. Theirs had been no ordinary coupling . . . and perhaps their bodies had known what their minds had not, or could not, yet realize.

A part of him didn't want to trust love again.

He'd told himself he was better off being a loner. He hadn't needed wife or brother.

Now his opinions were changing. Fate had placed Francesca in his path, and he was open to this second chance. She would grace his table, order his household, and raise his children all dreams he'd let die with his divorce.

The question was, could he trust love again?

He wasn't certain of the answer . . . but he started stacking his precious books, preparing to return to his ancestral home.

Chapter 18

The betrothal announcement appeared in the next morning's paper.

Francesca sat in the breakfast room, the small dining room the family used for most of their casual meals, with the *Morning Post* spread out before her. She stared at the words, needing several moments to realize they were written about her and not someone else.

She was not at her best this morning. She'd woken in the middle of the night in an absolute panic. *She didn't know Colster well enough to take a turn around Hyde Park with, let alone marry, him.*

Yes, he had done everything noble. Yes, he was the most attractive man of her acquaintance. And she *did* look forward to the freedom of being not

only a married woman, but also a duchess. She'd
enjoyed herself immensely being kowtowed to by
Madame Simone and her dressmakers.

She also placed a great deal of her trust in his
words: *If I hadn't wanted this marriage, I would not
have offered.* Yes, he was doing the right thing, but
he didn't seem angry about it.

Still, there was also a part of her that was very
afraid. It was the piece of her being that had sat
with her mother as she'd watched her door, longing for her husband, the man she loved, to come
spend time. Francesca had witnessed the disappointment and hurt. She'd also seen it on the faces
of other women whose husbands considered them
more possessions than people.

If Justin thought he would treat her that way,
he'd find out differently.

The vow still hadn't allowed her to sleep any
better, and finally she'd risen from bed, dressed,
and gone down to breakfast.

"Good morning, daughter." Her father's voice
from the direction of the doorway interrupted her
thoughts as he entered the room.

Francesca wasn't pleased to have the peace in
which she was indulging her worries disturbed,
especially by the culprit behind so many of them.

He didn't notice the lack of enthusiasm in her
murmured "Good morning."

Playfully he tapped her on the head with a copy

of the *Morning Gazette*, before setting the paper in front of her and pulling the *Post* out from the arm she had resting on it. "Colster doesn't waste time. An announcement in the *Gazette* and the *Post*. I like that man. By Zeus, I *like* him." He sat at the table while a footman poured him a cup of very strong coffee. Another servant, alerted by the sound of his voice, came out of the kitchen with the very rare beefsteak her father enjoyed every morning for his breakfast.

"So what do you think, daughter? Do you enjoy seeing your name in the papers?" Tucking a cloth napkin in his shirt for a bib and gesturing with his fork and knife, he didn't give her time to answer but said, "You've done well, daughter. Better than I would have ever imagined. Even your mother would have been surprised."

Francesca frowned. "Surprised? At which, Father, that I would be marrying a duke? Or that I would be marrying?"

"You are in a snit this morning," her father said cheerfully, washing his mouthful of steak down with a slurp of coffee. "Bring me an ale," he ordered a servant before turning his attention back to his steak and Francesca. "Your mother and I always knew you would marry. After all, you have all that lovely money. That's a man catcher, if ever there was one. But a duke! I don't even mind that you helped the matter along. You snagged yourself a fine one and it don't matter much what bait you used."

Francesca set down her cup. If he was saying what she suspected he was, she might have to box her own father's ears. "Bait, Father?" She was certain she would not like his answer.

She didn't.

He gave her a wink, "*You* know, tuck the ducky. Chase fox, catch the beaver." He laughed at his own wit. "It's all about competition out there. A girl has to use whatever she has to win the best man. The duke isn't the first to be trapped by his lust."

"You believe I trapped him into marriage?"

"I believe," her father said, tearing apart a hunk of bread and swiping it through the meat juices, "that it don't make much difference how you did it, you did well."

He popped the sopping bread into his mouth while Francesca grabbed the edge of the table, horrified that he spoke this way in front of the servants. With one look from her, the two footmen quickly withdrew.

"I did not trap Colster into marriage."

"It don't matter," her father answered happily, licking his fingers. "I didn't build my fortune by putting too fine a point on things. The end does justify the means, and I'm pleased. There is no telling how far my grandchildren and their children will rise. Ah, and speaking of children, here is my lovely wife."

Francesca turned to the door, surprised to see Regina. She never rose before noon, and yet here she was, radiantly ready for the day. Pregnancy must agree with her.

"Good morning, good morning." Regina greeted them with an exuberance she'd never demonstrated before this early in the day. Without waiting for an answer, she snatched the morning papers away from Francesca and began reading the announcements aloud, savoring the words . . . until her eye fell with disfavor on Francesca. She broke off in mid-sentence to say, "You can't wear that blue gown."

Francesca looked down at her day dress with its high, demure lace collar. "Why not?"

With exaggerated patience, Regina answered, "Because we are to have a host of company this morning. This dress is out of fashion." She turned to her husband. "See, Max? I *should* have gone shopping with her yesterday. I'm certain she has ordered all the wrong clothes."

"Madame will be over this afternoon to try on the patterns," Francesca said. "You can argue with my taste then. But why are you so concerned about this morning? Did you have something planned?" Francesca asked, not remembering anything scheduled. "I hope you don't because I'm certain there are preparations we must make for the wedding." She was not going anywhere with Regina. Not today, when she felt so sluggish. She didn't have the patience needed to deal with her stepmother.

Regina lowered the paper in her hand. "Do you not know anything?" She shook her head as if struck senseless by Francesca's naïveté and, acting as if she were a dozen years older and not a year younger than Francesca, announced, "As soon as the hallway clock strikes ten, we'll have callers."

"So early?" Francesca doubted it. They rarely had callers.

Regina let out a long-suffering sigh. "You have just landed the catch of the Little Season." She held up the paper as if to verify her position. "There isn't a matchmaking mother who won't want to hear the details. And their friends as well. By this evening, we will be the topic of conversation at everyone's dinner table."

Her father smiled his pleasure. "Well now, isn't that good news."

"Good news?" Francesca shook her head. "I hate to be the subject of gossip." Her mother would be turning in her grave. "Lady Bastone would certainly disapprove." She used the name of mother's dearest friend and arbiter of society as a buffer between herself and Regina.

"Sometimes, such as when you are about to marry a duke, gossip can't be helped, whether Lady Bastone likes it or not," Regina answered crisply, a reminder of how deep Her Ladyship's direct cuts had hurt. "However, I'm even expecting Colster himself to call. After all, he should, or do something to recognize the announcements in the paper."

Suddenly Francesca saw a reason to change.

She rose from the table, hating that what she was about to say would admit Regina was right. "Perhaps I should put on a different dress."

"Kathleen is waiting for you," Regina answered as if she had been certain all along Francesca would do as she expected. "Have Kathleen choose a more regal style for your hair. It's time you started wearing it up more."

"I *am* wearing it up," Francesca protested. She had tied it with a ribbon high on her head.

"Yes, but you have these—" She broke off and made twirling motions with her fingers around her hair. "You must start thinking of the image a duchess must project. Those curls are so annoying."

"My hair is curly," Francesca answered. "It's impossible to tuck every one of them in."

"Not for Kathleen," Regina replied serenely. "She's found a special cream that will smooth them all down. Now go, hurry. We'll have callers before you can blink."

Francesca went, telling herself she wasn't leaving because Regina wanted her to, but because she'd best leave before she exploded in a fit of temper. Thank the Lord, the wedding was in six days. She could barely abide another minute living with her stepmother, especially since her father bowed to the woman's every whim.

And it was silly to insist she change so early. It was just turning nine. No one with any social grace called before ten, and when they did come she'd wear her hair however she wished, thank you very much—

Someone pulled the bell at the front door, interrupting her thoughts. Francesca stopped by the back stairs, listening.

She heard Oleander open the door. A moment later, he was walking toward the breakfast room. Francesca moved swiftly before he could speak to her father and stepmother. "Who is it?" She didn't wait for an answer but snatched the calling card on the silver salver he held.

Lady Bastone.

Francesca stared, uncertain if she had read the card correctly. It was as if her recent mention of the powerful hostess's name had conjured her.

"She's in the reception room," Oleander said,

his voice low as if he didn't want Regina to over-hear him.

Thank you, she mouthed, and hurried toward the room by the front door where the family greeted callers. Oleander would have to take the card in to Regina, but at least Francesca might have a few moments alone.

Lady Bastone stood by the mantel over the cold hearth, studying a picture of one of the Dunroy racehorses. Her back was as straight as ever, and every hair beneath her fashionable bonnet was in place.

At the sound of Francesca's step, she turned toward the door. For a moment the two women took each other's measure, and then Francesca tossed aside all formalities to cross the room and throw her arms around her mother's friend. Tears came to her eyes. "I'm so happy to see you."

Her Ladyship gave Francesca a hug. She might seem imperial to others but she had once been a great mentor to Francesca. She pulled back and held Francesca at arm's length. "Quickly now, let us talk before that Other Woman joins us. Is the announcement I read in the papers true? Are you to marry Colster?"

Francesca nodded. "Yes, Tuesday."

Lady Bastone was shocked. "That's less than a week. What is the hurry?"

Instead of speaking of her own transgressions, Francesca was thankful to be able to answer, "My stepmother is to have a child."

Lady Bastone snorted in indignation. "Max is too old to be fathering children."

"Obviously not," Francesca said dryly, and Lady Bastone's sense of outrage gave way to a chuckle.

"The randy goat," she said without apology. She placed her hand on the side of Francesca's face. "But I didn't come about him but for you. Tell me, dear, are you happy for this marriage? I've heard rumors about Colster, although I've not met him yet. I did admire his brother when he had the title, but they say the twin is his exact opposite. I have not decided if I shall receive him or not."

Francesca had accepted Lady Bastone's banishment of her father and stepmother from her social circle well enough, even though that exclusion had included her as well. After all, Francesca had been in mourning and had wanted to see Regina and her father punished.

But Justin was blameless in any wrongdoing. Irritation flicked through her. She held her tongue. After all, this was Lady Bastone.

"He's a good man," she told Her Ladyship in Justin's defense.

"Yes, but society must have standards," Lady Bastone said gently. "For your sake, I have decided to meet him. This is a great concession. I hope you realize that. And truly, my dear, we have our standards for a reason."

"What 'rumors' have you heard?" Francesca asked, thinking, perhaps, she should give Lady Bastone the benefit of the doubt. After all, Her Ladyship was more experienced in life and society.

But before Lady Bastone could answer, Regina sailed into the room with her husband reluctantly trailing behind her. "My lady," Regina said in effusive greeting, "would you care to have a seat? Francesca, have you not ordered refreshment for Lady Bastone?"

Her Ladyship refused to look at Regina as she said, her tone clipped, "She offered all the amenities and I had to refuse. After all, I must be going. I shouldn't have called so early except I knew you would be overwhelmed with callers later. It was nice to have a private moment with my *dearest* friend's daughter. I miss Grace every single day." This last was thrown out almost as if a challenge to Francesca's father.

He didn't answer.

"Let me walk you to the door—" Francesca offered.

"No, I shall go," Regina cut in.

"Francesca will walk me to the door," Lady Bastone declared. However, at the doorway, she unbent enough to say, "I will hold a small dinner party in honor of Francesca and her intended to-morrow evening. This is short notice. I feel greatly put upon by having to plan quickly; however, I am left no choice." She spoke this last to Frances-ca's father so that all of them in the room knew she held him responsible. Her father frowned, and Francesca wondered if there had always been no love lost between them.

"I will send invitations to the Duke of Colster and his family," Lady Bastone continued. "You shall receive your invitation this afternoon."

Regina appeared ready to swoon at the excite-ment of such an invitation.

Lady Bastone smiled, the expression brittle. "Accompany me to the door," she ordered Fran-cesca.

In the hallway, away from Regina's prying ears, Lady Bastone said, "I don't like her."

"You may not, but you've made her very happy," Francesca confided. "She has longed for your approval."

Lady Bastone curled her lip in distaste. "Yes, I know. When he first married, Max came knock-ing on my door begging my endorsement of his marriage and his wife. I would not give it." She sighed heavily, the weary social arbiter. "Why is it so many second wives believe the first wife's friends should be theirs as well? Do they truly think we can forget a relationship built over years in a snap? Or is it that we should countenance everything the husband does?" She shook her head. "Men have too much power, and it is we women who must make rules. Otherwise society would crumble as it did with the ancient Romans."

She reached up and patted Francesca's cheek. "However, you have been wise, my dear. A duchess. Your mother would be proud of how lovely you've grown. I know it concerned her that her illness delayed your happiness."

This was news. Everything was such a blur after her mother's death. Then her father's remarriage had cast them into their own purgatory. "My happiness?"

"Yes, that you would not have your first season with the other young women of your age or find yourself married in a timely fashion. She used to worry over all those details she feared Max would bungle. And he did. You have missed so much."

But then, her mother's trusted friend hadn't come forward, either, Francesca found herself thinking. It was an outrageous thought. One didn't question Lady Bastone . . . and Francesca recognized she would not, either, except for Her Ladyship's hints about Justin. "Is happiness only to be found in marriage?" she wondered.

Lady Bastone's eyes widened as if Francesca had just called into question the Almighty. "For a woman it is. Marriage is the only acceptable course open to us, unless you want to be a governess or some put-upon companion, both miserable existences. A woman is only happy when she is married," Lady Bastone answered. "It's the only time she has true freedom. Once I gave my husband an heir, I could live my life as I desired. He's never interfered in what I wanted to do. He has his mistress."

Francesca knew mistresses were common . . . still, she didn't want to share her husband. "It wasn't that way for my parents." In her confusion, anger, and bitterness after her mother's death and her father's subsequent remarriage, she had forgotten this. They had been devoted to each other before her mother became sick.

"Are you so certain?" Lady Bastone asked, nodding to the maid who had accompanied her to rise from the chair where she had been waiting. "After all, he married Regina very quickly."

"That's true," Francesca answered, finding herself in the unusual position of defending their marriage. "However, Regina is from a good family and gently raised. I know there had been rumors, but I know they are not true."

Lady Bastone sniffed her indifference. "I'm surprised you defend her."

"I'm being fair." And she was remembering things she had forgotten—such as Lady Bastone not being a frequent visitor to her mother's sickbed, either. In fact, Francesca could count on one hand the number of her mother's friends who had stayed true to the end, and few of those were the society matrons.

Her Ladyship shrugged. "I don't like marriages where the wife is so much younger. I thought Max intelligent enough to see beyond a pretty face and a good set of teats. Oh, did I shock you?" she asked at Francesca's widened eyes. "When a woman's bosom is that big, 'teats' is the only word that will do. And they will only grow larger now that she is breeding. Max will be a happy man." She glanced back toward the reception room. "Is he planning for another son?"

"He hopes it is." Francesca dared not say more. The thought of replacing her brother hurt in places best left untouched.

"Then I shall pray he has a daughter," Her Ladyship said without sympathy.

Francesca gasped at not only her directness but her mean-spiritedness.

Lady Bastone caught the implied criticism. "Don't be a goose, Francesca. I'm only saying what you are thinking." She then kissed Francesca's cheek. "You will be a brilliant duchess, and you will know how to do it right. I expect great things from you."

She turned, ready to leave, her maid reaching for the door to open it, but Francesca wasn't ready to let her go yet. "Please, my lady, you mentioned something about rumors concerning Colster."

"You mean about his—" Lady Bastone started but was interrupted by the bell at the door.

Oleander and a footman appeared as if by magic to see to this new guest. The door was opened on two sets of visitors standing on the step, Lady Hewitt and her daughter, and Lady Whitcomb and her two daughters. Hard on their heels was the Countess Myzersky, Regina's closest friend.

The women came pouring through the door, their manners changing from cheeriness to deferential awe at the sight of Lady Bastone. Regina came out into the hallway while Francesca's father beat a hasty retreat to his study. In the welcoming, Lady Bastone did not have the opportunity to finish what she'd started to say and escaped with her maid before Francesca could question her further.

Regina was delighted these new guests had witnessed Lady Bastone under her roof. She led everyone into the reception room when the bell rang again. A few moments later, Oleander ushered in a footman carrying a huge bouquet of white roses that was almost as tall as he was.

"There must be over a hundred blooms there," the countess said in her low, sly voice. Only she would count. She'd buried three husbands and was currently on the search for a fourth.

"Let's see whose name is on the card, shall we?" Regina said. She held the card out to Francesca, who had to be prodded to take it.

The arrangement was for her.

The idea was shocking. No one had ever sent her flowers before. Her fingers trembled as she broke the wax seal.

The white rose is the most rare and fairest of them all. They reminded me of you.

Colster

This didn't sound like Justin. It lacked his droll, practical wit.

However, without asking permission, Regina grabbed the card from her hand and read it. "He said he chose white roses because they are the fairest flower of all, which is how he thinks of Francesca."

Her blunt paraphrasing robbed his words of their poetry. Francesca took back the card.

"Enjoy it now, my dear," the countess warned, "because after you are married, the flowers stop." The older women laughed their agreement before demanding all the details on how Francesca had managed to snare the catch of the season—and so quickly, too.

The questions made Francesca ill-at-ease. She

wasn't good at prevaricating. Regina didn't have a problem with it. She was happy to seize the stage and weave a fabulous story against the backdrop of her Arabian Nights ball. According to her stepmother, Colster had tumbled head over heels in love upon first sight and had *begged* her father for her hand.

"Look at her blush," the countess said to the others, indicating Francesca, and then laughed. "The rumors I've heard whispered among the servants could not be true."

Francesca's euphoria evaporated. "What rumors?"

The countess shrugged. "Rumors?" she answered as if she'd not brought up the subject. "I know no rumors although I am always anxious to listen."

"But you just said—"

Regina jumped in and changed the subject, recapturing everyone's attention by letting the news that she was with child slip gracefully from her lips.

The women made the proper noises of congratulation—but it was Francesca they envied, and both she and Regina knew it.

The bell rang again, and they were joined by more women eager to confirm for themselves the story in the morning papers.

And as the morning wore on, Francesca tried to

allow herself to be caught up in the excitement. She'd never felt the center of attention. Had never sought it.

You shall never regret this marriage. That had been Justin's promise. She wanted to believe it could be true, and yet, was this sort of watchful acclaim what it meant to be a duchess? No wonder he was uncomfortable with the role of duke.

The countess caught her eye. She motioned Francesca closer. "Don't look so worried. Enjoy this moment, my friend. After all, the first rush of love rarely lasts." With those reassuring words, she rose to say her farewell to Regina, leaving Francesca feeling more alone in a crowded room than she ever had before.

Chapter 19

I had roses sent in your name to Miss Dunroy," Phillip said to Justin. They had just been seated for luncheon at White's, Phillip's club and a stronghold of conservative thought combined with excellent pedigree.

Phillip had been pleased with Justin's decision to return home. While servants finished packing up Justin's apartments, Phillip had insisted they go to his club together.

It seemed an idle thing to do. Decadent even . . . as did so many of Justin's habits of late. He missed the long hours before his forge, the feeling of his muscles working and his mind busy with creating something practical. He was also aware of the glances thrown his way. He was an oddity, a piece of gossip.

Of course, Justin might have been in a better mood if he'd had a good night's sleep. His body and mind had vacillated between dark, erotic thoughts of Francesca, who kept changing into Moira, and the stark faces of his clansmen, people who had lost all and had nothing left to lose save their lives.

He was no fool. His dreams warned of how difficult his life had become. Yes, he wanted to help his clansmen, but he was also an Englishman, a duke. Would they accept his help? Especially if he refused to hand over the Sword of the Mac-Kenna?

Of course, his curse was that he understood Gordon's passionate rebellion.

The rooms of this club were growing increasingly crowded with men who could legislate changes that would make a difference in the lives of so many less fortunate than themselves. However, they appeared too busy stuffing themselves on shepherd's pie and trout to care.

Phillip cared, but he was a product of this world. He lacked the passion Justin felt from having lived among the oppressed.

His twin emphasized that uncaring stance when he continued, "I had a nice card put on them. Something about her being like these white roses. Thought you should know."

A surge of anger rose in Justin at his brother's complacency. "Do you think me some dumb Highlander? I can manage my own affairs of the heart. That at least I can do."

Phillip made an impatient gesture, showing his own annoyance with Justin's irritation. "I know you can. But there are little ins and outs of society, of *this* society," Phillip corrected himself, "that you are not familiar with and where I can help. By the way, the Dunroys will be joining us for dinner this evening, and Charlotte informed me before I left the house that we've received an invitation to Lord and Lady Bastone's for dinner in honor of your marriage." He reached for a roll and began buttering it. "This is good. Lady Bastone is one of the most powerful hostesses in London. If she approves of you, and she will since I understand she is very partial to Miss Dunroy, then you will have every door open to you."

Justin reached for one of the hot rolls on the table. "Don't I already have that as a duke?" he muttered. He tore the roll in half and the halves into fourths.

Phillip leaned forward. "Not around the likes of Lady Bastone and her ilk. They'd think nothing of cutting the prince, who is careful to mind his manners around them. The good news is that Francesca Dunroy knows her role. She's a godsend for you. Let her lead the way. She'll guide you through society with your colors flying."

Justin dropped the crumpled pieces of bread onto his plate. "I'm not some bloody eunuch."

"I didn't say you were," Phillip answered, his tone suggesting Justin was being unreasonable.

And Justin hated the fact that he might be.

However, before he could tone down his words, their meal was interrupted by one of Phillip's friends. Phillip had no choice but to introduce them.

"This is Lord Warren," he said with his easy grace. "Warren, my brother, the Duke of Colster."

"It's my pleasure, Your Grace," Warren said. He was of medium height, with a politician's smile. "I understand congratulations are in order." He looked at Justin as if expecting a response.

Caught with his mind still in his argument with Phillip, Justin asked bluntly, "For what?"

Warren blinked as if surprised Justin didn't know. "For catching *the* heiress." He leaned close. "There's been many a man toying with the idea of courting Miss Dunroy, but before any of them could knock on her door—she's a bit standoffish, you know—you snatched her up. Fetching thing, although I hear she is rather bookish. Her father used to complain about it a great deal."

"I like bookish women," Justin said simply.

"And how I wish we had more of them," Warren said, the words flowing from his mouth. "Especially those with fortunes."

Before he could continue, several other gentlemen approached the table for introductions. Justin had met one or two of them before. They paid him lip service before discussing important matters with his brother. He was left to push his food around his plate.

Of course, all of them made suitable comments about his marriage to Francesca. They assumed he was marrying her for her money . . . and for some reason he didn't yet understand, the assumption made him angry.

Or perhaps he was just angry to be ignored.

He pushed his chair back from the table. Heads were raised. Justin found himself the center of attention. He didn't like this, either. "I have an appointment," he lied as a way of apologizing for bolting—which was what he did. He didn't run from the room, but he didn't linger or glance back to see what Phillip thought.

And he didn't look up until he was going down the busy staircase leading to the front entrance. He thought to catch the eye of the porter at his desk in the front hall, hoping the man would see him coming and be ready to present his hat. Consequently, he almost bowled someone down and looked up to find himself eyeball-to-eyeball with Penthorpe, the last man Justin would have thought to enter the hallowed doors of White's.

For a second, the two of them faced each other, and Justin was seared by the bitterness in Penthorpe's eyes.

They didn't speak. Instead Justin used his ducal privilege to give the man a cut direct by continuing past him on the stairs without so much as a by-your-leave.

After all, dukes didn't have to excuse themselves to scoundrels.

The porter had seen him coming down the stairs and did have his hat at the ready. Justin tossed him a coin and pushed his way past a new group of gentlemen entering the club. He didn't draw a full breath until he was outside on the street.

There was a good deal of traffic as people saw to their business and made afternoon errands. Justin sought to blend in. He wanted to stretch his legs and escape the feeling that he didn't measure up, that he couldn't and wouldn't ever fit into this new world. Then again, what could he do? He couldn't go back to his old life, either.

Phillip caught up to him, placing a hand on his arm. "What the devil is the matter?" he demanded, ignoring any passersby who could overhear. He'd run out of White's so fast that he hadn't bothered with the hat or gloves he kept hammering to Justin were so important when a gentleman went out. He even still carried his table napkin in one hand. "I thought we laid *this* to rest yesterday."

"This?" Justin questioned.

"The animosity, the unreasonable anger you have against me. It wasn't my fault you were stolen, Justin. I'm not the criminal here. If you must be angry, then be angry at MacKenna."

"I *am* angry at MacKenna," Justin shot back with a vehemence that surprised even himself.

"Then do something about it," Phillip urged. "Give up the Sword of the MacKenna. Let us place it into the hands of those who will see it is never used for rebellion."

Justin yanked his arm out of Phillip's hand. He took a step back. "I thought this was about us as brothers. In fact, I was beginning to trust you. I thought I could."

Phillip held up a hand. "The sword has nothing to do with our trust as brothers. It's separate."

"Not as long as you want it."

"I don't want it for myself," Phillip answered carefully. "We've heard Lachlan is calling those who ran from Nathraichean around him. I don't want you caught up in this, Justin."

"I'm not," Justin replied bleakly. "But I am the keeper of the sword. As long as I have it, no one, and that includes MacKenna, can use it to stir up the Highlands. So no, brother, I will not give the sword to you, or Gordon, or Moira although she asked for it sweetly—"

"*Moira?*" Phillip frowned his opinion. "What is she doing in London? I thought she was in exile with MacKenna and the others."

So his twin had known MacKenna was in Italy. He had expected Phillip to tell him this information if he'd known it. Phillip hadn't. "How long have you known where the laird was?"

Phillip dismissed the question with a sharp motion of his hand. "Leave it be, Justin. I want to *protect* you, and besides, none of that Scottish business involves us now. I'm also growing damn tired of you not trusting me."

"Why should I?" Justin countered. "You've not trusted me enough to tell me the truth right from the beginning. And I'm no fool. You tell me that what happened at Nathraichean is no longer our concern, but then you ask for the sword. Who wants it, Phillip? You or the English government?"

"You may think what you wish," his twin replied levelly, "but I have only your interests at heart."

"You have the *Maddox* interests at heart," Justin gently reminded him. Phillip's first loyalty was always to his family name and the title.

"They are one and the same," Phillip said.

Justin began backing away. "And that is the problem. I have a foot in both worlds. I see the Scots' view and your view."

"I would think, since you are a Colster, you would understand your allegiance belongs to the Crown. You swore to that when you accepted the title."

"The Crown has my loyalty," Justin assured him. "However, that doesn't mean I will betray my friends. The Sword of the MacKenna is nothing, Phillip. It's cold steel without a heart or soul."

"But to some people, it's a symbol, Justin. You know that. You are well aware that there are men willing to lay down their lives for its cause."

"It's not the sword they honor," Justin said, "but the need for justice."

"That will come to them, but not if they rebel. They must be patient."

Justin shook his head. "There is no more patience or trust left, Phillip. Do you not remember the faces of those at Nathraichean? They are angry and done with waiting."

"All the more reason to not give them the sword. Rebellion means certain death."

"I won't. But I won't hand it over to you, either."

Phillip took a step forward. "Then where are your loyalties, Justin? You are the Duke of Colster. You must decide which world you live in. You cannot straddle both forever." With that, he turned on his heel and started back toward his club. As he walked, he noticed the table napkin in his hand as if just realizing he had it.

He paused and glanced back at Justin. For a moment he appeared ready to argue again, but then said, "Don't forget we dine with Miss Dunroy and her family. Half past seven."

"I'll be there."

"Do you need money?" Phillip's perennial question.

"I've what you gave me yesterday."

His twin nodded, then turned and walked on, his shoulders bent as if a great weight rested upon them.

Justin watched him until he'd gone into White's—and knew it wasn't the sword that kept them apart but his own discontent. Phillip would not betray him. He knew that.

And the rift between them was of Justin's making. He was angry with Phillip. Out of jealousy? Perhaps.

Phillip didn't have divided loyalties. Everything was so bloody clear to him. While everywhere Justin looked, there were more questions. They outweighed the answers—answers he was expected to know.

The flash of apple red hair across the street caught his eye. Its intense color reminded him of

Ian Munro. The lad had been the oldest of a family burned out by the Clearances. His father had lost his life defending their home, and Ian saw himself as the man of his household. He'd come to Justin's forge more than once for favors.

The lad with the hair even looked like Ian—

He *was* Ian. But Ian couldn't be in London. Why, the boy would have to walk to reach the city.

The boy gave Justin a small salute of acknowledgment, confirming his identity. The hand gesture was one Justin had always used on him in response to the boy's gratitude for favors. As Justin watched, Ian darted down an alley and waited for Justin to follow.

Justin glanced at the steps of White's. Phillip had gone in. No one else passing on the busy street noticed anything amiss.

Ian still waited for him.

Dodging traffic, Justin crossed the road and entered the alley.

With a sigh of relief, Ian confessed, "I wasn't sure you were going to come."

"I was certain it was you. What are you doing in London?"

"My mum sent me. Father Nicholas said he had to reach you, and she didn't want him to travel alone. He can barely see his hand in front of his face. She feared he'd end up in the sea before he reached London."

"Father Nicholas is in London?" The priest had lived with Justin in his cottage by the forge after the Lady Rowena had tossed him out of the laird's house in a fit of temper.

"Aye. He said he had to speak to you. Come, we've a bit of walking to do. I had to leave him at an inn several miles north of here. He's not feeling well, Tavis. He's weak as a puppy after the trip."

"You didn't walk all the way here from Scotland, did you?" Justin asked.

Ian laughed. "No, Father Nicholas paid for our fare on the post from the money you left for him. It was a wild ride, Tavis. We rode on top the whole way, and I swear it rained from the first mile to the last."

The wet weather could not have been good for the old priest's constitution. "So he's under the weather?" After all, for two years Justin had cared for Father Nicholas as if he were a family member.

"He caught cold and said he needed to rest. That's why he sent me for you. He wants to see you, Tavis. He says it is important."

"Then we aren't going to walk," Justin said. He took Ian's sleeve and said, "Come with me. We'll hire a hack."

An hour later, they arrived at the bustling Post House. The innkeeper was on the lookout for Ian. "Here now, boy," he barked at Ian. "Don't you leave that sick man in that room alone. Not without payment."

His admonishment confirmed Justin's worst fear. "I'll be responsible for his bill," he announced.

The innkeeper was a short man with black tufts of hair around the ears of his bald head. He gave Justin a look-over and relaxed, obviously noting the quality of his boots and the fine cut of his jacket. Still, he was the suspicious sort. "And who might you be?"

"The Duke of Colster," Justin said, using his title for one of the first times. He'd shied away in the past, uncomfortable announcing himself that way.

The innkeeper's manner changed immediately. "Your Grace," he said with a deep bow. "Welcome to the Post House."

Justin imagined how Phillip would respond and acted accordingly. "Present your bill and all their expenses for anything to my man for payment." He named Phillip's secretary, Thomas.

"Yes, Your Grace."

"Take me to Father Nicholas, Ian," Justin said.

Ian led him up the stairs to the inn's third floor. The hall was narrow here, and Justin doubted if the rooms offered much comfort.

In the hallway, Ian stopped. "Are you really a duke, Tavis?"

"Yes," Justin answered. "Surprised?"

Ian studied him for a moment and then answered, "No. My mum always said you were different from the rest of those who followed the MacKenna." On that unexpected statement he opened the door and confirmed Justin's suspicions about the quality of the rooms on this floor.

Father Nicholas slept on a narrow cot that took up most of the space. There wasn't a hearth, and the room's only light came through a small window close to the ceiling.

Justin closed the door. His old friend didn't move, and Justin's first fear was that he was dead, and then his eyes fluttered open.

"Ian, you found him," Father Nicholas said without turning his head. "I knew you would." He held out a hand, his movement weak.

Kneeling by the cot, Justin took it while laying his own hand on the priest's forehead. His skin was burning hot. Justin swore softly in Gaelic. "Has no one told you you are an old man? You should not have made that trip. If you'd sent word, I would have sent a coach and six white horses for you."

The priest smiled, as Justin knew he would. Slowly his head turned toward him. "I had to warn you."

Justin glanced at Ian, wondering if the boy should be here. Closing his eyes and with a nod of his head, the priest let it be known he should not worry. "The lad knows too much already. My tongue is loose in my old age."

"What did you want to say to me?" Justin asked.

"The sword. Do you still have it?" His breathing was shallow, making speaking difficult.

"You know that I do."

"Where is it?"

"Safe. And I am the only one, Father, who knows its whereabouts." He said this last for Ian's benefit, too. It was a sad state of the world when he trusted no one, including a lad.

"You must not let them have it."

Justin nodded. He understood.

Father Nicholas motioned him closer. "This is not why I came to see you. Not the sword." He wet his lips as if their dryness made speaking difficult. Justin looked around for a jug of water. There was nothing in the room and he wondered how long it had been since either the priest or Ian had eaten.

"Ian, go to the kitchen and order food for yourself and a bowl of soup for Father Nicholas. Bring back wine for the priest."

The boy stood rooted to where he stood. "I don't have money."

"The innkeeper will put it on my accounts," Justin told him, realizing that only two months ago, he would have been that naïve of the ways the world worked. They'd lived a sheltered life in Nathraichean. "Also, tell him to fetch a doctor. Our friend here needs one."

To his surprise, a tear formed in the corner of the priest's eye and his shoulders silently shook. Justin didn't believe the priest cried just from gratitude. "Go on," he told Ian. "Hurry then."

Ian opened the door and left. Justin leaned an arm on the cot over the priest's head. "My old friend, please. We have already come a long way together. Your expenses are a small recompense for the support you have given me over the years."

"*Mon fils,* once again I turn to you in my weakness and you offer me comfort. I am not worthy of such generosity."

"You are my friend." Perhaps his only loyal one in Nathraichean. "I will take care of you," Justin reiterated. "It would be my pleasure. Your friendship gave me purpose when Moira left. You taught me to read, man. Can you imagine what a poor duke I'd be if I couldn't even do that?"

Father Nicholas leaned over to use both hands to hold Justin's as if he did not want him to escape before he said what he had to say. His red-rimmed eyes burning bright, he confessed, "I did those things because I was responsible for what had happened to you. I could have made your life better."

"There are several in Nathraichean who could have done the same," Justin replied, pulling back slightly, but the priest's fingers tightened around his own.

"There is more." Father Nicholas leaned back, suddenly caught in a coughing spasm.

Alarmed, Justin braced the man as his body was racked with coughs. Beneath his clothes, the priest's body was far too thin.

"Has no one been seeing to you since I left?" Justin demanded.

"The lad Ian, and his mother," Father Nicholas answered when he was finally able to speak again.

"Then enough of this talk. You need to rest," Justin ordered.

"But I must talk. I have been a poor servant of God—"

"Enough," Justin interrupted. "This is not the time for blame. Later, when you are stronger, I will let you wear a hair shirt. For now, rest."

"I have much to tell you—" the priest started, but a knock on the door interrupted them.

Justin opened the door and a stout woman in a fresh starched mobcap bowed a deep curtsy. Behind her were two maids who curtsied after her. They held trays, and a very happy Ian brought up the rear.

"Your Grace, I am Mrs. Pembleton, the innkeeper's wife. We are so honored to have you patronizing our establishment. Here, girls, bring those trays in here—no, wait. There is little room. His Grace will need one of our *larger* rooms."

"Yes, you are right, but I am not the guest here," Justin said. "I want the very best for my friend."

Father Nicholas opened his mouth to protest. "You mustn't do this, *mon fils*—" Another coughing spasm broke off his words.

"I must," Justin answered. He liked making these decisions. He looked to Mrs. Pembleton. "Prepare that room. And Ian, eat," he ordered the boy.

The maids set down the trays on the room's small, rickety table. While Ian sat on the floor, Justin pulled up the one chair and fed Father Nicholas the broth Mrs. Pembleton had brought up.

The priest could not take more than a few spoons of it. He did drink a glass of wine mixed with water and then fell asleep. He didn't wake, even during the time Justin supervised the move to larger accommodations.

It felt good to provide this assistance to his friends. Helping them confirmed Justin's desire to help his clansmen. Being a duke wasn't a bad thing when one could use power for good.

He stayed to hear what the doctor said. Father Nicholas had a bad case of the ague but could recover with proper care. Justin authorized whatever treatments were needed.

The priest had argued. He'd said he was too old and that he should be allowed to die. He kept referring to his sins, but Justin refused to listen to his complaints. His friend was sick, and he held the power to help heal him.

Feeling more content than he had in years, Justin took a hack home. The hour was close to half past nine when he left the inn and ten when he arrived at his residence. He'd spent all of his ready coin and needed to go inside to fetch some from either Phillip or, if he were out, Mathers, the butler, who had access to family funds.

He had just stepped out of the hack and had started toward the lit doorway when Moira stepped from the shadows. She pulled down the hood of her cloak. "Tavis."

Justin stopped, frowning. He glanced to the door and then took a step toward her. "What are you doing here?"

"May I have a moment with you?" she asked, her manner completely different from the confident swagger of yesterday.

Curious, he said, "Of course, come inside. But first I must pay the hack driver—"

"No, I won't go inside. I met your brother earlier when I came to call. He practically tossed me out. He doesn't want me to speak to you."

Justin shrugged. "He doesn't hide his loyalties."

Her expression turned brittle. "He was more upset I arrived while his dinner guests were there."

Her words caused him to remember that he, Phillip, and Charlotte were dining with Francesca and her family. *How could I have forgotten such a thing?*

Swearing, he started up the steps, just as the door opened and Phillip came out. "Where were you?" he demanded. "I've been organizing the servants into a search party. I've been half mad with worry that Lachlan or MacKenna had done something to you."

"Francesca? Is she still here?" Justin asked, praying it was so.

"No. The Dunroys cooled their heels for two hours before Max Dunroy went storming out. Justin, where have you been? And your answer had better be you were close to death. Dunroy is furious. He is taking this as an insult. The man is very sensitive after being ostracized for as long as he was."

But he was speaking to Justin's back. Justin was already heading to the coach. "Where do you believe you are going?" Phillip demanded.

"To apologize to Francesca," Justin answered, tossing out the address for the Dunroy residence as he got into the hack—but then he remembered he needed money. "Phillip, you don't have a bit of blunt, have you?"

"You spent the money I gave you earlier. *You?*"

"Tavis, don't go," Moira ordered, coming out of the shadows she'd stepped into when Phillip had come out of the house. She hurried to his side and dug her fingers into his coat.

"I ordered you to leave," Phillip told her. Charlotte had come to the door now, as had Mathers and a few of the footmen Phillip must have been organizing into his "search party."

Justin was not pleased to have an audience.

Moria could not give a care. "I was wrong, Tavis," she said. "Wrong. I don't want you to marry."

Her words stunned Justin. He glanced at his twin, who had started to come down the steps. Phillip appeared equally taken aback.

"You don't have any hold over me," Justin told her—and it was true. He felt nothing for her.

"Watch her," Phillip warned. "She wants the sword."

"This isn't about the sword," Moira threw back and Justin believed her. He'd known her since she was a child. He'd seen all her moods. "Then what is this about, Moira? Have you decided you want to be a duchess?"

Her brows came together, her lips tightened, and she appeared to cry. "I don't want to lose you."

Justin understood. He knew her that well. "You don't want me, Moira. But you don't want another woman to have me, either."

"Besides, *you* don't have a thing to say about it," Phillip informed her. "You left him, remember?"

Justin frowned at his twin. "This is between us."

Phillip raised his hands as if washing himself of the whole matter and took a step away, staying close enough, Justin noted, to overhear everything.

Moira turned serious eyes on him. "I deserve his anger," she said. "I haven't been kind to you."

"It doesn't matter, Moira," Justin said, keeping his voice gentle.

"I don't want you to marry another woman," she said, a furrow forming between her brows. "You were mine."

"Not any longer," Justin answered. "You thought it a game, didn't you? You liked me pining away for you. But I'm gone now, Moira. I don't want to come back."

Her face appeared ready to crumple, and he knew she really had expected him to stay brokenhearted. That had been part of her power over him.

But he also knew she would recover. Moira was a survivor . . . and she loved herself more than anyone else.

"Good-bye, Moira. There's nothing more between us," Justin said.

Phillip gave a sharp bark of triumph but Moira was not a good loser. She dug her fingers into the sleeve of Justin's jacket. "You can't say that," she ordered. "I won't let you leave me."

"It's too late," Justin said, and pulled her hand from his sleeve.

His twin was already coming forward with coin for the driver and Justin wasted no time in climbing into the hack. He shut the door and signaled to the driver to go—but Moira ran up to the side of the coach, grabbing the window ledge with both hands. "You will not leave me," she vowed. "I'll see you ruined before I'll let you go to another woman—"

She broke off as the movement of the hack forced her to let go.

And Justin waved good-bye. He didn't even feel elated being the one to leave her this time. Yes, she had been part of his life—but he was the Duke of Colster now. He had a future.

And now he was going to find the woman who would be part of it and soothe her father's ruffled pride. He didn't give a damn what Dunroy thought, but he had to let Francesca know why he hadn't been there. She would have a clearer head—

Justin sat back against the hack's hard seat, stunned by the direction of his thoughts. He wanted to include Francesca. His life was no longer one closed road after another but included all possibilities.

And there was one person whom he trusted to help him understand what path he should take. One person who in a matter of days had become important to his understanding of the world. Her clear-eyed honesty was a balm to the twists and turns of his life.

The hack pulled up in front of the Dunroy residence. Justin hopped out.

"Shall I wait, Your Grace?" the driver asked.

"Yes, a moment," Justin answered and turned toward the door. However, as he prepared to knock, the door opened.

Max Dunroy stood there, his hair rumpled as if he'd pushed it back with his fingers, his face a mask of anger. "Well, you appear hale and hearty. What happened, did you forget you were to dine with my family this evening?"

A hundred excuses went through Justin's mind. But he wasn't political enough to use them. The truth mattered to him. He knew that now. No more deceptions in any form. "Yes, and I am deeply sorry—"

"How dare you show yourself here?" Dunroy demanded, liquor fumes punctuating each word. "Do you believe I am like the rest of London, that I must bow and scrape to you because you are a duke? I'm Maximus Dunroy. I have more money than all of you put together. It isn't enough I lost my son and my wife, but you and your kind have insulted Regina. She is upstairs crying right now because she thought to have dinner with you."

"I know and I am sorry that I was delayed," Justin started, but Dunroy cut him off, not even hearing the words of apology.

"There will come a day when men like me, men who know how to make money, will rule the world. And your sort," he said with disdain, "will grow weaker until you mean nothing."

"You could be right," Justin agreed, anything to make the man happy. "But I must see Francesca. I need to apologize to her, too."

"What? Do you believe *my* daughter will rise from her bed in the middle of the night at your beck and call? You can return at a decent hour and do your groveling then—but I doubt she will have you. We have our pride. With her money, she can marry any man. She doesn't need a duke." He punctuated his words by slamming the door in Justin's face.

Chapter 20

From the top of the stairs, wearing her night-dress, a dressing gown, and a shawl, Francesca heard the door slam. She'd heard everything her father had said, just as she could hear Regina's sobs coming from the bedroom.

Her father marched toward the stairs, but seeing her waiting, he stopped. He'd hit the bottle hard. Francesca hadn't seen him in such a tear since the night her mother had died.

He stopped when he saw her waiting. "Did you hear everything?"

She nodded.

"Are you going to take him?" he asked. "I'd advise you not to. They are all buggers, thinking they are so much better than the rest of us."

Francesca tightened her shawl around her shoulders. "I didn't believe he thought he was that way."

"Of course he is that way. It's in his blood." He started up the stairs. "Your mother wasn't that way." He stopped in front of her, his hand gripping the railing. "She defied all of them, for me, Francesca."

"And they accepted you."

"Did they?" he countered bitterly. "I was always an outsider. I went through with that ball we had the other night because it makes Regina happy, but I don't give a bloody damn. I'm a man who has made my own way in the world. Your mother understood that, and she loved me anyway. She made the blighters accept me."

A wealth of unguarded emotion colored his words.

"I haven't heard you speak of Mother. Not during her illness, not after she died."

His face tightened. He glanced down the hall. Regina had stopped crying. His gaze swung to meet hers. "I couldn't." He pinched his nose, holding back emotion.

For a second, Francesca thought he was going to push her away again. Instead he said, "It still hurts. I know you are angry at me. I know you believe I wasn't there for Grace when she was sick. You're right. It hurt too much, Francesca. I felt useless. I couldn't stop her pain. I couldn't bring David back. I couldn't do anything."

"None of us could, Papa," she said.

He nodded, studying some point beyond her down the hall, some point only he could see. His grip on the stair rail tightened. "I wasn't a good husband to her. Not when she needed it."

Francesca didn't know what to say. Here she was, at last witnessing his regrets, and instead of satisfaction, she felt pity. "Mother understood."

The lines in his face deepened. "I know. Doesn't make it better. And that's why I married a girl like Regina. She's simpler to understand. She doesn't sacrifice as much. If I fail, no one gives a damn about either of us. It's easier than being alone."

But is she worth it? Francesca wanted to ask, and kept her question to herself. Just as she accepted that he hadn't considered her company enough.

Her father drew a deep, cleansing breath and released it before changing the subject. "I'm not going to let Colster make a mockery of you. We don't need him, Francesca. If you wish to cry off, do so. I will stand beside you no matter how much Regina complains. In fact, I hope you do. I'd relish thumbing my nose at all of them, especially Lady Bastone. I wasn't looking forward to sitting at her table; I can tell you that."

He didn't wait for her response but patted her shoulder and moved on down the hall, going toward the bedroom he shared with his wife. He opened the door. Regina was still up.

"Where have you been? Was that Colster at the door? Did you speak to him?" Regina asked.

"Aye, it was Colster and I slammed the door in his face," her father answered, and Regina let out a howl of protest.

As her father turned to shut the door, his gaze met Francesca's, his eyebrows rising with a resigned acceptance.

Francesca stood a moment longer in the hall. Regina cried in anger now. This was the marriage her father had traded his peace for. He had not wanted to be alone—and yet, for the first time, he'd let Francesca have a glimpse inside his marriage . . . and she realized he was more alone than he had ever been.

Her gaze drifted to the closed front door.

Colster hadn't put up too much of a fight.

He'd apologized . . . but what did words mean?

Her father had claimed he'd loved her mother. His emotion moments ago had been real. Still, when her mother had needed him, when she'd called his name with her last breath, he'd not been there. So what did his regrets mean?

Nothing.

Francesca shook her head, uncertain. The note with the roses Justin had sent hadn't rung true. She preferred arguments, his stubbornness to that insincere sentiment . . . especially when he insulted her and her father by not even sending word that he would not be there for dinner.

And it made her wonder if all men were selfish. Did they all think of no one save themselves? Was there not one in this world whom she could trust?

She turned toward her room. The feel of Justin's body joining with hers was very clear in her mind . . . however, she was beginning to believe being alone was for the best. She would live among books. Perhaps even start a literary salon and dedicate her life to protecting her heart—

Francesca stopped in her tracks. Her heart.

She had lost her heart.

The moment she thought these words, the floodgates opened and she experienced a sense of loss and disappointment that threatened to overwhelm her. She wanted to believe in Justin. She wanted to believe that love was more than matches made for the sake of uniting fortunes with titles or for advancing treaties and business. She wanted to believe love meant having a partner who cared as much for you as you did for him. That it was the uniting of two souls against all odds.

She wanted to hold that belief, even having witnessed her father's horrible weakness. Having seen it in other men, like Penthorpe and those sadly lacking young lords lining up for her hand and her fortune.

Except she'd believed Justin was different.

Francesca slammed her hand against the door to her room. She'd sent Kathleen to bed. A lamp burned on her bedside table and a fire in the hearth. She turned down the lamp but didn't climb into bed. Instead she stood, her arms at her side, feeling used and useless. She could weep . . . but her pride wouldn't let her.

A scatter of sound came from her closed window as if hard rain or hail hit it. She glanced over to the window with a frown. The night had been clear when she'd come into the house—

Something hit the window again. It sounded as if someone was tossing the pebbles from around the terrace plantings at her window.

Francesca ran over and opened it. Her room looked out over the garden and the back terrace. At first she didn't see anyone, and then Justin stepped out from the terrace shadows into the moonlight.

"Come down," he whispered. He didn't wear a jacket or hat and his shirt appeared snowy white in the darkness.

She drew back. "I shouldn't."

"Please."

It was all he had to say.

Francesca carefully opened her bedroom door. The hallway was deserted, a single lamp lit against the darkness. Barefoot, she moved down the carpet toward the stairs. From her father's room she could hear murmuring. He and Regina were still arguing, but the sound of their voices was muted, as if they were talked out.

No footman guarded the door downstairs, nor was there a light. Francesca didn't need one. She'd grown up in this house.

She walked down the hall into the great room that also served as a ballroom. Oleander would have seen that the doors leading out to the terrace were locked, and he would have the keys. However, as she had done a few nights earlier to steal the necklace, Francesca unlocked one of the room's windows that reached almost to the floor and opened it. She stepped out into the night.

Justin was not where he had been a few moments ago. She walked across the terrace, expecting him to step out, and he didn't.

Then she heard him whisper her name. Turning in the direction of the sound, she saw the dark outline of his shape against the evergreens in the corner of the garden. Pulling her shawl around her shoulders, she went to him.

As she neared, he stepped deeper into the shadows, taking her hand and leading her to a private place close to the garden's wall. There was a stone bench here. Neither sat down.

He dropped his hand. "Are you as angry with me?"

"How did you come here?" she asked, ignoring his question. Her heart beat faster now that he was close, and she knew she must be careful.

"I climbed the wall." His teeth flashed white in his smile. "Are you angry?" he repeated.

"No," she answered. "Not after you've gone to so much trouble to see me."

He took her hand and pulled her down to sit beside him. "I'm sorry I missed the dinner party. I meant no slight by it."

"Where were you?" she asked. Her eyes had adjusted to the moonlit darkness and she watched him carefully, not quite trusting him.

"With a priest."

Francesca didn't know if she'd heard him correctly. "You were with a priest. Are you Catholic?" Catholics were not quite pariahs but she thought she would have known if he was one. It would have been part of the gossip circulating around him.

"No, I'm not . . . although he was the priest who married me."

"Married you?" Francesca pulled her hands from his. "You are married?" Her stomach twisted and she feared she would be ill. Her father had been right to refuse him.

Before she could bolt, he grabbed her hand and came off the bench to kneel in front of her. "Hear me out, Francesca. Don't judge me on half the story."

"What is the other half?" she asked tightly. "Or did you not appear for dinner because you knew you were a scoundrel and your conscience wouldn't let you?"

"Will you hear me out or not?" he demanded.

Francesca wanted to leave. She wanted to gather her pride and march proudly away.

But then another part of her, the part that realized she'd fallen in love, wanted to believe that all could be made right.

Yes, she was in love.

She could see it now. It had caught her unawares. No wonder her heart reacted whenever he was close. Even whenever his name was mentioned. "Are you widowed?" She prayed it was true, and knew deep inside that it wasn't.

He shook his head. "Divorced."

Now she stood. "Divorced?" The word seemed to suck the air from her. She knew of no one who had been divorced. It was a scandal. Shameful. It tainted everything.

Worse, it made her jealous.

He tightened his hold on her hand. She looked down. "Of course there would be another woman in your life," she said, speaking more to herself than to him. "You are too handsome, too bold to have been alone—"

"Francesca," he started, but she shook her head.

"I should have known better. I should have been more cautious—but who would have thought you could have this impact on me in such a short amount of time?"

He came to his feet. "What impact do I have on you?"

She wasn't going to tell him. It would make her appear even more foolish than she already was. "It's nothing. I just should have known." And then, because she couldn't help herself, she said, "Did you love her?"

The question sounded pathetic. Of course he'd loved her.

"Sit," he said instead of answering, his dark eyes watchful.

"I don't feel like sitting," she answered, too aware that she had been so anxious to see him, she wore her dressing gown and nightdress. "I need to go inside." She would have pushed by him but he swung her around into his arms.

"Please, Francesca, don't leave me. Not until you've heard all."

"Am I going to like the tale?" she dared to ask.

His lips curved into a sad smile. "I don't know. Phillip wanted me to annul the marriage. I wouldn't."

"Why not?"

He drew her down to sit beside him on the bench before saying, "Because she was part of my life. My refusal to buy an annulment—because that is what it would be, a purchase with *his* money—has been a sore point between us. She was my wife, Francesca. I meant those words when I said I would honor and cherish her."

"Then why the divorce?"

Justin's jaw hardened as he said, "She left me. She went off to live with another man. He was one of the laird's favorites and a kinsman. He had money and he had power and he wanted her. And what was I? A blacksmith. The laird, MacKenna, was a powerful man. Nathraichean is almost to the ends of the earth and only he ruled it. He ordered me to divorce her and made the arrangements."

"You loved her." He didn't need to tell her. Francesca *knew.*

Their hands were still clasped. She could feel the beat of his pulse through his fingers, and hers seemed to match its rhythm. Hearts beating as one—

"I did," he admitted.

Francesca thought her heart would stop. "Do you love her still?" She had to force the words out.

He leaned forward, lacing his fingers with hers, tightening his hold. "No."

That one word allowed her to breathe again.

He ran his fingers across the back of her hand. "I can't love her," he said quietly. "She was unfaithful."

She watched his thumb move across her skin as she said, "But you were forced to divorce her. You must have cared deeply at one time."

"I knew Moira since the day she was born. Her father raised me and taught me my trade."

Francesca frowned, realizing he spoke of his life after the kidnapping. She'd not thought of it overmuch. Like everyone in London, she knew he'd been raised among Scottish rebels, but she hadn't given consideration to what that had meant. "Did you believe him your father?"

"No," Justin said firmly. "It was made very clear I was the bastard of the village. From the first moment I can remember, I was thankful to Angus for giving me a roof over my head and food for my belly. I believe the laird's sister, Lady Rowena, the one who had kidnapped me, had meant for me to grow up in the streets begging for food, but Angus was a good man. He had a kind and generous heart. He and his wife were good to me. Moira was their only child, and I grew up watching and protecting her. She was sixteen when Angus died. His wife had died years earlier. It seemed only right I should marry and care for her. After all, I had taken over her father's forge."

"So it was a marriage of convenience," she said, feeling better when it was described that way.

"I suppose. At first. I did love her, Francesca. She'd once been a kind and loving child. We were young together . . . but then we started growing apart. I was blind to it. I had my work, and there was talk of rebellion. I wanted to be a part of it and so I spent time practicing with the other men, learning the arts of war."

He released his breath before saying, "I wasn't paying attention to her, and Bruce had noticed her. A man and his wife can grow apart if they aren't careful. She began to long for things I couldn't give her. Bruce could. Before I knew it, she didn't want me."

Francesca could not believe any woman married to this man wouldn't want him. And then another thought struck her, one born of her womanhood. "Why are you telling me this now? Does she want you again? Is she here?"

"I tell you because it is honest."

She didn't believe him. Studying him a moment, she murmured, "Will you not trust me?"

His gaze met hers and held. He didn't speak.

"You would rather I make this easy," she said. "You want me to accept what you say and not ask questions. We did this wrong, Justin." She gave his hand a squeeze. "We started backwards. We know each other without knowing anything."

"We know what is important."

"And what is that?" she wondered, doubting if it was true.

"I know the scent of your skin," he answered. "The texture of your hair. From the first moment we touched, we melded as one. Do you not feel it, lass? Can you not tell that it is different between us than with anyone else? More important, you are the first person in my life who actually listens to what I have to say. Who hears *me* when I speak."

It was true. She felt the same. In the short time they'd known each other, she'd stopped feeling so alone. "But is that enough?"

He looked into her eyes as if he could see her very soul. "Do we have an option? If I walked away from here right now, would you not feel as if letting what is between us go was the greatest mistake you'd ever made?"

"I don't know. I fear giving that answer." She squeezed his hand tight. "Where were you this evening? If I am so important, why did you not think of me?"

"Because I was thinking of myself." He sat upright and combed his hair back with his free hand. "Do you know what I always dreamed of being, Francesca? And don't laugh. I'm trusting you not to laugh."

"I won't," she promised.

"A hero," he confessed. "*Och*, I've wanted to be a warrior. I married Moira to be her protector. I wanted to always do what is right. To have a code, a standard of honor." He shook his head. "I never wanted to be a duke."

"But a duke can be a hero."

His eyes lit with excitement. "I know. I've realized that over these past few days. I mentioned the priest."

She nodded, letting him know she followed his thoughts.

"Father Nicholas had served Laird MacKenna and Lady Rowena well, but then the Lady Rowena took a sharp dislike to him. He was growing old and his eyesight failing. She threw him out and I took him in. He sent a lad to me this afternoon and let me know he was in London."

"Why is he here? Does he need a living?"

"He'll always need that. He escaped the Revolution in France and has depended on the clan. He married Moira and me and many others over the years." His brows came together as he said, "He's sick now. The travel wasn't good for him. He's not a young man but he came to warn me."

"Warn you of what?"

Justin glanced around as if fearing someone would overhear. "There is a sword that was used by the Mighty MacKenna centuries ago. It has led generations of the clan into battle. Highlanders will follow the man who carries that sword."

"Where is the sword now?"

"I have it."

Somehow Francesca was not surprised. "Does the priest want it?"

"Everyone wants it. My brother, the English government, MacKenna—even though he is living the life in Italy. He sent Moira here. He wanted her to seduce it out of me."

"Could she?" Francesca asked, knowing the answer even before he shook his head.

"No. I've a redheaded lass on my mind. Moira has been greatly insulted that her wiles no longer work."

Francesca sensed more to the story. "She's decided she wants you back."

"She wants a duke," he answered, his voice making it clear she'd not have him. "She wants me when she can't have me. I expect more from my woman. I expect loyalty."

The way he looked at her said more clearly than words that he knew he would receive it from Francesca. He trusted her.

"Why does the government want the sword?" Francesca asked.

Justin's sigh sounded as if the weight of the world rested on his shoulders. "They fear it could be used to start a rebellion."

"Should they have that fear?"

He nodded. "Gordon Lachlan was another of MacKenna's men, except his heart is true. He would use it to organize rebellion. He's a great leader, and with the sword, he could fire imaginations. Every young male in the Highlands would rally around him."

"Where is the sword?" Francesca dared to ask.

"I have a question for you first," he countered. He turned to her, taking both of her hands in his. "I want to marry you, Francesca Dunroy, because you are making me want to believe again. Because having you by my side seems the most right and natural thing in the world. However, it won't be easy, and I don't want you to be surprised later or feel that I betrayed you."

"Betrayed me about what?" she asked carefully.

"My intentions." He dropped his gaze to their joined hands before saying, "I want you to have the freedom to reject me. Don't think of the gossips or my reputation. This is about you, Francesca."

"What is it?" she asked, almost fearing his answer.

"Once we are married, I would leave London. I do not belong here, and from what I've seen, I could never help my clansmen. I'm not one for politics, Francesca. I am a man of action."

"What do you want to do?"

"I would take the land I own and that I receive from you in marriage and let those who have been turned from their homes by the Clearances come live on it. I'd help them build cottages and rebuild lives. I would take the task that MacKenna ran from. I would become their chieftain."

"How many people are we speaking about?"

"Hundreds. Perhaps thousands."

"Can we do that?" She could imagine such a thing.

"It won't be only us. These are good people, good farmers. They will work the soil and bring their knowledge to our land. They just need a place to live."

Francesca leaned back, letting the idea roll through her, seeing the excitement in his eyes—and then she understood. "They are your family, aren't they?"

He pressed his lips together, considering her words, and then smiled. "Yes. They are all I knew."

"And you would be their hero."

Now she surprised him. He shrugged, weighing her verdict in his mind. He shook his head. "Hopefully I've grown beyond that. What I wish now is to be a good man."

If Francesca hadn't already been falling in love with him . . . she would have now. The beauty of what he'd just said filled her heart with a sense of purpose and meaning that she'd never known. It manifested itself in the well of tears, tears of happiness in her eyes.

He saw those tears and raised his brows in alarm. "I understand," he said. "I knew my path might not be yours. I wanted you to have a choice, Francesca."

"And you believe I would choose against you?" she wondered.

"Have you not?" he said.

In reply, she freed her hands from his and pulled his face down to hers, giving him his answer in a kiss.

Chapter 21

ustin could have sworn Francesca was going to reject his proposal. He'd seen the
doubt in her eyes, the tightness around her lips.
She'd considered carefully all that he'd said—and
now here she was, in his arms, and kissing him
with love in her heart.

The anger that had for so long been a part of his
personality vanished. It disappeared as if it had
been nothing more than smoke.

He wrapped his arms around her waist, holding her tight. "I don't know what I would have
done if you'd turned me down," he confessed.

She pulled back. "Did you doubt me?"

Justin pressed a kiss against her forehead. "If

you were wise, you would run. You could do so much better than myself."

She tilted his chin down to look in his eyes. "I believe the world needs a hero . . . and I've not had much of a family, either."

"My brother will believe we've lost our minds." He had to be certain she understood what she was agreeing to.

Her response was to laugh, the sound actually carefree. "Can you imagine the look on Regina's face?" And then she kissed him as if she didn't care what anyone thought.

Justin wrapped his arms around her waist and pulled her into his lap. Burying his face in the wild riot of her loose curls, he vowed he would never let her go. She was *his*.

Her fingers brushed his hair. Her cheek pressed against his temple. And then he heard her whisper, "I love you."

A savage gladness spread through him. But he didn't want a whisper. He wanted her to shout the words.

He pulled back. "Do you truly?"

Her eyes widened. He'd been right. She had not been aware of what she'd revealed.

For a second, she appeared ready to deny it. He prayed she wouldn't. Her fingertips came up to trace the line of his mouth, following his jaw, touching the scar there before saying, "We've only just met—"

He cut her off with a bruising kiss. He didn't want excuses or artifice. That was for others. Here, between them, he wanted only what was important and real.

Her wayward curls formed a curtain between their faces and the world. Here it was private. Safe. He broke the kiss. "I don't believe anyone has ever given me so much of themselves as freely as you have. Or offered love so generously." He pushed back her hair, letting the moonlight fall on her beautiful face. "Francesca Dunroy, I've loved you from the moment we met. My body, my heart knew instantly what my mind is only beginning to understand—we were fated to meet each other."

Lips curving into a shy smile, she asked, "Are you saying Penthorpe was responsible for bringing us together?"

"It was his good deed of the century," Justin assured her.

His words made her laugh. "Let us not tell him. He'll extract a price for his services."

"Ah, but this is one I would willingly pay," Justin promised and kissed her again, their lips meeting as if it was the only right and natural thing to do.

Just as it was right and natural for him to want her.

She was enticingly naked beneath her night-clothes. He'd noticed that immediately . . . but he would not touch her. Not without invitation.

They kissed freely now, trusting each other, holding nothing back.

His hands ached to touch her. The weight of her body made him want to swing her around, let her straddle him, let him love her.

She bit his lower lip.

She had to know he was aroused. He kept his hands on her waist, not daring to move them lest he tear the clothes from her body. Instead he looked into her eyes and silently whispered the words he wanted to shout aloud, "I love you."

And he received his wish.

Francesca turned to face him, bringing her legs astride him. The hem of her skirts rode up to her knees. "I love you, too. You are my hero." She un-tied the sash of her dressing gown as she spoke and, reaching down, pulled her nightclothes up over her head.

It was a magic moment.

Moonlight turned her skin to silver. Her hair tumbled down her back as she threw aside all barriers between them.

Justin wrapped his arms around her, fiercely

wanting to hold and protect her for the rest of his life.

Her hands smoothed their way down his back as she leaned over to whisper in his ear, "Don't you want to make love to me?"

"More than anything I've ever wanted in my life," he vowed and, taking her face in his hands, kissed her deeply and fully.

Happiness gave Francesca a courage she'd never known. *He loved her.* This bold, compassionate man wanted her.

She kissed him back with all her being.

His hands came up her sides, taking the weight of her breasts in his palms. His touch held the power to turn her inside out. His kisses seared right through her, marking her for life. *She was his. She was no longer alone.*

Justin's mouth found and took her breast. Francesca could have wept from the pleasure. She curled the fingers of one hand in his hair— *wanting . . . needing*—while her other hand clutched the back of his shirt, tugging it upward.

He sat back. She made a soft moue of protest, until he yanked the knot of his neck cloth free and pulled his shirt up over his head.

Francesca went into his arms, reveling in the feel of the hard planes of his bare chest against hers.

Justin unbuttoned his breeches. The movement of his hands teased her. She was open and ready and aching for what only he could offer.

Perhaps there were other lovers who felt the same. Other lovers who believed theirs was the only world that mattered. Francesca didn't know; she didn't care.

All she knew was that what existed between her and Justin had power. It created them. It made them into one being.

And when he lifted her, when he slid into her, burying himself deep inside her, this love between them, this energy was all that was real, alive, and potent.

She leaned back, letting her hair fall behind her. His mouth kissed and loved her breast. The pull of his tongue went straight to where they were joined. She began moving, enjoying the feel of him.

His hands cupped her buttocks, guiding her and allowing her to do as she wished.

The garden, as she knew it, faded away. Here was paradise. They were Adam and Eve, creating a new world for themselves. Creating a new life between them.

Francesca moved more rapidly now. She couldn't stop herself from letting him know her pleasure with soft sighs . . . whimpers . . . gasps. She couldn't have kept quiet if they had been surrounded by people.

She braced herself with her hands on his shoulders. He no longer kissed her. His muscles were tense, his concentration complete. They worked together, moving as one, driving toward that glorious moment of union.

Her muscles tightened. Her senses heightened. For the span of one breath, sharp, delicious tension surged and then exploded. She leaned back, seeing the heavens above and feeling it inside, making her one with them.

His name left her lips. She dug her fingers into his shoulders, holding on, needing him for ballast.

Justin gathered her close. He held her tightly as rings of pure, glorious emotion waved through her.

This one moment made life worth living. He was still deep within her—and then she felt his release. It flowed through her, and all she could do was cling tight, wanting to never let him go.

His lips were against her neck. Neither moved. They couldn't. To move would destroy the perfection of this moment.

But all too soon, reality returned.

It came with the chill of the garden air.

While they had been making love, her skin had been molten hot. Now it cooled rapidly, making her all too aware of her nakedness.

He nuzzled her, his arms coming around her for warmth, and Francesca found her concerns about clothing fading. "I could stay here forever in your arms," she whispered.

"I hope you do," he answered.

Justin lightly ran his thumb over her nipple and released his breath with a long, satisfied sigh. "The sooner I make you my wife, the better for all of us." His hand slipped down to her belly. He pressed his palm against her. "If we continue this way, you shall be with child in no time. Our wedding can't come soon enough."

His words reminded her of his marriage. "Did you have children?"

He shook his head. "I wanted them but they did not come. It's a blessing, actually. She hasn't had children with Bruce, either."

No children . . . but he had cared for her. Not once had he denied it.

Jealousy did not set well with Francesca.

She pushed away, rising from his lap, now extremely conscious of her nakedness. She reached for her nightclothes and quickly put them on.

He took a moment to button himself but caught her hand when she would have turned away to tie the sash of her dressing gown. She looked down at his hand. It was easier than meeting his eyes as she said, "I would rather there had not been anyone else in your life."

Justin brought her hand to his lips, kissing the backs of her fingers. "I have many regrets," he answered. "And then again, none. I could wish that I'd never been kidnapped, that I had been born and trained with Phillip's gifts toward diplomacy. And yet, if I had, would I be as blind as he is to the plight of those who can't speak for themselves?" He gave her fingers a gentle squeeze. "Or would you and I have met the way we did? Both of us without the trappings of power? A man and a woman, two souls united by loneliness?"

Her pride melted. "I never imagined you a poet," she said, playfully pushing his hair back from his forehead.

"Love brings out everything good in a man. I never imagined myself such a thing, either." His expression sobered as he admitted, "In truth, my love, I would not have divorced Moira if I had not been forced. However, I never felt for her what I feel for you now. Our love will grow."

Francesca bent and pressed a hard kiss on his lips, wanting to seal that promise between them forever. "You needn't worry," she assured him. "Once we are wed, I shall be by your side every day of your life."

To her surprise, a tear welled in his eye. He swiped it away, bowing his head as if embarrassed. "What is it?" she asked. "What did I say?"

"Nothing," he answered, and then seemed to mentally stop. He faced her. "Not one person has ever made that promise to me before. No one has ever believed in me as you have."

"Not even your twin?"

A rueful smile twisted his lips. "He has doubts all the time. I've not told him of my plans about taking in the clan. He wouldn't understand."

"Are you certain? He cares for you very much."

"He cares for the family and the family name," Justin countered.

Francesca frowned. "You know better."

Justin stood abruptly, reaching for his shirt. He didn't meet her eye as he pulled it on over his head. In a flash of insight, Francesca said, "You don't want to trust him, do you?"

"I do trust him," Justin said, taking her arm and leading her toward the terrace.

She halted, not wanting him to brush this aside. "Have you told him where the sword is?"

He stiffened. "No. But then I haven't told you, either. It's best the secret stays with me."

"Because I'm English?"

Justin's mouth flattened. He stared at some unseen point across the garden. When he finally returned to her, he answered, "Where Phillip is concerned, yes. I know where his loyalty lies."

"With me?"

"I seek to protect you. There are people who would do anything to have that sword—Scots as well as English. If anything happened to you,

Francesca, I would not be able to live with myself. I've already lost too much in my life."

"And what if they hurt you? Will there be no one else to carry the secret, and will the sword disappear?"

"Perhaps it is best it disappears," he replied. "There is no place for bloodshed in this new world. Phillip is right in pursuing diplomacy. Peaceful means to resolving our differences."

Francesca smiled, slipping her hand in his. "You were wrong," she said.

His brows raised. "About what?"

"In your belief you won't make a good duke. I believe you will be a remarkable one."

Her reward for her confidence was another kiss before he led her to the terrace—and a few more at the terrace stairs.

At last they both knew they would need to part. "I'll see you on the morrow," he promised.

"Please call. Don't wait until we dine at Lord and Lady Bastone's," she said.

"I won't. If anything, I hate spending the few hours left of the night away from you." He backed away. "Go on. Sleep. Dream of me. Dream of being my duchess."

Francesca laughed. She was so happy, she doubted she would sleep a wink.

But they could not stand in the garden saying their good-nights forever. Reluctantly she went inside. The house was quiet. She picked up the lamp from where she'd left it. Glancing outside again, she caught sight of him going through the garden gate.

She started toward the stairs when her father's voice said from the hallway, "Francesca?"

The unexpected sound made her jump. "Father?"

He came to the doorway of the ballroom. "Were you outside?"

For a fleeting second she debated telling him the truth and then decided he didn't need to know. "I was. I couldn't sleep."

"Me, either. I came out in the hall and the lamp was gone so I thought to take a tour of the house to ensure all was well."

"It is," she assured him.

She could feel his gaze take in her appearance. "Is it Colster? Is his behavior tonight costing you sleep? You needn't worry. I shall handle the matter—"

"No," she cut in. "All is well with him, Father."

His gaze slid past her, moving toward the garden. Francesca was certain Justin was gone and, either way, knew the reflection of the lamplight in the windows would hinder her father's vision.

"Please, come with me," she said. "I have something for you."

She took his hand and led him upstairs toward

her bedroom. There she bade him to wait while she went for her jewelry box. She took out her mother's pearl pendant and turned to her father. She offered it to him.

"The chain is still broken," she said.

"I thought you were having it fixed?"

Francesca shrugged as she poured the necklace into his hand. "I meant to."

In the lamplight, he rolled the black pearl in his palm with one finger. "I do miss her," he whispered.

"She was a wonderful woman."

He nodded and then sniffed back his emotion. "So you will have Colster?" he asked, changing the subject.

"Yes," she said.

For a second, she saw something in his gaze that made her think he had caught her kissing Justin, but he didn't say anything other than "Good night." He returned to his room.

Francesca took the lamp into the bedroom and closed the door. To her surprise she quickly fell into a satisfying and dreamless sleep.

Out in the alley, on the other side of Dunroy's wall, Justin was surprised to see the Colster coach waiting for him. Clarens was at the reins. The hack was nowhere to be seen.

As Justin's step slowed, Clarens tipped his hat.

"Lord Phillip sent me. I assumed you'd want me to wait for you here."

"Where's the hack?"

"I sent him home, Your Grace."

Justin grabbed the handle on the side of the coach and swung up into the box beside Clarens. "You aren't going to give me another ride to the Three Princes, are you?"

The man's eyes met his in the dark. "Would it do any good, Your Grace?"

"No."

"Then I shall not. There is no one there who would wish to see you."

"So Gordon is gone from London, then?" Justin asked, playing on his suspicions.

Clarens snapped the reins, setting the coaching pair in motion. "I do not know a Gordon," he answered . . . and Justin did not press him for more.

However, he was glad he had not divulged to Francesca the sword's hiding place. Furthermore, he would do all he could to keep her safe. He understood how much Gordon would want the sword. Or MacKenna.

Any of them.

He and Clarens did not speak another word until the coach pulled up in front of the Colster residence. The lamps were still lit by the door, a sign that the household waited for him.

"Good night," Justin said as he swung down

from the box. The coach pulled away as he walked toward the door. He had reached the first step when Moira came out of the shadows.

"Your Grace," she said.

He stopped.

She appeared a forlorn creature, the hood of her cloak covering her head, the folds of the garment gathered tightly around her. "What is it, Moira?" he asked, wary.

"You truly aren't going to return to me, are you?" she said.

"Did you always believe I would?"

Moira nodded slowly. He understood. After all, he'd had a hand in spoiling her.

"Return to your husband," he said, his voice as patient and kind as he could make it. "We once meant a great deal to each other, but now it's over."

"I never thought it would be," she answered. "I always thought you would never abandon me."

"I'm not abandoning you," he said, letting his voice grow firmer. "You are the one who chose another. Now I see that you were right. We didn't love each other, did we? Good night, Moira."

He walked up the step, opened the door, and went inside without looking back. He was not surprised at Moira's supposed change of heart. She'd always wanted what she could not have.

A footman had fallen asleep waiting for him.

The rest of the house was quiet. He came awake as Justin closed the door. Rising to his feet, the servant said, "Your Grace," in greeting.

"Go on to bed," Justin replied—however, at that moment there came a screech from outside. *Moira*. She slammed the door with her fists.

"What is that?" the footman asked. "It sounded like a harpy." He referred to those mythical creatures that were birds with women's heads, which would pick men's bones clean.

Justin found the description apt.

"I shall see you to hell," Moira threatened. *"You shall be sorry."*

Justin knew he wouldn't be.

"Should I send her away?" the footman asked, his wide eyes saying louder than words that he'd rather stay on this side of the door.

"No, she's gone," Justin answered.

The footman cracked the door as if needing to see for himself. "She is," he reported.

"Harpies never linger once a man stands up to them," Justin said, and started for his bed, but then stopped. "What is your name?" Other than Biddle, he'd not bothered to learn the names of the family servants.

"Jeremy, Your Grace."

That name was familiar. Justin turned. "The footman who helped his mistress sneak about London in breeches?"

The servant's face paled. "You had someone search me and my wife out, Your Grace. You gave orders to hire me."

"So I did." Justin studied him a moment. "You deserted your mistress once."

"Yes, Your Grace."

"I don't expect you to do so again."

Jeremy's relief that he wasn't about to be sacked on the spot was palpable.

"Did you see the woman who was here in front of the house earlier?" At Jeremy's nod, Justin said, "She was the one on the other side of the door. See if you can follow her. Her name is Moira MacKenna. She may also call herself Lady MacKenna. I want to know where she stays and who she speaks to."

"Yes, Your Grace." Jeremy left.

Justin went to bed, feeling as if he'd done all that he could.

However, in the morning, he was disappointed to learn that, although Jeremy had managed to find Moira walking on the street, he could only follow her until she was picked up by a huge black coach drawn by a pair of matched grays.

After that, the footman lost the trail.

Chapter 22

The dinner the following night given by Lord and Lady Bastone went admirably well.

Francesca was proud of Justin. He often faulted himself for knowing less than he should about manners, but his natural intelligence and innate kindness stood him in good stead. Lady Bastone was pleased.

And if Her Ladyship was happy, then Regina, and consequently Francesca's father, were happy.

The days leading up to her wedding passed in a whirl of visitors, dress fittings, rides through the park with Justin, and dinner parties to honor and celebrate the two of them. Francesca was becoming accustomed to being referred to as a duchess.

One of the best moments was when Justin introduced her to Father Nicholas, who was recovering nicely from his illness. Justin had moved him to his old set of rooms over by Penthorpe. The priest was almost overwhelmed by Justin's generosity—while she and Justin enjoyed delicious amusement over what Penthorpe would say when he met his new neighbor.

However, it was young Ian Munro, who had served as Father Nicholas's eyes on the trip to London, who impressed upon Francesca exactly what it was Justin wanted to do with their combined resources of land and money.

The lad was far too serious for his years.

When asked, he'd told Francesca without emotion that his father had been killed by English troops while attempting to protect their cottage and possessions from being set ablaze. She understood the English viewpoint. The land that the crofters had lived on for generations was not theirs but belonged to the landowner.

Still, how did one give up a home?

After meeting Ian, she and Justin sat out in her father's garden for a long time discussing how they would manage their situation. They wanted to be fair, and also to avoid the problems that had created the current situation.

Francesca had also enjoyed the opportunity to know Charlotte better. Charlotte had agreed to stand up with her during the ceremony.

"I wish my sisters could be here," Charlotte said. "They would adore you as much as I do."

"Where are they?" Francesca asked, wondering if they were as lovely in person and spirit as Charlotte. They were sharing a quiet moment the afternoon before the wedding. Her father and his solicitor were in the study with Justin and Phillip signing the marriage documents. Regina had not been feeling all the thing, what with her pregnancy, and the two young women were enjoying this cozy chat.

"My sister Miranda is married to Alex Haddon, who owns a shipping company with his friend Michael Severson. You will meet Michael and his wife, Isabel, at the ceremony. Alex likes to travel, so he sails with his ships."

"Does Miranda like it?"

Charlotte smiled, stirring milk into her tea. "She's happy wherever Alex is." She set her spoon aside. "My youngest sister, Constance, is in Scotland at a boarding school for young women."

"Which one?" Francesca asked.

"Madame Lavaliere's Academy for Young Women. It's in Ollie's Mill, outside of Edinburgh."

"Will she be here for the wedding?" Francesca wanted to know.

Charlotte made a face, taking a sip of her tea before confessing, "You and Justin are marrying so quickly, there really hasn't been time to make the proper arrangements. Constance is not fond of Madame Lavaliere's and will be upset when she realizes she has missed an opportunity to spend some time in London."

"This is terrible," Francesca said. "I would want her here."

"I know, but the truth is, she isn't a good pupil. The school is excellent and I arranged for her to attend because I wanted her to have a bit of sophistication before she met the *ton* and found herself on the marriage mart. You know how it is."

Francesca did. However, to be fair, she said, "Justin has been learning on his own."

Charlotte shook her head. "Justin is a duke and male. The world is much harder on females. Miranda, Constance, and I were raised in the Ohio Valley. We hunted for our own food and wore moccasins or went barefoot."

"You have certainly adapted to England." Charlotte appeared as refined as the bluest blood in the land.

"I *wanted* to change," Charlotte said. "Constance does not. She isn't completely happy here, and I'm hoping that if she makes some friends at Madame Lavaliere's and has some time to learn all the social graces, then her success when she is presented will make her happy."

"I pray it is so," Francesca said.

"I do, too," Charlotte agreed fervently. "At least

I hope she grows happier at being forced to wear shoes."

Francesca didn't know if she was being teased or not. She didn't think so. Charlotte's expression was completely serious.

However, at that moment, they heard the door to the study open. The men's footsteps echoed in the hall as they made their way to the sitting room.

Phillip arrived first, followed by her father. "It's done," Phillip announced. "Now all we need is the ceremony."

Justin said farewell to the solicitors before joining them. He crossed straight to Francesca's side. A sense of the rightness of things went through her. They'd not kissed, barely touched since that night in the garden, and she could tell by the way his gaze followed her that he missed the close intimacy as much as she did.

Her father spoke. "My daughter and I mustn't stay longer. After all, Your Grace, she will be yours on the morrow."

"I look forward to it," Justin replied in his warm, rolling brogue.

There was nothing left then but for Francesca and her father to take their leave.

She couldn't wait for the next day.

Francesca woke feeling completely alive and refreshed. She'd gone to sleep hugging her pillow, knowing that in hours she would belong to Justin forever.

Kathleen brought in hot chocolate and rolls. "Good morning, miss. We need to set to work if we wish to have you ready to leave for the church in two hours' time."

"I'm all yours," Francesca replied, too excited to be hungry.

As she bustled around, laying out items for Francesca's toilette, Kathleen said, "It's a pleasure to serve you, miss."

"I have appreciated you, too," Francesca answered, giving up all pretense of eating, and rising from bed.

"Perhaps if you need a lady's maid, you might think of me?" Kathleen shyly suggested.

Francesca stopped, flattered that the maid thought enough of her to wish to be in her service. Or perhaps she wanted to escape Regina or the move to the country. "My maid Rose will be serving me, but if there is a position, I shall think of you. I know Lady Maddox's sister is away at school but she will be joining us in London. Considering that she must face the rigors of the marriage mart, she could greatly benefit from a lady's maid of your talent."

Kathleen blushed and bobbed a curtsy, obviously pleased that her request had met with some success. She started helping Francesca to dress, taking some time out to hurry and help Regina. Francesca didn't mind. This gave her a moment to be alone with her thoughts. She was nervous, but also excited.

When the maid returned, Regina came with her. Francesca's stepmother was dressed, and around her neck was the black pearl pendant. Francesca had offered it to her father as a gesture of goodwill and he had apparently wasted no time in giving it to Regina.

Now, seeing her stepmother wearing the necklace, Francesca felt no remorse, and then the thought struck her: The pearl wasn't her mother. It wasn't even a true symbol of her mother.

Living her life fully and with love was a far better tribute to her mother than a piece of jewelry.

So when Regina asked if Francesca liked the way the pearl looked around her neck, Francesca could say truthfully that there was exactly where the necklace belonged. Her words pleased Regina . . . and Francesca discovered the anger she'd nursed so long had disappeared.

She and Regina would never be close friends, but for the sake of Maximus Dunroy and for the sake of that baby who would be Francesca's half brother . . . or sister . . . they could be companionable.

For her wedding dress, Francesca and Madame Simone had chosen a dove white muslin with silver trim over wide rows of lace. Francesca was tempted to wear her hair down but in the end allowed it to be styled up, especially when Regina offered her diamond pins shaped like stars as adornments. Francesca liked the notion of the stars, remembering making love to Justin in the garden.

Kathleen used them to pin the eight-foot-long lace scarf to the center of her head. The ends of the scarf were draped loosely around Francesca's bare arms. She pulled on kid leather gloves so fine and soft, they molded to her hands like skin.

Downstairs, her father waited impatiently. Oleander stood off to one side holding his hat.

At the sound of her footsteps on the stairs, her father stopped his furious pacing and looked up. His mouth dropped open momentarily, before he closed it and climbed the bottom two steps to meet her and take her hand.

"You *are* a duchess," he said. He escorted her the last few steps down before making her do a pirouette for him. "Your mother would be so pleased."

Such praise brought tears to her eyes and almost sent her father into a panic. "No, don't be this way. You must be happy, girl. It's your wedding day." He took his hat from Oleander. "Is the coach ready?"

"Yes, sir."

"Doesn't she look fine, Oleander?"

"Very fine, sir."

Francesca took a moment to say to the butler, "Thank you for all you've done to aid in my happiness."

He had the good grace to blush. "All the servants in this household wish you well, Miss Francesca."

The good wishes warmed her heart. Today everything was as it should be. The world that for so long had not made sense, that had seemed lost in chaos, now appeared part and parcel of a divine plan.

"Then let us go," her father said, offering her his arm. He offered his other one to his wife. Oleander went with them to direct and officiate over any details where his eye might be needed.

Outside, to Francesca's delight, a white coach drawn by four matching bays waited for them. Her father said, "I hired this rig so we could all arrive in style. There will be a crowd waiting for us. Everyone in London will want a glimpse of a new duchess. We'll give them quite a show."

It *was* a show. As the coach drove them through the streets of London, passersby stopped and stared. It was a beautiful day with a clear blue sky. They rode with the windows open and waved at children who watched their passing in wide-eyed amazement.

Her father had been right about people crowding the road outside the church. They were there from every walk of life.

Originally it had been thought the wedding would be an intimate affair. However, as the days had passed, her father had given out invitations to everyone. Now a line of coaches waited. Street boys called out, offering to help coachmen with horses. Women stood in the churchyard and along the street, craning their necks for their first glimpse of Francesca.

There was even a businessman here and there, selling pies or flowers and trying to make a penny or two off the grand occasion.

Her father had thought ahead to send footmen to help keep the onlookers at bay as the coaches unloaded guests. The Duke of Colster had also seen that he had men there to ensure not only the safety of this momentous occasion, but to pass out donations to the poor to mark the event. His generosity not only touched her deeply, but made her proud.

The white coach moved forward to the walk leading to St. Paul's front door. Regina offered her hand to the footman, who helped her down to where one of her father's many cousins waited to escort her in.

Her father sat back in his seat. "Well, well. It's just you and me now. Are you still ready to do this?"

"With all my heart," Francesca answered.

"Good," he answered.

At that moment the door reopened. "Are you ready, sir?" Oleander asked.

"We are," her father said.

"Then it is time."

Her father climbed out of the coach. He held out his hand. Francesca took it, marveling at how much had changed so quickly.

The crowds in front of the church gave a collective sigh of approval at the sight of her. Oleander handed her a posy of white roses. "His Grace asked you to carry these."

White roses. Of course.

Inside, the church was cool and quiet. Charlotte waited to lead the way to where Justin stood with the bishop in front of the altar. Phillip stood beside him as groomsman.

The brothers were both particularly handsome. They wore coats of deepest blue superfine over white knee breeches. The blue set off their dark, handsome looks . . . but Francesca found she favored Justin. He appeared less refined and more intense than Phillip.

She was so intent on him, she barely registered the faces of the family members gathered as witnesses for the ceremony. The majority of the guests would be coming to the wedding breakfast.

The bishop started the ceremony. Listening,

Francesca was so conscious of Justin beside her that she noted his slightest movement. The scent of the roses in her hands mingled with the spiciness of his shaving soap—reminding her of that first night together. When he took her hand to pledge his vows, she imagined him hammering and forging steel into something useful, something safe.

That was what he'd done to her. Before she'd met him, she'd had no direction, no purpose other than her anger.

Now she was not only his duchess but also his partner, his trusted companion in creating new lives for others. She repeated her vows, meeting his eye, pledging to love and honor and obey.

And then it was done. She was married.

The bishop turned them to face the witnesses. "May I present His Grace, the Duke of Colster, and his duchess, Francesca. Let it be known that what God has joined, let no man tear asunder."

His words echoed against the stone walls and ceilings of the church.

Justin placed her gloved hand on his arm and they prepared to walk out, but at that moment a woman came striding in from the vestibule. She marched straight for them.

The guests frowned at her boldness.

Francesca watched, mesmerized by her beauty. The woman had black, black hair and flawless, creamy skin. Her eyes were so blue, they could have been chips of stained glass.

Justin's hand on Francesca's arm curled into a fist and he moved to stand protectively in front of her as the woman announced in a clear voice, "I'm sorry I wasn't here sooner. I would have stopped this marriage."

"Moira, you have no grounds," Justin said.

Francesca recognized the name. Here was her husband's first wife. The faithless one.

"Grounds?" Moira laughed. "I'm your wife, Your Grace. What better grounds is there than that?"

"We're divorced," Justin said, speaking to the bishop.

Confused murmurs, shock, and dismay met his announcement. Philip stepped forward, addressing the guests. "It's true, they are divorced. It was legal in Scotland, regardless of what we think of the matter here."

Moira smiled, unruffled by the brothers' declarations. "He *believed* we were divorced," she corrected, addressing the guests. She pulled out a sheaf of documents. "However, the papers were never properly done." She waved the papers in her hands. "Nathraichean, the village where we lived, was so very far from civilization. The laird never managed to properly file these documents with the courts. They were left in his desk."

"You lie," Justin said, taking a step forward as if he would strangle the truth from her. Phillip caught his arm, holding him back, as did Francesca.

"Do I?" Moira asked. She smiled, pleased with what she had done. "You may be disappointed," she said to Justin, "but our marriage is legal and valid."

"No, it is not," a French-accented voice said from among the guests. Francesca turned and saw Father Nicholas. He sat close to the front. She'd been so focused on Justin, she'd not noticed him.

"Why do you say that?" the bishop demanded.

The priest moved out toward the aisle, excusing his way past other guests, and keeping one hand on the chairs to help guide him. When he stood out where everyone could see him, he said, "I know that the marriage between Moira and the man known as Tavis was not legal because I married them."

"Then you would know it is legal," Moira countered.

"It can't be," Father Nicholas said, "because I am not a priest."

The wedding guests had all fallen silent, riveted by the drama being played out before them.

"Of course you are a priest," Moira said. "You performed a countless number of marriages."

"Oui, and they are all invalid," Father Nicholas said. "Let me explain. When the Revalidation first started in my country, priests were given a choice to forsake their vows or be beheaded. I was weak. I renounced my calling." Tears started to run down his cheeks, and his hands were shaking.

Phillip came forward, offering his arm to the man who accepted it gratefully.

Father Nicholas continued. "I escaped France, but what I truly escaped from was myself. You are right, Moira, Nathraichean is far from civilization. I could pretend to be a priest there. It gave me importance."

"So they were never married?" Phillip suggested.

"Non," the priest answered. He faced the bishop. "This is my sin. I had thought to live to the end of my days in Nathraichean. I had thought no harm would come from my deception. It gave me peace." Father Nicholas turned blurry eyes to Justin. "I'm sorry, *mon fils.* I have wronged you several times. I knew of your past and I kept quiet, as did so many of us. I also knew I should not perform the marriage."

"What is this about?" Moira demanded. "I was married to him for years."

"You *thought* you were married to him," Phillip answered. He said to the bishop, "Do you have anything to say, sir?"

The bishop scrunched his face and wagged his head back and forth before smiling and announcing, "Only that this marriage is legal and binding, for surely I am a man of the cloth."

Applause broke out from the wedding guests as if they had just watched the end of a very satisfying play.

"It's done, Moira," Justin said. "We are quit of each other."

And Moira had no choice but to turn and walk away.

Francesca felt a moment's empathy for her, a moment that quickly faded.

The bishop raised his hand over their heads. "Let us finish this God-ordained sacrament. As I was saying, what God has joined, let no man tear asunder. Ladies, gentlemen, the Duke and Duchess of Colster. May you go in peace, and may your union be one with God."

With those words, they were man and wife.

Justin offered Francesca his arm. Together they walked down the aisle, followed by Phillip and Charlotte, who escorted Father Nicholas.

The white coach Dunroy had hired waited for them in a sea of spectators. The word of what had happened in the church was starting to spread. Soon it would be on everyone's lips. There would be gossip. Perhaps scandal, but Francesca didn't care. The dark forces that had reigned at that place called Nathraichean no longer had the power to hurt their love.

Justin helped her into the vehicle and then climbed in after her. He shut the door and signaled to the driver to go.

At last they were alone. They rode in silence until Francesca had to say, "She is very beautiful." She held her hand up, begging him for understanding. "I couldn't help myself. I had to notice."

If she expected him to deny her words, she was mistaken. "Aye, she is lovely. But she has no soul. She's greedy and lacks warmth, compassion, understanding. All qualities a man looks for in a woman." He moved closer, his arm coming around her. "You have all those qualities, along with the beauty. A man would be a fool to choose her over you."

"And we know you are no fool."

His lips curved into a sly smile. "Absolutely not."

Before he could say more, the coach came to a halt in front of the Colster residence. Because his home was larger, it had been decided to hold the wedding breakfast here. Even then, the house was full to overflowing with guests. Francesca didn't know half of them. They were acquaintances either of Phillip or of her father.

Justin looked at the happy crowd, most of them with wine or punch glasses in their hands. They waited to cheer for them, toast them, and celebrate them with a party that could go for hours.

"I don't want to wait," he said. "I've already been waiting too long."

The heat of desire skittered along her skin. "Too long for what?" she dared to ask.

He didn't answer but gave her a look that seared her with his need for her.

Just as she wanted him.

"I have an idea," he said. "It's our wedding day. We should enjoy it and leave Phillip to the entertaining."

"What are you going to do?"

"Watch me." He nodded for the coachman to open the door. He climbed out and then turned to help her. However, as Francesca put the first foot on the step, Justin swept her up into his arms.

Their guests roared their approval.

Grinning, Justin carried her up the front step and over the threshold. The guests made room for them.

However, instead of going in the direction of where the feast for the wedding breakfast was laid out, he started up the stairs to the bedrooms.

For a second, Francesca was nervous. She didn't know what to make of the laughter and the catcalls. "Ignore them," he said.

"But they are guests—"

"My brother will see to their needs. You and I

have something far more important and better to do. This day is about *us*, Francesca."

Her protest died on her lips. He was right.

He carried her down the hall. "I chose this room for us because it overlooks the back garden," he said. "You know how I like gardens." He opened the door on a magnificent room in shades of cream and green.

Kicking the door shut, he set her down, and their lips immediately found each other. Their tongues met, stroked, tasted. Justin nibbled his way to her neck. "I don't believe I'll ever tire of kissing you."

"I pray you don't," she answered.

He grinned, cupping her breast with his hand, but Francesca was more impatient than that. She began unbuttoning his jacket, pulling his shirt from his waistband, her movements sure and demanding.

Clothes began flying every which way. They kicked off shoes and undid laces until they were both gloriously naked in the afternoon light.

Francesca turned shy. She still had the diamond pins in her hair, so didn't have even the benefit of her curls for protection. Justin caught her hands at the wrists and spread her arms so that he could admire every inch of her. Her skin turned pink and rosy with her embarrassment.

And then she spread his arms and gave him the

same careful, approving scrutiny. "You are such a beautiful man."

"I've never been so hard for a woman in my life," he answered. "Do you see it, Francesca? He has a mind of his own, and he wants you."

He swept her up and carried her to the bed. The coverlet was of the softest cotton. He laid her down upon it and stretched out over her, resting his weight on his arms.

"You are my wife. My beautiful, vibrant, giving wife."

Francesca brought his weight down on her, her body curving to receive him. "And you are my hero. My warrior."

Fierce pride lit his eyes. He kissed her as if he'd never let her go, sliding deep inside her as he did so.

"I like this," Francesca whispered.

"Good," he answered, "because I plan on spending a good portion of our marriage exactly this way."

He began moving then, thrusting deep.

As in life, Francesca was no passive partner. She wrapped around his hips, holding him deeper and tighter.

Together they moved, experiencing the climax at exactly the same moment, the same intensity.

His seed flowed into her, and she was lost.

This was as it had been meant to be. She was

truly, completely his—not only in body but also in name.

Later, snuggled under the covers as their bodies cooled, Justin laced his fingers with hers. "Francesca Maddox," he said, testing the name.

She smiled drowsily. "Do you like it?"

"I've never heard one finer."

Francesca laid her head in the hollow of his shoulder, her fingers lazily stroking his chest, his abdomen. "Can we always be like this?" she wondered.

"We will," he vowed—and so they were.

They never did attend their wedding celebration. Instead they had one of their own.

In this room they were not duke and duchess, but man and woman.

Still, Francesca had one question. "Will you be safe?" she asked. "Or will they continue to hound you for the sword?"

He shook his head. "They can't harm us, Francesca. Not as long as we have each other."

And as the moon rose high in the sky, Francesca realized that he was right. They had each other . . . and at last, she had found where she belonged . . . in his arms.

Epilogue

There was nothing to do after the humiliation of the wedding but to leave.

He was lost to her. Completely.

Moira was surprised at how keenly she felt Tavis's loss.

The wind off the Thames was chilly this time of the evening as passengers boarded the ship bound for Italy that would leave with the tide in the morning.

Moira stood waiting for her bags to be unloaded from the hired vehicle and taken aboard the ship.

She'd failed. In all ways.

Laird MacKenna would not be pleased. Nor would Bruce. They had expected her to succeed, counted on it. The English government was offering a fortune for the Sword of the MacKenna. The men had thought to sell it.

She had thought she'd not cared one way or the other. The sword was a means to an end. Now she found herself wondering why she had not seen earlier that Tavis was a much better man than Bruce . . . even better than the laird.

"Bruce will be displeased to see you home without the sword," a Scots voice said from the shadowy darkness beyond the torchlight.

She recognized the voice—Gordon Lachlan. Turning toward its sound, she demanded, "Where have you been while I've been attempting to gain the sword?"

Gordon stepped out of the shadows, the light hitting his golden hair and beard. "Watching. I tried to find it before you. I failed, too."

"Tavis won't give it up," she said. "I know how stubborn he is. He'll go to his grave with the secret of where he has hidden it." She pulled on her gloves.

"Moira, is that admiration I hear in your voice?" Gordon asked.

She didn't want to answer. Tomorrow she'd be stronger. Tonight she needed to lick her wounds. "You can trust him, Gordon. He won't give it to the English either."

"How can you be so certain?"

Moira smiled, and for the briefest moment allowed herself to remember a time when everything was good. "I was the man's wife . . . no matter what that priest said. I slept in his bed. I know him better than anyone. He'll keep the sword, Gordon, but he'll keep it safe."

"He's no longer one of us." Gordon's voice was edged with bitterness. "There is no telling what he will do."

For a second, Moira thought to argue, and then shook her head. "Well, if you find it, or convince Tavis to give it to you, bring it to the laird. He will see you are handsomely rewarded. He always liked you, Gordon. I tell you this knowing that Bruce would not be pleased."

Gordon's smile was flat and without mirth. "Your husband is not here. He's not fighting his own battles, Moira, he's sending you."

He was right, and, deep inside, Moira resented Bruce for it.

"Be honest, lass," Gordon said, his voice as seductive as Satan's, "you gave up a good man in Tavis. You backed the wrong horse. Was there not a moment during that scene in the church when you wanted him back? Even just a little?"

Yes. But she would never admit it.

"And what of you?" she asked. "What do you intend to do now?"

"I'm going to claim that sword."

Moira doubted it. "Tavis is stubborn. He will win, Gordon."

"Not if I make him choose between the sword and something that is equally valuable."

"And what would that be?" she asked.

"His family. Tavis was an orphan. He values family above all else. Do you not remember how carefully he cared for the priest? How he waited for you when any other man would have tossed you aside?"

Moira ignored his jibe. "Do you think to kidnap his wife?" She laughed. "He'll not let you near her. I've already heard Tavis and his twin are planning to hire men for their protection. You will never be allowed close enough to her."

"It's not her I shall use," Gordon assured her.

"Then who?"

Gordon's teeth flashed white in the darkness. He wasn't going to tell her. She knew it.

Instead he answered, "Godspeed to you, Moira. Someday both you and Bruce can return to Scotland, a free one. I'll be waiting on the shore to bid you welcome. And until then, tell your husband he can kiss my arse."

"Where will you be if he wishes to reply?" she asked.

"At a girls' school close to Edinburgh." He stepped back into the dark edges of the dock and disappeared.

If you loved this Cathy Maxwell book,
then you won't want to miss any
of her other delicious Avon Books!

Following is a sneak peek
at some of Cathy's
other amazing love stories . . .

The Price of Indiscretion

*The granddaughter of an earl must charm the ton
and secure a good match for herself and her sisters.
But her true love is a renegade
and a most improper marriage prospect.*

The dark room opened onto a deserted area of the terrace
that had been set up for privacy. There was no light
save for the moon.

Large pots of conical junipers, gardenias, and tiny trailing flowers shaped like white stars lined the edge of the lattice wall that separated this part of the terrace from the rest
of the house. Red roses climbed up the trellis against the
support columns. Their heady scent mixed with those of the
gardenias.

Beyond the lattice came the music and conversation and
laughter from the party. No one would hear them here.

It was the perfect spot for what Alex had in mind.

He could feel her coming. She walked quietly, but he
could hear her kid leather dancing slippers move quietly on
the tile floor. He stepped into the shadows and waited.

Miranda came out onto the terrace. Moonlight turned her
hair to silver and her skin to alabaster. Her eyes were wide
and dark. She looked around the terrace, her gaze stopping
when she saw him.

Alex stepped forward into the moonlight. "Having a
good time this evening leading all those men around by
their noses, Miranda?"

Veral Cameron's daughter took a step back before

pulling herself up as regal as a princess. "Is that why you wanted me out here? Is that what you wished to say?"

Oh no, there were questions he wanted answered, and this time there was no one with a horsewhip to protect her.

"Men must come across as fools to you," he continued conversationally.

"You don't." She took another step back. She *should* be afraid.

"I should," he said, answering his own question, letting her hear his anger in the depth of his voice. "I was the biggest fool of all."

Almost defiantly, her face pale, she demanded, "What do you want, Alex? An apology? Would one erase what happened between us?"

No, nothing could do that.

And it made him angry that even now, after all these years, the sound of her voice made his heart skip a funny beat. She had no right to still have control over him. He should leave.

Instead he walked toward her.

She took a step for the door, but then stopped as if rooting herself in place. Miranda was many things, but she was no coward

How much he had once loved her . . .

He stopped in front of her. With a will of its own, his hand came up to rest on the trimness of her waist. Time might have passed, but some things had not changed. Memories rushed through him.

Alex went hard with a force he'd not experienced since last they'd met. He caught the scent of her hair. "You smell of the forest and of the spring wind in the valley," he whispered. "I'd forgotten how sweet it was."

He hated having her in his blood. She was a curse, a weakness that had almost destroyed him, and he'd best remember it—

Miranda leaned toward him, her shoulder against his chest. Her lips formed his name.

Pulling her closer, he let her feel how aroused he was. Her lashes dropped seductively over her eyes. Her nipples hardened . . .

But the innocence they'd once shared with each other was lost. He brushed his lips against her ear as he said, "And I think you are a pert tart to be dangling for a husband, when the man you married is standing right here next to you."

Miranda's eyes flashed. She pushed away, trying to free herself from his hold at her waist, but he kept her close. She attempted to strike out with her other hand. He captured her wrist in an iron grip. She had always been a fighter—in all matters save confronting her father.

She lashed out with words. "We were never married."

Alex gave her a little shake before pulling her closer. "Why?" he demanded. "Because you don't believe promises between yourself and an Indian carry weight?"

Her breasts pushed against his chest. "There was no church, no preacher— "

"There was *us*, Miranda." Alex was all too conscious that her curves had grown more womanly over the years. Their bodies fit together well. He focused on his anger. "*We* were all that mattered back then, or have you forgotten? Do you not remember that night? How we stood beside the river and followed the Shawnee way? Do you remember what I whispered to you?"

She shook her head, refusing to look at him. She tried to wrest her wrist free, but he held fast.

"You are lying," he accused quietly. "You can't forget."

"How do you know?" she threw back at him.

Alex smiled. "Because I can't," he admitted sadly.

Temptation of a Proper Governess

*A governess should be mild, modest and
keep to herself. And she must never attract
the attention of any male in the household . . .
but Isabel Halloran is too beautiful
for Michael Severson to miss!*

$\mathcal{M}$ ichael watched the woman walk to him, her expressive eyes wide with apprehension—and longing.

Yes, this is what I need. Mindless sex would relieve the tension and frustration that had been building in him ever since he'd returned to England.

Elswick had shut him out. For close to five months, Michael's every effort to reclaim a place in Society had been thwarted to the point he'd had no other venue to pursue than the likes of Riggs, the profligate nephew of a duke whom few people accepted, and the drunken, fawning Wardley.

Not even his brother returned his calls. The butler, whom he had known since boyhood, seemed to enjoy informing him they were "not at home."

Michael knew Carter was there, and his wife Wallis, too. He could feel them watch him as he left their doorstep. They wanted him to stay out of their lives.

Meanwhile, Alex had returned from a profitable trip to Spain. Their shipping venture was already returning their investment fourfold. He had suggested Michael go with him on their next trip. Michael refused.

There had been a time, before Aletta's death, when he would have taken the easy route, when he would have forgotten the past. Now, he was a man who got what he wanted.

And at this moment, he wanted this woman.

She offered a much-needed diversion—and an excuse not to return to feigning drunkenness with Wardley and his ilk. He'd had enough.

Nor was Michael unaccustomed to women presenting themselves to him. He wasn't vain about his looks, but he knew their power. Furthermore, money was a potent aphrodisiac. In spite of the rumors swirling around his name, women in London eagerly sought him out. But the incident with Aletta had taught him discretion. He'd not taken what was freely offered. Even in Canada, he'd rarely had lovers. He'd been too focused on building his fortune and preparing for the day when he'd return to clear his name.

However, this woman attracted him in a way he'd not felt for a very long time. Her shining hair hung in a loose braid almost to her waist, reminding him of the proud Indian women back home. She was tall, her straight back and high cheekbones giving her an aristocratic air. A most unusual woman for a servant . . . but then, in Canada, he'd met many who had been bold enough to carve a place for themselves in the world. He'd just not expected to find such pride under Wardley's roof.

The woman stopped as if unable to take the last step toward him. The flickering candlelight cast dancing shadows around the room. Her skin was smooth and without the artifice of the cosmetics that so many women used in London. Her full, black lashes framed apprehensive sherry gold eyes. Seductive eyes. The sort that lured a man with their innocence.

His mind warned she could be a trap. His instincts didn't believe it. She was as leery of him as he was of her . . . and yet as caught up in the moment as himself.

He lifted his hand toward her hair. She drew back. He held still.

"I want to touch your hair," he whispered. "I want to know if it is as silky and heavy as it looks."

This time, when he raised his hand, she didn't flinch. He took his time, slipping his fingers into the clean, shining mass. She smelled of soap, fresh air, and woman.

Just this light touch was enough to make him hard with a force that was astounding, and he knew he was going to have her. She shifted away, shying from him. He brought his other hand to cup her face. Her skin was softer than he had anticipated.

"Don't be afraid," he whispered. "I won't hurt you. I'd never hurt you."

Her gaze held his. "I shouldn't be here," she said, her voice so low he could have almost imagined her words.

"But you are," he responded just as quietly.

She nodded.

"What is your name?"

She wet her lips, the movement almost bringing him to his knees. He wanted to smell, touch, and bury himself in her.

"Isabel."

"Isabel," he repeated. Even the sound of her name was magical.

A pounding began in his ears. It was the beat of his blood propelled by the force of that blessed need that made him a man.

Go easy, he warned himself. *Take care.* But he could not heed his own advice. "I want to kiss you."

She didn't reply, her gaze solemn, and he took that as permission, placing his hand on her waist and gently bringing her closer. She didn't balk . . . or turn away when he lowered his mouth to cover hers.

His mind registered a moment's resistance, a hesitancy, but as he fit her to him, her lips softened. She sighed her acceptance, and he could finally kiss her properly.

Elswick, Riggs, Wardley, *the world* disappeared. For too long he'd kept his guard up, his drive for vindication taking precedence over other desires. Now, the urge for release pushed him as it never had before.

He could tell she'd not kissed many men, but she was an apt pupil. As their kiss deepened, her own uncertainty vanished. Her arms came up around his neck.

Adventures of a Scottish Heiress

Miss Lyssa Harrell longs for love,
but knows her duty lies in marriage . . .
she is promised to a lord, but does the unthinkable—
and ends up in the arms
of fortune hunter Ian Campion.

Dumbfounded, Lyssa stared after the Irishm—

Her mind stumbled over the appellation as she
broke off the thought. *Campion*. He wanted her to call him
Campion.

She frowned. The pride in his voice nagged at her conscience. The man had saved her life, but he was too high-
handed by half. And at this moment, he was walking away
as if he didn't care if she followed or not.

No. He *expected* her to obey.

Which she did, because she had no other choice.

She picked up her skirts and followed, but rebellion
brewed in her mind. Think what he may, she was *not* returning to London.

She would *not* marry Robert or go through another humiliating Season of idle, patronizing chitchat from those
who only pretended to like her to please her stepmother or
even her father. She was too old for such nonsense.

She wanted purpose in her life, and she knew she would
find it here, in Scotland, the birthplace of her parents.

In the meantime, she would contrive to be everything a
proper, biddable young woman should be. After all, when
they reached Amleth Hall and she refused to return to London

with him, the Irishman would be cheated out of a great deal of money, and he wasn't going to take it very well.

So, Lyssa did her best to "march," but keeping up with him was a challenge. He had a long stride and moved as if he planned to cram the two days of travel inside this one night. She wasn't about to complain. Living with her father had taught her it was best not to pull on the watchdog's whiskers, and this man was definitely a watchdog.

Of course, it didn't help that her stockings were wet from their dash through the stream, and that water had seeped into her tight shoes, causing blisters to form on her feet.

She ignored the increasing pain each step caused her, and focused on placing one foot in front of the other.

She stumbled over a root growing over the path.

For a second, she was in midair, heading for the ground. But Campion turned, with that uncanny ability of his to know everything that was happening, and in the next instant, her cheek was against the solid wall of his chest. He set her on her feet. "Are you all right?"

"I'm fine." She took a step away from him. He wasn't the only one with pride. "I'll be better when we arrive someplace where we can hire horses."

"We won't be hiring horses."

Lyssa almost stumbled over her feet again in surprise. "You don't mean to *walk* all the way to Appin?"

"How else did you think we would travel?"

"With Charley and Duci, I had the wagon."

"There is no money for a wagon either, unless you have some."

She didn't. Her money had been hidden in the wagon that was burned to the ground. "You came after me without a shilling?" She'd never imagined herself without money.

"What little I have can be better spent than hiring horses."

"I doubt that."

Her flat reply startled a laugh out of him. "Oh, come now, people walk the distance across Scotland and back all the time, Miss Harrell. We shall manage."

"But not with my—" She stopped just in time. She'd been about to complain of her blisters, but she wouldn't give him the satisfaction. She'd heard the touch of satisfaction in his voice over having the power to make the rich man's daughter walk. Oh, no, like the noble Joan of Arc, she vowed to keep her personal sufferings private.

"Not with your what?" he prompted.

"Not with the present company," she improvised. "I'm certain walking is more pleasant with better company." He didn't like that response one wit, and she liked getting a bit of her own back—even though each step was agony.

And yet, she kept on, refusing to complain. She was her father's daughter for a reason.

The Irishman led the way, holding back low-hanging branches that would have swiped her in the face or helping her scramble up the often steep climbs in the forest path. She hid her suffering. Behind his back, she would hobble like a troll, but once he turned, she forced herself to walk upright.

In truth, the longer they traveled, the friendlier he became. As the first rays of the sun signaled the approaching dawn, he appeared ready to smile—until he caught sight of her limping.

"What's the matter?" he demanded.

"I've a blister. Nothing more, nothing less." They had come to a smooth road, which she hoped would make the walking easier. She attempted to pass him, her head high . . . but parts of her feet felt like hot coals.

He held out his arm, blocking her path. "Sit down on that rock and take off your shoes."

"I have no intention of doing any such thing." And she would have ducked under his arm and continued on her way, except he hooked his hand in her elbow and swung her around to face him.

Lording his height over her, he asked, "What? You'd rather walk until you have nubs instead of feet?"

"That won't happen," she said.

"It will and it has," he shot back. "I've seen grown men lose *all* their toes because they didn't take care of a blister."

Lyssa frowned, slightly unnerved by his accurate diagnosis of her problem and yet not believing such a preposterous statement. "You're hoaxing me."

He shook his head. "Sit on that rock. We've been walking most of the night and the time's come to take a breather."

Her pride tempted her to nobly wobble on in spite of the pain. She wondered if he would be more contrite if she *did* end up with nubs instead of feet.

However, what won her over was the idea of sitting. He was right. They had been moving all night. Letting down her guard, she gratefully sank onto the round, flat stone half buried in the hillside beside the road.

Who would have thought "sitting" could be such heaven?

He dropped to his knees in front of her and reached for her shoe. She pulled her foot back. "What are you doing?"

The Lady Is Tempted

When a well-bred lady, Deborah Percival,
becomes stranded at a country inn,
the Earl of Burnell tempts her with the chance
to fulfill all of her dreams . . . in his arms.
She knows she should say no—
but how can she resist?

Deborah's mind went blank. She should protest, proclaim her innocence.

But then, another part of her, a part born from curiosity and unfulfilled lust, wanted to mew like a hungry kitten for more. Mr. Aldercy's kiss was a far cry from her husband Richard's perfunctory pecks. This was a full-lipped, on-the-mouth, real-man-behind-it kiss.

Lust won out.

What harm could a little taste do? After a marriage to a man who'd been more of a father figure than a lover, she was more than a touch curious about what she had been missing.

With a soft sigh, she let down her guard.

Mr. Aldercy's hand went to her waist and pulled her closer.

The kiss changed. His lips became more searching, insistent. She hesitated, uncertain . . . and then decided that if she was going to experience kissing properly, she must throw caution to the wind. She kissed him back for all she was worth.

But—

Something was wrong.

He broke contact. She would have pulled away, but he held her near, his arm still around her waist. The light of a thousand devils danced in his eyes. "Mrs. Percival, what are you doing?"

Hot embarrassment flooded her cheeks. She wasn't sure how to answer. "I thought you knew what we were doing," she replied stiffly.

A low hum in the back of his throat was his answer. "If that is all you know of kissing, then, with all due respect to your late husband, you have been sorely neglected." He took her hand and pulled her toward the door. "Come."

Apprehensive, she asked, "Where are we going?"

"To a place where I can teach you to kiss properly."

Deborah hung back. "I don't see why you can't show me here."

He turned. He was so tall, so strong, so overpowering, and yet his reassuring squeeze on her hand was gentle. "I don't want Roald or Mrs. Franklin to walk in. Not if we are going to be after a proper kiss."

That would not do.

As if to lend credence to his words, a footfall sounded behind the pantry door. It started to open.

"Come." This time she didn't hesitate but hurried behind him. She couldn't help herself. Her hand felt safe in his . . . and she did want her kiss—if for nothing more than to satisfy her curiosity.

After all, she couldn't very well ask anyone in Ilam to teach her. Mr. Aldercy was providing an excellent opportunity.

However, she did have second thoughts when he started for the staircase. She balked. "Why not the sitting room?"

He paused, one foot leading up the stairs. "Too public. At least for the kiss I have in mind."

She shouldn't.

Upstairs were the bedrooms. She wasn't so naïve that she didn't suspect his intentions—

Roald's low voice came from the dining room. "They've left the table. I'll clear it now."

Deborah panicked. What if he looked out in the hall and saw the two of them standing there in this ridiculous pose like she was a reluctant mule Mr. Aldercy had to coax forward?

They could dash into the sitting room—but then, she wouldn't get her kiss. And she wanted one very much.

With a glance over her shoulder to ensure no one saw them, she charged up the stairs. Mr. Aldercy fell into step behind her, and they hurried like schoolchildren afraid of being caught in a prank.

However, at the top of the stairs, games stopped. He whisked her up the last step, twirled her around until her back was against the wall, and kissed her.

*And don't miss these other
amazing love stories
by Cathy Maxwell*